My skin prickles and it feels like I'm suddenly alone in a boat in the middle of an ocean. Uncharted territory. I've never talked about Ari behind her back to our other friends. It's just not something we do.

It's Ari and Kaylan.

Kaylan and Ari.

Original BFFs and everyone else is just fluff—ruffles on the side of a perfect cotton sweater.

"Um, well, the thing is." I stop myself. Once I start going in this direction, I'm not sure I'll ever go back to the before.

Cami says, "All I'm saying is that she's seemed a little off since her bat mitzvah. I don't know the reason, but it's like she doesn't want to hang with us so much. I mean, you're different and she still wants to hang with you. But, like, she doesn't really care about the rest of us."

A knot forms in my stomach and I feel nauseated and hungry all at once.

Has Ari been distant? I guess, sort of. Not with me. Only a little with the others, I guess.

And if I go on this trip, will that make her even more distant?

ALSO BY LISA GREENWALD

11 Before 12

12 Before 13

13 and ¾

TBH, This Is SO Awkward

TBH, This May Be TMI

TBH, Too Much Drama

TBH, IDK What's Next

TBH, I Feel the Same

TBH, You Know What I Mean

A FRIENDSHIP LIST NOVEL

13 and Counting

LISA GREENWALD

Katherine Tegen Books
An Imprint of HarperCollinsPublishers

Katherine Tegen Books is an imprint of HarperCollins Publishers.

13 and Counting
 For information address HarperCollins Children's Books, a division of HarperCollins Publishers, 195 Broadway, New York, NY 10007.
www.harpercollinschildrens.com

Library of Congress Control Number: 2018965818
ISBN 978-0-06-287525-9

Typography by Aurora Parlagreco
20 21 22 23 24 PC/BRR 10 9 8 7 6 5 4 3 2 1
❖
First paperback edition, 2020

For Zeyda, a Miracle Man

KAYLAN

"I KIND OF EXPECTED SOMETHING crazy to happen the minute we turned thirteen. Didn't you?" I ask Ari. We're side by side on my bed, watching *Freaky Friday* for the zillionth time.

"Not really." She laughs. "You expected aliens touching down on your front lawn? Or what?"

I whack her with a pillow. "No, nothing like that. Forget it. I don't know."

All of a sudden it hits me that we really are thirteen. That we've been friends since fourth grade, when Ari moved to Brookside. It's been a long time already.

"I know what you're saying." Ari sits up. "We waited so long to be teenagers and now we are and it's been two months of just, like, regular life."

"Yup. Regular life. And winter. And blah. I guess my

main hope for the next few months is that we have a lot of snow days." I pause. "Yours?"

"Ummmm." Ari rubs her eyes. "I kind of just want to relax. The first half of the year was all bat mitzvah stress. And my dad has a new job now so that agita is over, too. Can this half of the year just be chill time? Except for the insane amount of homework I have."

"Nice use of the word *agita*, Ar." I laugh. "And yes, chill time sounds fab. Ohhhh, and can we finally do that beach-themed sleepover we've been talking about forever? We can turn the heat super high and wear our bikinis and stuff. I feel like we need that to get us through winter. Like trick our minds that it's maybe summer?"

Ari claps. "Yes. Def. Next sleepover is totally beach theme. Do you realize we just had our fourth sleepover of winter break?"

I think about it for a second. "I didn't realize you were counting. But, yeah. *Wahhhh!* I am so sad we're going back to school tomorrow."

Ari frowns. "Break went so fast. Didn't it?"

"Kaylan!" we hear my mom yell up the stairs before I have a chance to answer. "Mail!"

"Mail?" Ari crinkles her face. "You get mail? Like real letters? From who?"

I shrug. "Sometimes."

"Are you expecting something?" Ari asks, hopping off

the bed and sliding her feet into the fluffy slippers she leaves at my house.

"Um, maybe?" My heart pounds because I kind of *am* expecting something.

We get downstairs and find my mom at the kitchen table, surrounded by a pile of mail and a steaming mug of tea.

"This came for you," my mom says, handing me an envelope, her glasses perched at the edge of her nose.

Ari leans over my shoulder, trying to read the envelope.

Return address: *Laurel Lake Camp for the Arts.*

"What is happening right now?" Ari whispers in my ear as I stand perfectly still with my eyes closed, holding the envelope in my hand. I've suddenly become frozen in place. "Are you all right, Kay?"

I nod, and look over at my mom, who appears not to have read the envelope and is clearly not even paying attention to us at all. Maybe it's better that way.

"Let's go into the den," I say quietly.

We sit down on the couch and I'm still holding the envelope in my hands. I wasn't even expecting a real letter. I figured I'd get the answer by email. And to be perfectly honest, I wasn't expecting anything right now. I thought I'd hear in February, maybe even early March. I planned to have more time to come up with some kind of reason why I didn't even ask my parents if I could apply, why I didn't tell Ari or anyone in the world about this.

"Kaylan," Ari says in her quiet, concerned tone, putting a hand on my shoulder. "Are you okay? You haven't said anything in a really long time. Your skin looks kind of gray."

"It does?"

"Yes." She raises her eyebrows at me. "Would you like me to, um, open the envelope?"

I nod, slowly. I'm not sure I really want her to, but I don't think I can do it myself. I already see sweat droplets on the paper; something has to happen soon.

Plus, if there's anyone I'd want around me when I get bad news, it's Ari. And if it's good news—she's the person I want beside me then, too.

"Hold my hand," I whisper.

Ari crinkles her face again and then tries to hold my hand and open the envelope at the same time. She's about to rip it apart with her teeth when I let go. "Okay, that won't work. Just open it."

Time creeps by from the second she tears open the envelope to the second we're reading the letter. But then I see:

Congratulations! We're happy to welcome you to
Laurel Lake Camp for the Arts' Comedy Intensive!

I stop reading. I fall back on the couch with my eyes closed.

I got in.

I didn't tell a single person about this because I truthfully didn't believe I'd get accepted. I had to send a two-minute video of a comedy routine and write an essay about what comedy means to me. But when I realized that they didn't require any adult signatures, I decided to just go ahead and do this on my own and see what happened.

"Kay?" I feel Ari's presence super close to me, almost like she's trying to peer into my brain somehow. "Are you all right?"

I sit up and open my eyes. "Yes. I'm fine. Shocked. But fine."

Ari drapes an arm over my shoulders. "Um, I'm a little concerned, FYI. Also, please explain what's going on."

I turn around to make sure my mom isn't eavesdropping. I'm going to have to tell her about this sooner or later, but it needs to be finessed in a certain way. It's not the kind of thing a mom should overhear.

"Well, first of all, this kind of came about because of your Camp Silver obsession. Just so you know." I eye-bulge at Ari and she nods, encouraging me to keep talking. "And so I did some research on summer comedy programs, and I found this one. But I didn't tell my parents because I figured they'd try to talk me out of it, and when I found one where you had to, like, apply and maybe not get in, I didn't want to tell anyone because I didn't want to jinx it."

"Wait," Ari interrupts me. She picks the letter up from the floor and reads it over. "So we're both going to camp this summer. Apart. Away from home? This says the session is four weeks. I'll be gone for seven."

I nod. "I think so. I don't think anyone stays all summer at Laurel Lake. But, yes. We are both going to be away, at camp, apart. I'm going. Even if my parents say no and I have to run away, I'm going."

"This is so amazing." Ari's smile widens. "Now you'll know how great camp is. You'll really and truly get it! You'll get to live the magic."

I look at her sideways, remembering when we stayed up all night and I found it so hard to understand the whole camp thing. Maybe she's right—maybe I really will get it now.

Ari's quiet for a moment and then she says, "You know what this means, Kay?"

I tilt my head to the side. "Um, that I'm actually super funny?"

Ari cracks up. "Yes, but something else, too. . . ."

I don't know what she's talking about and I'm not really into guessing games, especially at a time like this. "Just tell me. I'm not thinking clearly."

She flicks my forehead. "The list. Our next list. We need to start it right away because we're both going to be away for the summer for the first time in our lives and we need a list to prepare us, and we won't really be able to do a summer one . . . and—"

I cut her off. "Ar, relax. You're right, but also the first thing on the list probably needs to be *tell Kaylan's parents she's leaving for the summer and they need to pay this camp tuition and she's sorry she didn't even tell them she applied.*"

"Right." Ari smiles. "So we're not ready to make the list yet. But we agree we need to do a list, right? And start soon? Deadline first day of summer break?"

"Yes, definitely. Agree." I sit back and think for a minute. I'm completely shocked and overwhelmed at the moment. But the thought of a new list feels oddly calming.

I guess that makes sense since it's how the lists started in the first place.

"I know we said we weren't going to make the list yet, but I just had a brainstorm and I have to share." I widen my eyes. "What do you think about the list items sort of coming to us naturally? Like, let's not overthink it. Let's just see what comes into our heads."

I rest my head on her shoulder and breathe in her crisp, cucumber-smelling organic shampoo. I hope she uses this shampoo for the rest of her life and always smells like this. It's the most comforting smell in the world.

"I like that. An organic list." Ari ponders this for a second.

"Like your shampoo!" I pick my head up from her shoulder. "But first, list or no list, I need to figure out a way to tell my parents about this."

"Yes," she says. "You do."

My phone buzzes on the table and I pick it up.

"Oh, Cami texted. They're all going to that indoor water park. You know the one where they have that new spiral twisty slide?"

"Um, maybe?" Ari crinkles her nose.

"She wants to know if we're coming."

Ari deep-sighs and exhales. "You know how I feel about indoor water parks. . . ."

"Yeah, but this could be really fun and everyone's going, and I heard they remodeled it and it's way cleaner now," I tell her, sort of lying but also sort of not. I didn't study the reviews or anything but I heard Ryan tell my mom once that it was pretty cool. So that's something. "Plus it'll take our minds off the dreaded *school is starting again tomorrow* thoughts."

"I thought we had to work on telling your mom about the comedy camp thing?" she asks me.

"Sssshhh. Not right away! And yes, we do. But I feel like this could be fun and I have to do something with all this nervous energy. Come on, let's go with them!"

Ari makes a face at me.

"Would you kill me if I don't go?" she asks. "I just don't know if I feel like getting into a bathing suit. My period is still kind of here; you know when it's at the end but still hanging on? And I haven't shaved my legs in a decade and—"

"Ari! Hello! Remember we regretted not adding *saying yes* to the last list? The whole *you regret the things you don't do more than the things that you do do.*" I crack up. "Do-do."

"Good to know your maturity level is still not quite at your age level." Ari rolls her eyes at me. "Kay, I really don't want to. You can go and have fun, and it's fine. And I can do something else. For real."

"You're lame," I say. "What are you going to do? Spend all day reading about neuroscience or something? You've become such a brainiac now that you're in the honors block."

"Have not." She moves away from me a little bit and lies down on the couch. "I'm pleased with myself, thankyouverymuch."

"Well, I'm pleased with *myself*, thankyouverymuch."

"Good. Have fun." She air-kisses me. "I'll spend all day thinking of a game plan on how to tell your mom about comedy camp."

"That's a good idea. I still wish you were coming, though, Ari," I whine. "Pleaaasssssee."

"Kay, I'll come next time." She smiles and pulls a sweatshirt over her head. "Promise, promise. I'm just not feeling it today."

"Fine." I text Cami back that I'm coming but Ari's not.

“But definitely text me pics and stuff so I can see how much fun you’re having,” Ari instructs. “I’m hungry again. Can we have a snack before you go?”

“Totes.” I look up at her. “But, um, one last thing—can I borrow the bathing suit you left here last summer?” I scrunch up my face, feeling a little silly that I never returned it. “That polka-dot bikini. I just love it.”

“Sure,” she replies. “What’s mine is yours, dahling.”

2

ARI

AFTER CAMI'S MOM PICKS KAYLAN up, I walk home. It's actually mildly warm for January and I can be outside without needing to be dressed for the Arctic. I feel fine in my fleece jacket and scarf. The air smells smoky, like someone's making a fire really close by.

I sit outside on my front porch before going in, pondering how Kaylan can tell her parents about the comedy thing and contemplating a few potential list items in my head.

I should probably go inside and finish the winter break math packet, but I just can't muster up the energy.

"Yo," Jason yells from across the street, holding a basketball.

"Yo," I yell back.

He stands there with his hands on his hips, holding

the ball under his armpit. After staring at each other from across the street for a few minutes, he walks over to my house.

"What's up, Nod?" he asks.

I laugh. "Is that my new nickname?"

He squints. "I think so. It works, don't you think?"

"My last name *is* Nodberg." I shrug. "So. Sure."

He pulls over one of the Adirondack chairs close to mine and sits down. Our arms are on both the armrests, so close that they're sort of touching. I look over at him, suddenly confused, like he doesn't seem like the Jason he's always been.

"So talk to me. Did you have a good break? What's happening?" he asks, not sounding like his usual Jason self. I don't know what's different, though. Now I can't remember how he usually sounds. I just know that something is off.

"Not much," I reply. "You?"

"This, that, the other." He smiles and looks at me a minute while bouncing the ball. "All right, good talk. Later, Nod."

He gets up and dribbles the ball as he crosses the street.

He's just not as Jason-y as I remember him. But I don't know what that means exactly.

My phone vibrates in my pocket, and without even picking it up I can see that it's a selfie of Kaylan and the girls in M.W.'s dad's sprinter van all cheery, making goofy faces.

I type back a quick: *Nice! Have fun!*

I close my eyes and try to scrounge up the energy for the day. We stayed up too late last night. All I really want to do is get back into bed and close my eyes and sleep the afternoon away.

My phone buzzes again and I expect another Kaylan group selfie.

But it's Golfy.

Hey Ari. Just saying hello. Talk later.

He's pure goodness. Kindness. Friendliness. He should run a class for all the boys our age so they can see how to act. I don't think anyone would sign up for the class, but it's still a good idea. Maybe I'll suggest it to him one day.

But the thing is, lately I haven't been getting that heart-flip feeling when he calls or texts. Sometimes if we miss a day or two without communicating, I don't even realize it right away.

After my bat mitzvah, we talked and texted constantly. He was all I could think about. I replayed the slideshow in my head—how it felt to have his hand on my back when we slow-danced, how he gave me the quickest kiss ever in the temple's coatroom right before he went home.

I had a check-off calendar on my desk, counting the days until we'd be back at camp together.

And then one day, my parents, Gemma, and I were

out late visiting cousins in New Jersey, and Golfy and I missed our nightly call. And I swear, after that, things changed.

Is that how relationships fizzle? Just a scheduling glitch, a routine change?

I mean, I still like him a ton. But that utter, maddeningly obsessive infatuation has kind of faded. I hate to admit that, but it's true.

I type back: **Hello. Bye Bye. Talk later.**

I open the screen door and yell "I'm walking over to Bubbie and Zeyda's" to anyone who's close by. I don't really need to ask permission but my parents should know where I am.

"See you later!" my dad yells back.

I tie my gray paisley scarf around my neck and zip up my puffer coat, pulling my hood tight around my head. How did it get so much colder in the last hour? It sort of feels like it may snow all of a sudden.

I start to realize that I'm kind of in this no-man's-land part of the year. I'm not super excited about going back to school tomorrow. Camp is still really far away, so even though I can look forward to that, it's not exactly a close looking forward to it kind of thing.

"Hello, my darling girl!" Bubbie greets me at the door, barefoot, despite the fact that it's winter. The only time she wears shoes and socks is when she's outside. Never at home. She wraps me in a hug and holds me there and she says, "You really didn't have to do this, you know. I'm sure you have more exciting things to do than spend an afternoon with two old people."

"You're not old." I smile, pulling back. "Anyway, I wanted to do this. You know how I am with old pictures."

"Only you." She laughs her contagious laugh. "You're amazing."

That's such an overused word and I think people only really mean it about a quarter of the time. But when Bubbie says it, she means it.

"So does it look any better in here?" she asks me, hands on her hips, surveying the rooms of stacked boxes.

"Well, you have the lion doorstopper/pillow thing on the couch, so that's a start." I shrug. "You really never used it as a doorstop?"

"No. Too nice to be a doorstop. Too heavy to be a pillow. *C'est la vie.*" She sits down at the table and sips a half-full glass of seltzer. "Relax for a minute and then we'll get to work."

"Okay."

"So talk to me," she says after another sip.

"Um." I giggle. "I don't really know? I'm happy you guys are here, though."

"It's a lot of work." She shakes her head. "I think we see ourselves as younger than we actually are. So we figured we could handle this move while we were strong and fit. But guess what? I don't think we're as strong and fit as we think we are."

I roll my eyes. "Don't say that. You're definitely strong and fit. And can I tell you something? In my eyes, you don't age. I think you're still, like, in your sixties."

"Sweetheart, we age. Believe me, we age."

I look at her crooked for a second, wondering if she's trying to tell me something. Bubbie has this cryptic way about her. Like she says things without saying them. But then sometimes I think there's really no deeper meaning and I'm just reading into it. And every time I try to get up the courage to ask her what she's really saying, I choke back the words and smile instead. Maybe she says what she wants me to know, and that's it.

"So should we get started on these pictures?" I ask her.

"Yes!" She attempts to hop up from the chair in her usual Bubbie way, but her hop is slower than it used to be. "It's the top box in the first row of boxes in the den."

I laugh. "Okay, wow. There are a lot of boxes in the den. Are you sure we can't get you more help to unpack? When my friend June's aunt and uncle moved here last year, they hired these two guys to unpack them and they were done in, like, three hours."

"No, no." She walks in front of me. "Your father will help us, and we can do it. We'll let you know if we need to hire extra people."

"Okay, whatever you say, Bub." I open the top of the box and see all the framed photos stacked neatly, in bubble wrap. "I think we should try and re-create the order you had in the old house, on the wall leading upstairs. We want this to look as authentic as possible."

Bubbie laughs. "You're delicious. Do you know that?"

I wonder if it's only grandmother types who refer to people as delicious. I never hear young people do it. Maybe it's something that comes with age.

"Okay, so if I'm remembering correctly, when you first started walking up the staircase, it was the photos of you and Herbie as kids . . . right?"

"You think I remember?" she cracks up. "I lived in that house for fifty years and I have no idea!"

"Yes, you do! Come on. Let's ask Zeyda."

I call out to him; he's working in the bedroom.

"You think he remembers? You've got to be kidding! He doesn't remember what he had for breakfast and we only got up a few hours ago!"

I fall back on the recliner, laughing.

"Ari, there's a box in the garage I need you to get," Zeyda instructs. "It has all sorts of hanging materials. I'm going to try and get some of these pictures up on the wall."

"Oh, no, you're not." Bubbie laughs in a sort of sinister way. "We're not as young as we think we are."

"I'll grab it, so it'll be all ready when the guy comes to hang stuff up, but Zeyda, I can't allow you to do it yourself." I hop up and walk through the living room, taking a piece of biscotti out of the jar on my way to the garage. Clearly their priorities are in order—most of their stuff isn't even unpacked, but they do manage to have baked goods for the taking.

When I make it out to their garage, I find rows of boxes stacked to the ceiling and random other things like an exercise bike and the sign-in board from their twenty-fifth-anniversary party.

My dad said they were getting rid of all the stuff from their basement in the old house, but so much of it is here. It's hard to throw things away.

I find the box Zeyda was talking about and I'm about to head inside when my eyes land on something else. Something I never saw in their old house.

A unicycle.

Confused, I walk back inside.

"Um, guys," I say. "Did you join the circus and not tell me? Why do you have a unicycle?"

"You found it!" Bubbie yelps, clapping. "We discovered it when we were cleaning out. Apparently your dad wanted to learn to unicycle at some point! He never succeeded. We forgot all about it, but we brought it with us to surprise you."

I nod. "Well, I'm definitely surprised."

"Someone in the family needs to learn," Bubbie tells me. "It's brand-new! I mean, it's probably thirty years old, but it's new."

I laugh.

"Take it!" Zeyda exclaims. "If anyone can learn to unicycle, you can."

I sit back down on the recliner. "But I'm not sure I want to learn to unicycle."

"Oh yes, you do, Ari." Bubbie smiles. "My money's on you," she says, using one of her favorite expressions. "Take it; you and Gemma can practice together. It's good exercise."

"What?" I crack up, intrigued by this, but also realizing I'm not going to be able to say no.

And then it dawns on me: our first organic list item. I text Kaylan.

Me: K, are you ready for this?

Kaylan: just got off a waterslide. Ready for what?

Me: our 1st list item . . .

Kaylan: ????

Ari: learn to unicycle!!!!!!!!!!!!!!!!!!!!

Kaylan: wowwwwwwwwiiiieeeeee

Me: ummm, don't u want to know how this got on the list????

Kaylan: yes! Tell me later! One more slide to go!

I go back to organizing the pictures. I help Bubbie unpack a box of sweaters and fold them as neatly as I can in her dresser drawer. And then I get another text from Kaylan.

Kaylan: where r u?

Me: @ B&Z's

Kaylan: oooh! can I come over and say hi? Bub & I totally bonded @ ur bat mitzvah. I miss her!

Me: Ok! Come! They're in Woodbury Cove, the development across from Fox Hollow Hotel. Unit 703!

Kaylan: K! Be there soon!

I feel a little bubble of happiness that even though Kaylan went to the water park with the lunch table girls, she still wants to come and hang out with me and also see Bubbie and Zeyda. I think if I took a poll of all the BFFs in the world, I wouldn't find many who would want to hang with the other's grandparents.

Kaylan shows up pretty soon, her hair wet from the water park. "Hiiii," Kaylan sings, walking into Bubbie and Zeyda's house.

"Kaylan," Bubbie says, pulling her in for a kiss like they're old friends. "You've gotten taller since Ari's bat mitzvah."

Kaylan nods. "I have, right? All of my pants are short on me."

"You're gorgeous," Bubbie says. "Two beauties."

Kaylan looks around the apartment. "Wow, you really love lions," she says. "You don't even have a ton unpacked yet, and there are lions everywhere."

Bubbie replies, "Well, I'm a Leo."

"She is. And she's basically a lion," I tell Kaylan. "Strong and fiery and loyal and powerful and . . ."

"Okay, okay." Bubbie shakes her head. "Enough flattery for one day!"

Kaylan laughs and suggests, "You should call this The Lion's Den. . . . What do you think? Get a sign for the door or something. . . ."

Bubbie and Zeyda look at each other, smiling a little.

"Do you feel like since you love lions, people always buy you lion stuff, though, and it's kinda too much after a while?" Kaylan talks like she's a stand-up comic. "Because I went through this phase a few years ago where I was obsessed with rainbows and it was like, that was all anyone bought me for every occasion and it became wayyyyy too much. Rainbow pins, rainbow sweatshirts, rainbow stationery, even rainbow underwear." She pauses. "I mean, where does it stop? Rainbow toilets? Come on, people . . . ya know? Maybe that's where the whole *too much of a good thing* comes from. . . ."

Bubbie laughs so hard she starts coughing a little bit and I rub her back.

We spend another hour in the den, talking and organizing.

When it starts to get dark, Bubbie says, "You guys should go home now. Really. I'll worry otherwise."

"Someone could pick us up in a few hours. Really," I mimic. "And then we could take the unicycle."

"You'll take it another day. I'm glad you want it." She

pauses. “Please listen to me. Thank you for coming and thank you for going.”

We all start laughing, and Bubbie and Zeyda hug and kiss Kaylan and me, and we start the walk home. It’s not even that dark yet, and today is one of the warmer winter days, but you can’t say no to Bubbie. When she tells you it’s time to go, it’s time to go.

“That was so great,” Kaylan says. “I really had no idea about the lion thing.”

“Yeah,” I reply. “It’s intense.”

“I like it. Also, she kind of looks like a lion in a way, with her red hair.”

“You think?” I ask.

“Totally. So what do you think about the comedy routine I tried out on Bubbie? It just sorta came to me. I want to be the kind of comic who talks about everyday stuff. . . .”

“The thing about the rainbows?” I ask. “Did you plan that ahead of time?”

“Not really, sort of . . . I think it’s a good bit.”

“It was funny, Kay! Bubbie certainly cracked up.”

She nods, all proud. “Do you think I could be an honorary Nodberg granddaughter now that they live here?”

“I don’t see why not,” I answer. “You’ve known them as long as you’ve known me. Welcome aboard.”

“Should I call them Bubbie and Zeyda, though? Even though I’m not Jewish?” she asks.

I scoff. "Yes, of course. Those are basically their names. It's Yiddish for Grandma and Grandpa, but anyone can use the terms."

"I kinda figured that. But wanted to check." She links arms with me. "Did you think of any ideas for how to tell my mom about comedy camp?"

I look over at her. "I guess just be honest? It's really the only way."

We mull it over the rest of the way home, and when I'm inside I realize I never even asked Kaylan how the water park was. But then I realize I don't actually care all that much.

I don't have that terrible left-out feeling like I did over the summer when I didn't get invited to the ice cream place.

I'm okay with doing my own thing, and I'm feeling pretty good about that.

3

KAYLAN

THE NEXT DAY, WE'RE ALL at lunch, telling the other girls we're about to embark on a new list as soon as we come up with the items, or the items come to us.

"Oooh, can we help come up with some?" Cami asks, popping a sweet potato fry into her mouth.

Ari looks at me, and I look at her, but we don't say anything.

"What about if you two do most of the stuff, and we help finish it out?" June suggests. "Because, like, you need thirteen things this time, right? That's kind of a lot."

I nod. Ari is only half paying attention. She's more focused on buttering her bagel.

Marie jumps in. "Yeah, we'll do the polishing items. Stuff you haven't thought of, and give you an outside perspective." She nods like she's trying to get us to agree with her. "Please."

I say, "Ari? Thoughts?"

"Oh, um." Ari looks up from her bagel. "Sure, okay. But Kay and I have the final say."

"Okay, then." Cami rolls her eyes. "We didn't think we'd, like, be in charge of the list or anything!" She laughs, but more in an annoyed sort of way.

"Calm down, guys," I tell everyone. "I like this plan. We'll keep you posted on our progress."

"You guys, what's the deal with that active shooter drill thing they talked about in homeroom today?" June asks, picking the lettuce out of her tuna wrap. "I am so confused."

"It's gotta be done," Cami replies. "That's the world we're living in. Can you even believe it? I mean, I can but I can't, ya know?"

Ari makes eyes at me from across the table. She's such a zombie at lunch lately, barely talking, just nodding occasionally and usually studying for something with books on her lap.

I make eyes back at her, but truthfully, Cami's not that bad. Yes, she's kind of a know-it-all but she does know a lot of stuff, so maybe it's okay?

"They'll explain everything, I'm sure, before it happens," I tell June, but really the whole table. "It's just something schools have to do now because of all the dumb shootings, but it's better to be prepared, right? Also, kids are really taking an active role in combating gun violence. Have you all read about it?"

Everyone nods, sort of halfheartedly, like this is something they haven't thought about much.

"It's totally ridiculous," Ari finally chimes in. "I mean, what is wrong with this country? Why are people so insane about their guns? This doesn't happen in other countries with this kind of regularity."

Ari's fired up and I love when she gets like this. Her words are fast and she's talking with her hands like her whole body wants everyone to agree.

"I totally don't get it," Marie adds. "But I have an uncle who owns guns and goes hunting all the time and it's really intense, but the thing is he knows how to properly secure them and stuff. That's important. I think people are careless with guns and that's the main issue."

"I don't agree. I'll never understand why someone would want to own a gun. I'm sorry, Marie. You know I love you, but I don't get that." Ari shakes her head and gathers all of her lunch remnants. "I'm so glad all of those teens have spoken up and are taking an active role and trying to make a difference. They're going to Washington to protest and organizing marches and everything. Anyway, I'm gonna go a few minutes early. I need to cram for this Spanish test."

I hop up from the table and follow Ari out of the cafeteria.

"Ari." I put my hands on her shoulders. "Another thing for the list."

"What?" she asks, a little impatient-sounding.

"Start a movement," I answer.

Her eyebrows curve inward and she waits for me to tell her more.

"Like you said, about the teens and gun violence and stuff . . . we could start our *own* movement."

"What would it be?" she asks.

"That's what we'll figure out!"

Ari nods. "I like it! I really do need to go study for Spanish, though. Can we discuss more later?"

"Of course!" I give her a quick hug and walk back to the cafeteria, and when I get to the table Cami asks, "What's up with her? It was weird she didn't come to the water park and she's weird again today."

She's asking the whole table, but I feel like she's directing the question right to me. Because even though we're all one solid group of friends now and Ari and Marie are pretty close, it's still Ari and Kaylan as a solid unit and then everyone else. We just go together. I think it'll always be like that. No matter what.

"She's fine," I tell everyone. "You know how she gets with studying and the crazy honors block. And the water park thing—she just doesn't like them."

They all shrug halfheartedly and then move on to other discussions.

When it's time to clean up from lunch, we all throw out our stuff and walk to our next classes. I'm not super worried about Ari and her out-of-it-ness at school lately.

It's more the hot and cold. Like sometimes she's super into something and fired up and other times she's just sort of blah.

I don't see Ari again until sixth period, when we're sitting in our creative writing elective—our favorite time of the day. I think it's because we can really express ourselves and get all of our feelings out on the page. Plus there's no homework or tests or stress.

It's bliss.

Our teacher, Ms. Graham, lets us write pretty much whatever we want. She'll sometimes give us a prompt and then we go from there, but it can be any kind of writing—Kenny Youn is always writing these bloody horror-thriller pieces and Ms. Graham is fine with it.

"As long as it's school appropriate," she says.

So I always try to write something funny and then when everybody laughs, I feel like I can conquer and, like, heal the world with happiness. That's kind of my goal in life.

I'm halfway into my piece about a hamster who becomes addicted to television when Ms. O'Leary, the new secretary in the main office, knocks on the door.

“Is Arianna Nodberg in this class?” she asks. “I know there’s been some elective switching and I’m not sure I have the most up-to-date version of the schedule.”

“Yes, she’s here,” Ms. Graham says. “Ari?”

I crinkle my eyebrows at Ari, my heart pounding. People only get called out of class when something bad happens, or the administration thinks something bad has happened.

“I have no idea,” Ari mouths to me. I grab her hand as she walks past me, about to leave the classroom. I wish I could go with her.

“Please take your things, Arianna,” Ms. O’Leary instructs. I’m thinking there should be some kind of course for people at schools who need to yank students out of classes. Shouldn’t she be saying something like *don’t worry* or *you’re not in trouble* or *this isn’t a big deal? Grab your things* is pretty much the worst thing you could say.

I try to get back to my piece but the words aren’t flowing anymore. I have the hamster addicted to the Cartoon Network and that’s pretty much it.

I’m too worried about Ari being called out of class to think about anything else.

4

ARI

I'M SHAKY AS WE LEAVE the classroom, like I could fall over and I need someone to help me stand up straight. My skin feels clammy—like I'm burning hot and freezing cold at the same time.

"What's going on?" I stammer as we walk down the hall.

"Your mother is picking you up early. I'm sure it's nothing to be concerned about," Ms. O'Leary tells me, staring straight ahead. This woman needs a lesson or two on speaking to people, maybe teenagers especially. She's like seventy years old and it seems like she may have only had three or four conversations with humans in her entire life.

"How come? My mom never picks me up early."

"She didn't say."

We walk quietly to the main office after that and all I can hear is the click-clack of her itty-bitty heels against the floor. I find myself wishing that the hallways were at their usual noise level right now; the quietness only makes me more nervous.

Finally, we get to the main office and I find my mom sitting in one of the brown armchairs, holding her head.

And then the world seems to crack into a thousand pieces.

"Mom? What's going on?" It feels impossible to get the words out.

"Ari, hi, we gotta go. Come out to the car. Hurry," she says, grabbing my backpack from me before I have the chance to tell her that we should probably stop at my locker for some things.

As we're about to get to the main doors of the school, I ask again, "What's going on? Also, I need my coat."

"Right. Go get it."

"Mom!" I yell. The hallway monitor turns around, about to tell me to quiet down, but then she sees that I'm with my mom and stays quiet. "You have to tell me what's happening. This is insane!"

"Ari, it's Bubbie. She fell. She might've had a stroke. We're not sure. We want to get to the hospital right away. I knew you'd want to see her."

"Wait. What?" I ask. "See her because, like, she may not be around that much longer? Or see her because she's upset? Or see her because—"

"I don't know," my mom says, worn-out sounding. "Please just get your coat. We can talk more in the car."

After that, everything slows down. The three seconds it would normally take to walk from where I'm standing to my locker feels like it takes a decade. The drive to the hospital that would normally take ten minutes seems to take three hundred years.

Even though my mom said we'd talk in the car, we don't talk at all. I thought I had questions to ask her, but it turns out my mind is blank. I know I don't know anything that's going on, and yet I can't even think of what to ask.

I hear my phone buzzing in the bottom of my backpack and I dig through my binders and books to try and find it.

Kaylan: What's going on? Are u ok?

At this moment, even replying to a text seems like a major effort. I don't want to write very much. And I don't want to write anything that will keep Kaylan asking questions. Because the thing is, I don't know the answers.

I ignore her text for now and I know that will frustrate her. But it is what it is.

We pull into the hospital parking lot. "You're not picking Gemma up?"

"No, not right now," my mom says. "Dad is already here. Gemma can go to Extended Day at school. We need to see what shape Bubbie is in before we bring Gemma over."

Sometimes I wish I was the younger sibling—shielded and protected from everything. Gemma's the one who people look out for. They debate if she's old enough to know things, what she can handle. But being the oldest, it's like, well, of course Ari can handle it. I'm like a miniature grown-up. And I don't know if I want to be that. No one asked me if I wanted to. It shouldn't be automatic that the older kid has to shoulder all the heavy stuff and the younger kid just gets to skateboard through life, covered head to toe in helmets and knee pads and elbow pads.

The older kid is practically mountain climbing without a harness.

Birth order is pretty unfair when you think about it.

"This hospital doesn't have the terrible hospital vibe as much as others," I tell Mom as we walk down the hallway. "Like the time Zeyda got that knee infection. That hospital was over-the-top hospitalness."

Mom laughs for a second. "I guess."

"Do you know what I mean?" I ask her, like this is the most important conversation in the world. "This one's small and so it feels a little more homey and it doesn't have that disgusting tuna-salad-in-a-hospital-cafeteria smell."

"I didn't realize you've thought this much about

hospitals." My mom squeezes my hand tight and then lets it go.

"I didn't realize I had either."

When we walk into Bubbie's hospital room, she's lying there in the bed and my dad and a few nurses and doctors are standing around her. She has a clear oxygen cord thing in her nose. We all need oxygen and I guess some people need help getting a little more, but when you see the things in someone's nose, it's just so scary. It's like even though you don't know all the details, you know that something is very, very wrong.

"Hi, dolls," Bubbie says softly. She introduces my mom and me to the nurses and doctors in the room and we all exchange hellos.

Well, if she's introducing us, she can't be that sick, I tell myself.

She's totally with it and knows what's going on.

She's fine.

This isn't bad at all.

My parents step out of the room with the nurses and doctors, probably to get some more information. I hear Zeyda's voice and crane my neck; he's by the nurse's station. I sit down on the edge of the salmon-colored fake-leather chair next to Bubbie's bed.

"How are you feeling?" I ask, scrunching up my face as if my whole body is preparing for bad news. I reach over to hold her hand, careful not to disturb the thin tube used for the IV.

"Not great," she says. "Very tired."

She closes her eyes, not saying anything. I can't stand the silence. It's so un-Bubbie-like.

"I told you to let someone else help you unpack!" I fake yell, laughing a little.

She half smiles with her eyes still closed.

We spend another hour there, and my parents and Zeyda chat with everyone and try to get all of the information, and I pretend to watch whatever's on TV. Some rerun of one of those daytime talk shows. I let Bubbie sleep but every so often I look over to make sure she's breathing.

"Please don't let her die," I say in my head over and over again. I think back to my bat mitzvah and all the debates we had about God's existence. I'm not even sure how or why I debated it. I'm clearly praying to God right now, even if it is only in my head. Maybe it's more than that; maybe I'm saying it because I know that God will hear me.

5

KAYLAN

"SO WHAT'S GOING ON?" I ask Ari over the phone later that night.

"Ugh, I don't know," she answers. "She's in the hospital. They think she had a mild stroke so she'll need all kinds of therapy and there may be other stuff going on, too. I don't know. It's all like confusing medical talk."

My stomach sinks. "I can't even believe this. They just moved here. Maybe the move was too much for them."

"I know." She pauses. "But listen, I think this is happening right now for a reason. I just realized this a few minutes ago."

"Why?" I ask her, intrigued.

Ari sighs. "The list. Our new list. The whole organic part of it, more stuff just keeps coming to me, and I know we have the unicycle and the start a movement . . ."

"Yeah?" I know a lot is going on inside her head right now, so it's okay that it's taking some time to get it all out.

"And so two more list items came to me totally, one hundred percent organically," she says. "One is, spend more time with Bubbie and Zeyda. I mean, because they live so close now and also because time is precious. We never know about the future."

Goose bumps prickle all over my arms when she says that. I lean back on my bed. "That's very true."

Ari goes on, "Also, figure out how we feel about God. I know I've had my doubts and so have you and my bat mitzvah sort of made things a little clearer but also more confusing, and I kind of miss my meetings with the cantor where I can talk all of this out." She pauses.

"Yeah?" I ask. "Go on."

"So, now that this crisis has fallen in my lap, and I've already prayed to God ten times since I got to the hospital . . ." Her voice trails off again and it's hard to tell if she's crying or just thinking. "I think now we need to finally figure out once and for all how we feel about the subject."

"About God? Figure out how we feel about God?" I ask, confused and a little overwhelmed.

"Yeah, I mean. Discuss it and stuff," she replies.

I hesitate to answer because it feels like a lot to take in at once, but I really think Ari is onto something. "I'm in."

"Are you sure?" she asks. "I know I'm sort of like throwing these list items at you, but they just came to me and I feel like they're super important."

"I'm sure," I reply. "We had so much fun at Bubbie and Zeyda's the other day. I want more of that!"

Ari cracks up and then she's quiet before responding. "Well, yeah, we will def have more of it. I mean, the doctors haven't said anything really, but I think Bubbie's going to bounce back. She's totally going to bounce back."

I perk up a little. "Okay, well, that's good."

"How was the rest of school?" she asks.

I hesitate. "Um, fine? I can't even remember now. Is that weird?"

Ari laughs. "Not really. Have you told your parents about the comedy thing yet?"

"No. I'm too nervous to do it, but also too nervous to keep it hanging over my head."

"I know that feeling." She sighs.

"Yeah." I pause. "I gotta go start homework. Keep me updated on Bubs. Oh, and when we were packing up at the end of the day, we talked about maybe all sleeping at Cami's this weekend." I pause again. "You in?"

"I don't know." She hesitates. "Maybe. Let's see what's going on with Bub and all that."

I think she may be using the Bubbie thing as an excuse, but I let it go. "K. Love you."

We hang up and I wonder if Ari's ever going to be

totally honest with me about how she feels about the lunch table girls. It's like she's only half into them. Like they're fine and she'll deal with them but it's never her first-choice thing to do. She was so upset when she wasn't included last summer for the ice cream date and for Lizzie's bat mitzvaḥ and now she's included all the time but she doesn't really want to join.

I guess it's not a big deal. But we do spend a lot of time in school and we have many, many years of school ahead of us so she should probably try and lean in, as they say.

I wonder if it's possible for Ari and me to stay strong-as-ever BFFs if I'm closer with the school friends than she is. It'd be sort of like we're twins but have a different group of friends. And we're super, super close when we're together but we get that we can be okay apart, too.

I go down to the basement to see if my red cardigan is dry from the laundry yesterday, and I realize how drab it is down here. There's so much more we can do with the space. I think back to last year's list and our doodle-a-day, wondering if my mom would let Ari and me doodle on the walls, when an even better idea comes to mind, completely out of the blue.

Organic, as Ari says!

I run up the stairs to tell my mom about my brilliant idea. When inspiration strikes, you need to grab on to it!

But when I get to the kitchen, she's at the table filling out a stack of forms. It seems a good one-third of her life is spent filling out forms and I'm not even sure what they're for. Sure, we have the usual school stuff, but it's January. What forms are required at this time?

"What's for dinner?" I ask, my enthusiasm fizzling.

"I think rotisserie chicken if I have a moment to run out and get it," she says, not looking up from the pile of paper. "This stuff is endless."

"What is it?" I ask, peering over her shoulder.

"Insurance stuff, a permission slip for Ryan's eighth-grade overnight. I don't even know. I make a pile as things come in and then I go through it when I have time. And it seems I never actually have time." She sighs and finally looks up. "Anyway, how are you?"

"Good," I say, realizing this isn't the time to ask her for something. "I love you, Mom."

She smiles and leans over to kiss me on the forehead. "I love you, too. You're welcome to keep me company while I work on this and get started on your homework."

I agree to her plan, and run upstairs to grab my folders. I'm gathering all my stuff when my phone buzzes.

It's Cami.

"Hey, girl." She pauses and crunches some snack that sounds super loud through the phone. "Why did Ari leave school early? You never told me."

"Oh, um, her bubbie's in the hospital," I tell her, walking down the stairs.

She gasps. "The one who just moved here? OMG."

"Yeah."

"That's so terrible. Is she gonna be okay? What's going on?"

I try to start my vocab crossword puzzle as she talks.

She groans. "Hello? Where are you? Are you there?"

I close the folder and walk into the den. Clearly I can't do homework and talk to Cami at the same time. "Yeah. Sorry. Um, I think she's gonna be okay, yeah. I'm not sure. I don't have all the details. Cam, I gotta finish this homework, okay? Can I call you back?"

"Sure," she answers, reluctant sounding. I wonder why she's not trying to finish her homework, too, or maybe she did already. "Oh, wait! I called for another reason. . . ."

I roll my eyes at the phone. "What?" I try to sound interested.

"How would you like to go on vacation with my family? Feb break. This super-fab resort in Turks and Caicos . . . all expenses paid! Say yes! Say yes!"

"What?" I yelp. "Are you serious?"

I peer into the kitchen to see if my mom is paying attention. Luckily or unluckily, she's still busy with the paperwork and doesn't seem to notice anything else.

That's when it hits me: another thing for the list. Get good at the act of persuasion, especially when it comes to my mom . . . since there seems to be something new to convince her on every day.

"Yes! Totally serious! Please come. We'll have the best

best best best best time."

"Um, I need to ask my mom, Cam," I whisper. "So, um, can I let you know?"

"Sure," she answers. "I am praying you can come. My mom's going to call your mom, B.T. Dubs. So don't ask her yet until my mom calls, okay?"

"I can't even believe this!" I whisper.

"I know. I can't either!" Cami sings. "Oh, one more thing. Can I just say something?" Cami speaks in a quieter tone all of a sudden. "Do you think that's why Ari's been kind of distant lately? Like her bubbie was sick and she didn't want to tell anyone. 'Cuz, like, she has been distant, right?"

My skin prickles and it feels like I'm suddenly alone in a boat in the middle of an ocean. Uncharted territory. I've never talked about Ari behind her back to our other friends. It's just not something we do.

It's Ari and Kaylan.

Kaylan and Ari.

Original BFFs and everyone else is just fluff—ruffles on the side of a perfect cotton sweater.

"Um, well, the thing is." I stop myself. Once I start going in this direction, I'm not sure I'll ever go back to the before.

Cami says, "All I'm saying is that she's seemed a little off since her bat mitzvah. I don't know the reason, but it's like she doesn't want to hang with us so much. I mean, you're different and she still wants to hang with you. But, like, she doesn't really care about the rest of us."

"Yeah. Maybe. I don't know." I pause. "I gotta go finish homework, Cam, for real. Thanks so much for the vacay invite. Talk later, k?"

"K," she replies. "Love ya."

I type out a quick text to Ari.

Me: new list item—work on the art of persuasion . . . especially with my mom.

Ari: ooooh. I like. B/c of comedy stuff?

Me: Yeah, and other stuff, too

Ari: What other stuff?

Me: IDK. Just saying.

I sit there for a few minutes wondering if I should tell Ari about the trip right away. But I don't even know if my mom will say yes, so how can I tell Ari before I know for sure? Maybe I should tell her about my idea for the basement and how that ties into the art of persuasion.

A knot forms in my stomach and I feel nauseated and hungry all at once, replaying the Cami conversation in my head.

Has Ari been distant? I guess, sort of. Not with me. Only a little with the others, I guess.

And if I go on this trip, will that make her even more distant?

6

ARI

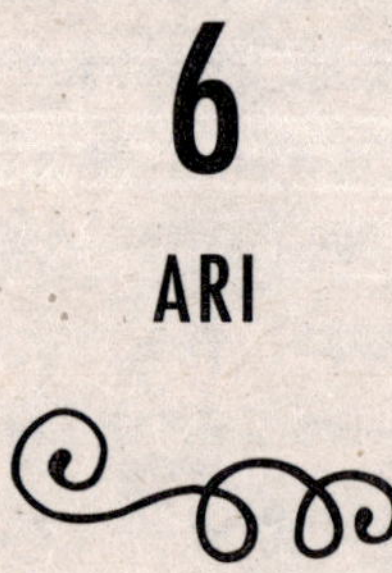

EVERY DAY THAT BUBBIE'S IN the hospital feels like ten years. So when it's three days later and she's still there and we don't have any more answers than when she first got in, I feel myself starting to go a little crazy. Why does every doctor take forever to get back to us? Why does it seem like they're never really working?

"Ari, obsessing and worrying isn't going to help her get better quicker," Dad tells me as he passes the platter of chicken cutlets.

"Do you even realize that for most of my life I wasn't a worrier at all?" I ask, forceful sounding. "I mean, I was the chill one. People would call me Chill Girl Ari."

Gemma bursts out laughing, spitting cucumber all over the table. "OMG, that is kind of a lame nickname, Ar," she says, still laughing.

I glare at her. "First of all, stop. Second of all, I'm worrying and obsessing because we don't have any answers. Do you get that?" I look at my dad and then my mom and they just stare at me openmouthed. "Why aren't you demanding more answers?"

In a warning kind of way, my mom says, "Ari, please."

"You could be doing more." I look down at my plate and scarf a few bites of mashed potatoes. "You can't just let her rot away in the hospital!"

"Ari!" my mom yells this time. "Get ahold of yourself."

I shake my head. "I'm full. May I please be excused?"

They nod reluctantly and I push in my chair and carry my plate to the sink. When I get upstairs to my room, I pace around, trying to think of something else to keep my mind occupied.

I start searching online for anything I can find on strokes. Having information calms me. It's when I don't know what's going on or how things will turn out that I end up feeling anxious and uneasy.

To stay Chill Girl Ari, I need to also stay Informed Ari.

I don't know why it's taken me so long to realize this.

So I keep reading online about strokes and recovery times and different therapies and strategies and then something entirely different comes up: a 5K for stroke awareness. And it's in a town only twenty minutes from us!

My heart speeds up as I read over all the information.

I don't even know how long a 5K really is so I have to search for that, too, and find out. Okay, it's only a little over three miles. We could totally do this. But it's not like it'll be super easy. We'll need to train, at least a little bit.

We can totally do this!

Kaylan and me!

Another organic thing for the list. I add it to my rough draft.

New Ari & Kaylan Friendship List

1. Learn to ride a unicycle
2. Start a movement
3. Figure out how we feel about God
4. Spend more time with Bubbie and Zeyda
5. Perfect the art of persuasion, especially with Kaylan's mom
6. Train for and run a race

I hit the "favorites" button on my phone, where I have only one number listed: Kaylan.

It's true that I have more favorites now: Alice, Golfy, Hana, Zoe—okay, all Camp Silver people.

But I haven't added them as favorites in my phone.

"Hey, how's Bub?" Kaylan asks right away, not even saying hello.

That's how you know you have a true, one-of-a-kind best friend. They cut right to the important stuff, what they know is on your mind. They don't even waste time with hello.

"Eh, I don't know. It's like we're not even given answers."

"I don't get it. Why?" She coughs. "Like they don't have the information or your parents are keeping it from you, or what?"

"I don't know."

We're quiet for a few minutes, and I don't even realize it until Kaylan says, "Soooo what else is going on?" which basically means she's asking me why I called, like if there was any specific reason.

"Oh, right." I laugh for a second. "I called because . . . drumroll, please, another list item."

"OMG, Ari," Kaylan says. "You are on fire. What is it?"

"We're going to run a race! It's a stroke awareness race. They think Bub had a stroke, by the way. So yeah, it's a meaningful cause. And a 5K is really only a little over three miles, so totally doable. But I think we'd still have to train." I pause. "What do you think?"

"Um. Wow. You just talked really, really fast, by the way," Kaylan starts.

"Sorry," I reply, not actually feeling sorry.

"When is it?" she asks. "I don't want to run outside when it's freezing, or ever, really . . . but if it's for a good cause, maybe?"

"Hold." I put down the phone and go back to the website. "June."

My mouth drops when I look at the date and then up at the school calendar tacked on my bulletin board above my desk. "OMG. Actually, you're never going to believe this. It's on the last day of school. Hello! The day we need to finish the list. This could be the final thing. This is a sign! I just sent you the link."

"This is an absolutely crazy sign," Kaylan replies. "Like it's all coming together, the reason we are doing a winter list, the deadline, the items, all of it." She pauses. "It makes so much sense."

"Yay!" It feels so good when Kaylan and I agree, like all is right in the world.

"Can I ask you a question?" Kaylan says, all tentative. "And don't be mad, okay?"

"I hate when people do that," I tell her. "It's like setting someone up to be mad."

"Okay, but still."

My happy, successful feeling disappears. "Whatever." I sigh. "Fine. What is it?"

"Can you just be honest about how you feel about our

friends? Like, if you don't like them, it's okay. But I want to know."

"Kay," I groan. "Haven't we discussed this a bunch already?"

She laughs. "I don't know. Have we?"

"I think so. It seems familiar." I sigh. "Anyway, it's all good. I like them. I just don't need to be twenty-four/seven BFFs with them. They're good in-school friends, and that's still a big thing. Ya know?"

"Got it." She laughs again. I'm not sure why, though. None of this is that funny.

"All right, I gotta go, Kay." I clear my throat. "But I'm feeling good about the race and the list and stuff. Are you?"

"Yuppers, yuppers," she says. "Let's do our sleepover Friday to discuss and see how many things we have. Okay?"

"Okay," I say. "Nighty-night."

"Nighty-night."

I sit there for a moment and my enthusiasm about the race starts to fade a little. It's like it only helps for a second because when I think about the reason we're doing it, my insides turn gray.

I start to feel trapped inside my room, inside my house, trapped with worry and frustration. I run downstairs and grab my coat and go out to the front porch. I sit back on the Adirondack chair with my hood up, and breathe in and breathe out, breathe in and breathe out.

I focus on the crispness of the air and pray that things will be back to normal sometime soon.

A few minutes later, I'm in that state where I'm kind of asleep but also having real thoughts, not dreaming, and then I hear someone say "Hey" in a soft half-serious, half-jokey kind of tone.

I open my eyes and look over at the person in the rocking chair next to me.

Jason.

"Oh, um, hey." I laugh, totally caught off guard. "How long have you been sitting there?"

He considers it for a moment. "I dunno. Not long."

I look at him sideways. "Oh-kay."

"So what's up? Heard you guys are doing a new list . . ." He raises his eyebrows. "Well, more like I overheard Kaylan talking to Cami about it."

"Yeah, we are." I look down at my boots, curling my toes inside them. Maybe it's too cold to be out here.

"Hello! Earth to Nodberg!" Jason laughs. "You sound like you're on another planet."

I sigh. "No, just a lot on my mind."

"Yeah?" he asks, genuinely sounding concerned and wanting to know what's going on. "Like what?"

I start talking. "Well, my bubbie fell, and she's in the

hospital, and I'm all twisted up now. Like I can't really focus on anything else."

"Oh." He nods. "Yeah. That sucks."

I wonder why I just told him all of that, but I also wonder why his response feels oddly comforting. He didn't even say anything. But he acknowledged the suckiness level of this kind of thing, and that sort of feels like a lot.

"It does suck," I say. "They just moved here, and we had all these plans, and all I want is for her to get better so we can move forward and also go back to normal."

"I get that," he says. He moves over the tiniest bit, and for a second our elbows are sharing the arm of my rocking chair.

It's the weirdest thing ever, but when he moves his elbow away, I'm sort of disappointed.

We sit there talking for a few more minutes until Jason declares, "Okay, it's freezing out here. I'm going home."

I look over at him and realize all he's wearing is a fleece jacket.

"Yeah, you need to bundle up more, Klee." I laugh, not even sure where that just came from. I've never called him Klee before. I barely call him Jason.

"Yeah, noted." He gets up from the rocking chair and starts to walk down the steps, toward our front path and across the street. "Nodberg, if you ever want to, uh, talk, you know I'm here. Yeah?"

“Yeah,” I answer.

I watch him walk away, back into his house. I see him through the long window next to his front door, hanging his fleece up on the coat tree. And then I catch a glimpse of him, running up the stairs.

I stay on the porch for a few more minutes, staring at his house, sort of hoping he’ll come back outside again, or that he’ll wave from his window.

He was just here, and he’s just Jason, and I know I’ll see him tomorrow, but there’s a little part of me that misses him.

7

KAYLAN

A FEW DAYS LATER, MY mom and I are in the den together, cozy on the couch, relaxing after dinner. She hasn't said anything about the Cami trip yet, and neither have I. It's been this crazy-intense waiting game, making me realize how super, mega important the art of persuasion thing really is. It probably should have been on our first list.

Cami tells me every day that the moms have been playing phone tag, but we have no idea when they'll finally connect.

"I talked to Cami's mom earlier today," she says.

"Oh!" I sit up straight, wondering if she just read my mind or if moms have the ability to do that. I really hope they don't. "And?"

"It's certainly a lovely invitation." She looks at me, and

I wait for her to continue. "And I think it's a great thing. You haven't been away from home for that long before."

"I know," I reply, wondering why she's dragging this out so much, and when she'll finally get to her answer.

I can't take it anymore. "So? Can I go? I was going to bring this up sooner, but then I figured it'd be best if you talked to Cami's mom first."

She hesitates. "We'll miss you. But I think you can go. Drink a fruity umbrella drink for me."

I laugh. "For real? You mean it?"

"Yes!" She pulls me into a sideways hug.

"Thank you, thank you, thank you, thank you."

I stay in the hug for a moment, not saying anything. I guess I didn't really need to work on my art of persuasion there. I got off easy on that one—the other things will be more difficult, I think.

My mom slow-dips her tea bag into hot water. She never seems happy drinking tea, at least not the way she is when she's drinking coffee.

"Um, Mom," I say, mustering up feelings of courage and kind yet forceful persuasion vibes. "Um, so, there's something I didn't tell you."

"Kaylan," she warns, her voice rising at the end.

"Mom, remember a long time ago, when you talked to Ryan and me and you promised to be open to whatever we had to say and not get mad because you really wanted us to be honest with you?"

She side-eyes me. "Go on."

"So I kind of did this thing, and I didn't tell you. . . ." I wait for her to interrupt me, but she doesn't. She just sits there. "Um, well. I read about this comedy camp last summer when Ari came home from camp and was obsessed with it and I was so jealous, and I kinda mentioned it to Dad on our trip and he said something like *follow your dreams or whatever*, not paying attention that much. But anyway, I signed up for their emails and when the notice went out to apply, I applied." I pause, realizing I've been rambling on and on for a long time. My mom is still sitting there, quiet and frozen. "I didn't think I'd get in, really. I had to submit a short video. Anyway, I really want to do it. I got in, by the way." I burst out laughing from how insane this is, but my mom just stares at me. "So, yeah. That's it."

"I see." My mom slow-nods, taking it all in. She's silent then, for what seems like forever. Finally she says, "Well, congratulations on getting in, but I just don't understand why you didn't talk to me about it, or tell me you were applying or anything. You talked to Dad, but not me?" Her voice catches at the end.

I move closer to her on the couch and rest my head on her shoulder. "Well, I didn't really talk to Dad. I just happened to mention it to him because he was there when I first read about it online." I play with my mom's hair, trying to butter her up a little, but also trying to be close to her. She feels really far away. "Also, I didn't even know if I'd get in! I didn't want to make it a big deal. And I've never gone away for summer before . . . I was afraid you'd say no." I pick my head up and look at her, finally. "It was a lot of things."

My mom says, "Got it," in her soft, trying-to-figure-things-out tone. "Well, now that you did get in, you're going to have to discuss this with your father again, you know." She sniffles. "I'm proud of you, Kaylan. And also disappointed that you handled it this way. Lots of mixed emotions right now."

I perk up. "So that means I can go?"

"We don't know what this costs, the dates, the transportation, anything at all." My mom raises her eyebrows. "We'll try to find a way to make it work, but I can't say for sure." She gets up from the couch.

I follow her out of the den, already drafting an email to my dad in my head.

Let's just hope he remembers that *follow your dreams* conversation, and that he's going to help pay for me to do it.

8

ARI

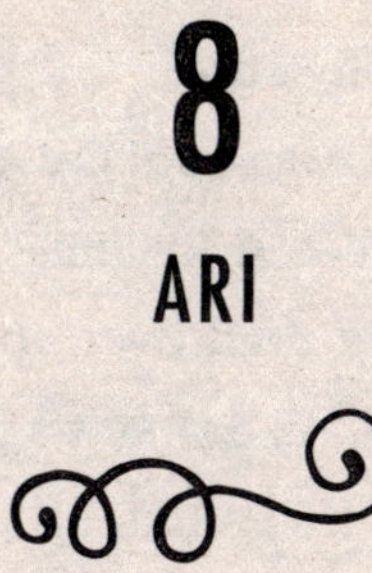

I WAKE UP TO A text from Golfy:

Any updates on the Bubster?

I crack up and write back:

Me: LOL. Cool nickname. No real updates, though.

Golfy: I sent you something for Valentine's Day, btw. I know it's next month but it takes a long time to ship . . .

I don't have the heart to tell him I don't really celebrate Valentine's Day.

Me: Ooooh. What is it?

He doesn't respond again after that because he's not the best texter. It's like he starts a conversation and then forgets he's in the middle of it, and puts his phone down and moves on with his day.

On the bus ride to school, I get a string of texts from the camp girls.

Alice: how is bub

Me: eh, ok. Not really sure

Hana: we love her! And you! Obvs!

Zoe: keep us updated Ariiiiiiiiiiii

I scroll back up and read over chunks of our texting conversations, and I realize that it's hard to give updates on the Bubbie situation. It's like I don't want to tell anyone any of the bad stuff because if I say it out loud it becomes real. And also, I don't know a ton of information. All I know is, she can't really walk. She can't get out of bed on her own. Her speech is all slurred. Her head is tilted to one side.

Other than that, she's the same Bubbie. She still has the same clever sense of humor. She still knows everything that's going on with all of her friends. She still asks a million questions, and wants to be informed, and is up-to-date with politics and everything happening in the world.

On the way to our lockers after gym, Kaylan asks me a thousand questions. "So when can she go home?"

"I don't know. They're saying she needs to go to some kind of rehab facility. But why can't she just do all the exercises and physical therapy with someone at home?" I ask Kaylan like she'll have an answer when obviously she won't. She probably doesn't even know what I'm talking about. It's not like I had an idea about any of this before we found ourselves in this situation.

Somehow with Kaylan, it feels easier to talk about all of this, easier to ask questions, not only to her but to the universe. Maybe that whole honorary Nodberg granddaughter thing is really true, and that's why it feels different.

"Um," Kaylan starts to answer. "Maybe she can. I'll ask Mrs. Etisof. I remember when her sister got sick two summers ago. There was a lot of discussion about rehab and therapy and stuff. My mom was always talking to her about it, but I didn't really pay attention. I can find out, though."

Okay, so maybe Kaylan does know more about this than I thought she did.

"That would be great." My skin prickles in a good way, thinking that maybe Kaylan's neighbor Mrs. Etisof could solve all of our problems.

Kaylan says, "I forgot to tell you. I am going out with Cami's family for hibachi tonight. It's Cami's mom's birthday but she invited me, too, for some reason."

"Of course she did," I respond, even though I'm not even really sure what I mean by that. It's a nice thing that she invited Kaylan. But it makes me so angry for some reason. That whole group just makes me so angry and I don't even know why. It just feels like one of those things that once you start feeling annoyed with someone, you can't stop.

"Ari, what's that all about?" Kaylan asks me.

"I don't know," I say. "I'm sorry. I gotta run. Let's talk later."

"Sometimes I don't get you," Kaylan says a little louder as I walk away.

Sometimes I don't get myself, I want to reply. But I don't. I just keep walking.

When I get home after school, my mom is at the kitchen table surrounded by a thousand little slips of paper with random phone numbers and notes and every time she puts her cell phone down, it rings again.

She holds up a finger as she answers the phone. "Yes, hi." She pauses. "Right. I see. Okay." Pause. "Well, we can discuss it. Okay. I'll be in touch."

"What's happening?" I ask her after she hangs up the phone.

"All sorts of craziness, Ari." She deep-sighs. "They want to move Bubbie to a rehabilitation facility. We think she can get the help she needs at home. There are all sorts of forms that need to be dealt with." The phone rings again. "I'll try and explain later."

I run upstairs to check email and am so thrilled to see a group email chain from the camp girls.

Hey loves. I know we texted this morning but I just miss you guys soooooo much. How are things? How many days are we down to? I need to be back

at camp PRETTY MUCH YESTERDAY. And now it's winter and wahhhh . . . I just miss you. Xoxoxoxo AlKal

Hiiiii. Same same same. Sleepover soon? Maybe over Feb break? Love forever, Zoe

Yes! Sleepover! I cannot wait for this. LOVE YOU ALL BEYOND WORDS, Hana

Sorry I am replying so late. Feeling miserable with Bubbie in hospital. Ugh. They just moved here. And why do I hate my school friends? I mean, I don't hate them. But they just annoy me so much. Please help. Not Kaylan, though. Actually, for the first time in forever I feel like we are tight and things are great between us. Can't wait for the sleepover. Smoooooooches! Ari

Ariiiiiiiii. We LOVE you and we're here
4 u 100% 24-7! NEVER FORGET THAT.
Xoxoxoxoxoxoxoxoxoxxoxooxoxoxox Al Kal

In a world full of chaos, at least there's Camp Silver and my girls and countdowns to summer and a February break sleepover to look forward to.

9
KAYLAN

EVERY DAY, I PLAN TO tell Ari about the vacation with Cami's family, and every day, I chicken out. I just don't know how she's going to react to it. There's so much other stuff to talk about, anyway.

Especially with Bubbie being sick, it feels kind of crazy to talk about a luxury vacation. And it's probably, most definitely, not what Ari needs to hear right now.

Plus if she responded so weirdly to a hibachi dinner, how is she going to respond to a whole vacation?

I hit the button to call Ari and it goes straight to voicemail.

"Hey, Ari, it's me. I was going to text this but it feels like too much to type and I am feeling very lazy right now. I talked to Mrs. Etisof and want to update you. Also, at the hibachi place they had the coolest thing—all different varieties of fruit water. It was like the most delicious thing I've ever had. Okay. So much to share. Call me back. Love ya. Bye."

I hit the end button on the phone, and wonder if she'll call me back or just text back that she's tired and I'll fill her in in the morning.

"Hey." I answer the phone three seconds later when I see that it's Ari calling.

"Hey, how was hibachi?" she asks me.

"It was good. Their fruit-infused waters were insane. Really, really good."

"I don't know what you mean. What is fruit-infused water?"

"Like water with fruit in it!"

"Just floating in the cup?" Ari asks. "I'm so confused."

"No. I mean, sort of. But not like whole pieces. Just sort of infused in the flavor. Strawberry mango! In the water!" I yelp.

"Wow. I've never heard anyone get this excited about water before." Ari laughs. "But yum!"

"Does making fruity water count as cooking?" I ask.

"No, I don't think so." Ari giggles.

"Ooh! Brainstorm," I shout. "What do you think about adding it to the list?"

"Um. Sure." Her words come out slurred and it sounds like she's holding a pen cap in her mouth. "I'm adding it to the draft."

"Fab!" I pick at my peeling nail polish. "Also, Mrs. Etisof said she can walk your parents through everything. She's going to call them."

"Oh. Great." Her voice sounds normal again. "I'll show you the rough draft of the list tomorrow, okay?"

"Awesome, yeah." I pull back my covers and go under them, suddenly feeling chilly. "Ooh, imagine our water varieties are so good we convince the cafeteria staff to have them? Like a healthy alternative to fruit juice?"

"Genius, Kay!" Ari shouts. "What if they're so good we end up having a company and it becomes a new kind of bottled water, but bottles made from recycled plastic?"

I sit up on my bed, my heart fluttering with energy. "Start a business needs to be on our next list. But this ties into persuasion, too! Persuade the cafeteria staff and the administration to add this to the menu at lunch!"

"Woo!" Ari yells. "Fire! Fire! We are on fire!" She makes up a silly song, and then I join in.

"We are on fire," I sing back, and stand up and do some kind of a solo kick line. "I'm out of breath from singing and dancing on my bed, by the way."

She replies. "Same, and I still didn't finish studying for my math test. I better go."

"Nighty-night, Ari my love."

"Nighty-night, Kay."

I fall back on my bed, about to burst from all of our

genius ideas, but my glowy feeling fades a little when I realize I still didn't tell Ari about the Cami trip. I'm not sure if I forgot about it, or if I chickened out again.

Maybe a little of both.

My mom knocks on the door at ten o'clock and I think it's because she wants to make sure I'm asleep. So I pretend to be asleep even though I feel my eyeballs pounding around a little bit under my eyelids.

"Kay, are you awake?" she whispers.

I still pretend to be asleep but I'm not sure why. It would be okay for me to be awake lying in my bed. But somehow I'm keeping up with this pretending to be asleep thing. It's like the kind of thing that once you start it, you really need to lean in and follow through entirely, the whole way.

She sits on the edge of my bed and starts stroking my hair and then she leans down and rests her head on my chest. "I love you so much," she whispers. "You're growing up so fast. And you're leaving for the summer. And I just don't know where the time has gone."

She starts to cry a little and now it's really weird and awkward that she thinks I'm asleep but I'm not asleep and she's crying and I feel terrible that she's crying. And I can never let on that I know this happened or that I wasn't actually asleep.

"It seems like just yesterday you were a toddler and

now you're a teenager." She sobs. "I really don't know how it's even possible."

I start to pray that she stops talking, and that she leaves the room, because I'm not sure how much more of this pretending I can do. It's actually much harder to pretend to be asleep than people realize. I feel like my eyeballs are moving all over the place under my eyelids. And I'm forcing myself to stay still.

She sighs and kisses me on the forehead. "I love you so much, my Kaylan doll. Please don't grow up too fast. You already have."

She gets up, finally, and leaves my room, closing the door softly behind her.

After that, I'm really awake, tossing and turning, unable to fall asleep no matter what I try.

I get out of bed and grab my laptop and type out a quick email to my dad.

Dear Dad,

I want to talk to you about my summer plans. Remember the comedy camp thing I told you about last summer when we were on our trip? And you said *follow your dreams*. Anyway, I'm following them now. ☺ Let me know when you're around to chat.

Love, Kaylan

My heart pounds after I hit send. It's there, out in the open. This thing is happening. I mean, I think it's happening. My dad can't say no, or veto this.

At least I don't think he can.

10

ARI

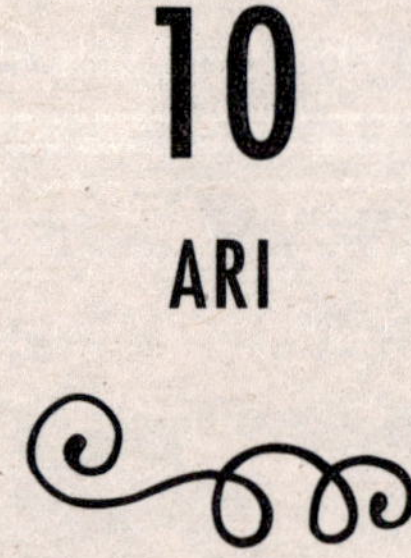

IT'S EARLY IN THE MORNING and Kaylan's on her way over for our beach-themed sleepover. We planned to get an early start so we could finish and polish the list. We'll turn my room into a beach tonight—complete with a fake sand floor, my heat turned all the way up, and our fave bikinis from this past summer.

While I wait for her to arrive, I straighten up my room and flip through my camp photo album and check my email.

A few minutes later, I hear the screechiness of the front door and then Kaylan pounding up the stairs.

"Hey," she says, all out of breath. "It's frigid out there. I ran over but I'm seriously freezing. So excited to feel like I'm at a beach tonight! Woo!"

"Woo," I say back, trying to sound enthusiastic. "Check

this out. I found it online. It's a mat that looks like sand! We can put it on my floor!"

"Whoa, Ar." Kaylan claps. "Imagine if we become sleepover consultants and we plan sleepovers for people? Like as a job when we're older. We can start training now with Gemma and her friends."

"Okay, so now we have a fruit water business idea, and we're becoming sleepover consultants. We're on the verge of becoming full-on entrepreneurs." I laugh. "Would people really pay us for the sleepover thing, though? I think everyone likes to come up with their own ideas."

"Just think about it," Kaylan instructs.

She hangs up her coat on one of the hooks on the back of my door and flops forward onto my bed. "Do you feel like this list process is different because we're older or because it's a winter list?"

I curl up on my beanbag chair, pulling a throw blanket over me. "A winter list. We're slower. Your body moves differently in colder temps."

"Yeah, true," Kaylan replies. "It may be like the coldest winter on record, but like no snow. That's what I heard, anyway."

"Yuck. That sounds awful."

She nods. "You're never going to believe this."

"What?" My throat tightens, expecting to hear bad news.

"So Cami's family invited me to go away with them for

February break to Turks and Caicos. Kinda last minute, I know. Apparently they got some crazy deal. But they're billionaires so maybe they just say that." She raises her eyebrows, like waiting for me to respond. "I found out last week but then I had to ask my mom. And I was kind of nervous to tell you!"

"Nervous? Why?"

"Because, like, I'm going away without you. With Cami." She moves farther back on my bed, leaning against all my throw pillows. "So what do you think?"

I hate to hear she was nervous to tell me something. It shouldn't be that way.

"How long is the trip?" I ask.

Going away with someone else's family is a big thing. A huge thing, really. An experience reserved for special friends, VIPs. This trip could be that line in the sand. The situation that divides the before Ari and Kaylan with the after Ari and Kaylan.

"A week." She sighs. "It sounds so awesome. And it'll be freezing here."

"Your parents said yes?"

Kaylan pauses. "My mom did. I didn't ask my dad. Actually, Ryan said something about my dad visiting then, but I haven't heard anything, so I don't know if it's true."

I shrug. "Well, sounds like it'll be a great trip." I get up and fold the blanket. "Wait, what happened with the comedy thing? Your parents said yes to that, too? You never told me that either! Why are you keeping so many secrets?" I fake some anger, but maybe a little of it is truthful.

Kaylan rubs her eyes, the way she always does when she's overwhelmed. "My mom said yes, but she said I had to discuss that one with my dad. He has to help pay for it! And he hasn't emailed me back yet!"

I scrunch up one cheek. "That's weird. Right?"

Kaylan nods. "Yeah. Who knows? He's always on trips with his girlfriend now."

"Listen, I know you're going on vacay with her, but don't bring Cami into the list, please." I shake my head, almost feeling like I'm about to cry but not even sure what's causing it. It feels like some kind of imbalance where all my feelings are filling up a beach bucket and they're about to spill over. Like I'm having so many feelings all at the same time and they don't know where to go or what to do.

"Ar, for real? Like I'd ask her to do the stuff?" Kaylan scoffs. "No. But, like, we did say they could add some items. Remember?"

"Yeah. But that's different," I reply. "A whole group thing. I mean, like, don't actually do the list with her on the trip."

Kaylan rolls her eyes. "Obv not." She hops up from the bed and hugs me. "I think we've switched roles, by the way. You're like the old anxious version of me, and I'm the old, chill version of you."

"Like an awkward *Freaky Friday* kind of thing." I bulge out my eyes. "Spooooky."

We laugh about that for a few seconds, and then walk downstairs to get a snack, still cracking up about how we've pretty much switched roles.

We walk past the den and see my parents wearing bathrobes, watching some kind of news show, looking at their phones and reading the newspaper all at the same time. Their glasses are perched on the edge of their noses.

"Oh, is that Kaylan?" my dad asks.

"It is," she says, all cheery and high-pitched.

"Well, I have to thank you, and your neighbor Mrs. Etisof. She was very helpful to us in terms of lining up services for my mother at home," my dad explains in a super adult-sounding way. "Thanks for connecting us."

Kaylan nods. "No problem. I like to think of myself as a connector." She bows, all over the top, and my parents and I start laughing.

"And Arianna Simone, I have some good news for you," my dad says, standing up to face us. "Good news for all of us, actually . . . Bubbie is coming home today!"

"OMG!" I yelp. "This is the best news ever ever ever ever!"

I squeeze Kaylan tight and we dance around in a circle and I'm not sure anyone can understand the complete joy I'm feeling at this moment.

I don't care about Cami and the vacation or that Kaylan was nervous to tell me or anything at all. All I care about is that Bubbie is well enough to leave the hospital. That she's coming home. That things are going back to normal.

"Can you drive us over to their place later?" Kaylan asks. "We can help her settle in and stuff."

I laugh that Kaylan asked that before I even got the chance to.

"Um." My dad smiles. "I'd like to give her a few days to settle in before she starts getting visitors. But that's a lovely thought!"

I wonder if that applies to me, if I'm really considered a visitor. But I'm okay with waiting to go over there. As long as I know she's home, and the hospital torture is behind us, I'm fine with pretty much anything.

"Okay, tell us when we can go see her and I'll be ready that second," I announce.

I grab Kaylan's hand and lead her into the kitchen. I exhale a deep, heavy breath I've been holding from the minute I found out Bubbie was in the hospital. She's coming home. It's happening. I can relax again. "We need snacks. Official list organization starts now."

"Yes!" Kaylan salutes me like I'm some kind of senior official, and then starts laughing.

I grab a bunch of bags of mini pretzels, a box of graham

crackers, a few apples, and some mini carrots, and we head up to my room.

"Your mom is cool with us snacking up here?" Kaylan asks.

"We'll be neat." I go over to my desk and take out the notebook where I've jotted down the rough draft list.

I sit with my legs crossed on the beanbag chair. "The amazing thing is, all this stuff just kinda came to us. Like based on actual life stuff." I look over at Kaylan, who appears to be texting and not paying attention. "Kay! Listen!"

She throws her phone across the bed and looks up at me. "I heard everything you just said."

I nod. "Okay. Well, here it is, our most organic list yet. We just need a good name for it. Look."

New Ari & Kaylan Friendship List

1. Learn to ride a unicycle
2. Start a movement
3. Figure out how we feel about God
4. Spend more time with Bubbie and Zeyda
5. Perfect the art of persuasion, especially with Kaylan's mom
6. Train for and run a race
7. Come up with lots of fruit-infused water varieties

"OMG!" She grabs my Hula-Hoop off the floor and then jumps up on my bed, hula-hooping. "I'm in love with our list. Brilliant."

"Ooh! Something just came to me!" I scribble down a note at the bottom of the page. "Let's up the ante on number one . . . hula-hoop on a unicycle!"

"What?" Kaylan cracks up. "*Up the ante?* Who are you?"

I giggle. "Ms. Yelsin says it every time she hands out a math worksheet . . . we're really going to *up the ante* here. But seriously, look how good you are at hula-hooping!" I shimmy around a little bit, all fired up. "We need to challenge ourselves as much as possible. That's the over-arching theme of this list, I think."

She shrugs. "Okay. I'm in!"

"Yayyyy," I sing. "Okay, any more ideas to add?"

Kaylan sits back down and drums her fingers against her forehead. "I need to tell you about my other idea . . . it ties into the persuasion thing. . . ."

I smile. "That seems to be your fave one, I think."

"Yeah, well, I really want to, like, spruce up my house and add new things. I feel like since my dad left, it's just the same as it always was, but we need to really make it ours." She pauses. "I want Mrs. Etisof to paint a mural in my basement. I mean, I didn't ask her yet. And I didn't ask my mom, obvs. But that ties into persuasion." She raises her eyebrows.

"Yeah!" I tap my feet excitedly against my rug. "And

maybe she can incorporate some of our doodles from the last list!"

"Oooh, yes!" Kaylan finally stops hula-hooping and runs over to hug me. "Especially that hot dog one. That's my favorite."

We look over the list. "Okay, so far we have seven things," I announce.

"And our friends get to do the polish, the final few items. We'll pick a day to have them all over and stuff," Kaylan reminds me of how we talked about that at lunch. "But what should the breakdown be?"

"Right. I think we come up with eight, and then let our friends come up with five. One for each of them." I do a quick count in my head, making sure I've remembered everyone. "It's still so weird that Sydney moved away out of the blue, isn't it?"

"Yeah." Kaylan nods. "So weird. She seems happy in Florida, though. I mean, based on her social media vibes."

I laugh. "Yeah, true. Sad she doesn't really stay in touch, with, like actual communication." I think about my camp girls, and what it would be like if we just lost touch, weren't part of each other's day-to-day lives. It'd be impossible to muddle through the gloom of winter without them.

"I know. Okay. Back to the list," Kaylan instructs. "So then that means we need to come up with one more item on our own. Like right now?"

I look over the list again. "Yeah." I hop up from the beanbag chair. "Why wait for tonight? Time to turn this room into a beach! Right now!"

I open up the sand floor mat and turn the thermostat in my room up super high. I open my bottom drawer and take out my turquoise-and-green color-blocked two-piece.

"Um, I wanted to be prepared, so . . . I'm already in a bathing suit! Your polka-dot bikini." Kaylan falls back on the bed.

I shrug. "What else do we need? We could put some sunblock on. Just for the fragrance. I still have some in the medicine cabinet."

"Eh, I can live without the sunblock," Kaylan says. "Just being in a bikini makes me feel beachy."

"Same," I reply. "And doesn't the floor mat make it even more realistic? Ooh, let's get towels and lay them out on the mat, like we're really sunbathing."

"Yes!" Kaylan claps. "Oh, can I go get us lemonade from downstairs? Do you have mini umbrellas to put in the drinks?"

I crack up. "I don't think so, but that would have been great. You get the lemonade. I'll get the towels."

When we're all stretched out, tall glasses of lemonade next to us, Kaylan bolts up. "Oooh, epiphany alert! I know what we need to add!" She pauses and takes a sip. "Now that I'm getting my brain to be in a summer mode . . ."

“What?” I ask, tucking my feet under my legs to avoid seeing how badly I need a pedicure.

“Thank our teachers! Properly. Like in a big, meaningful way . . . before the end of the year.” Kaylan raises her eyebrows, waiting for a response. “Since this is a winter list, and we’ve always done summers, we’ve never had the opportunity to do it before. Could be awesome!”

I think for a second, not really sure what she has in mind. “Yeah, like a gratitude kind of thing.”

“Yeah, they work so hard. This would be really special.” She pauses. “And, like, Ms. Graham—she’s so amazing how she lets us express ourselves and write whatever we want to, and she gives such great feedback on our pieces. I want her to know she’s appreciated!”

I write it down. “Love it, Kay.”

Kaylan says, “We’re crushing this,” and I can see the gears turning in her brain. “Wait! That’s our list name!”

“What?” I giggle.

She stands up and curls her fist into a microphone like she’s making a bold proclamation. “Thirteen Must-Dos to Keep Crushing It as Thirteen-Year-Olds!”

She dances around in a circle, and I stand up to join her, and soon we’re doing a mini hora like we did at my bat mitzvah, only without music and by ourselves.

We fall back on the towels, out of breath, laughing, and we sip our lemonade, trying to get ahold of ourselves.

Kaylan says, “Would you hate it if we had the lunch

table girls come over *today* since we're on such a roll? Maybe they're free?"

I think for a minute, and don't answer her.

She continues, "I could text them to say they're in charge of coming up with the last five, reminding them what we discussed at lunch. I just kinda feel like we're in such a good groove, ya know." She smiles at me.

I think she's right. Why wait to finish the list? "Okay. That makes sense."

I get up from the towel and go to type it up with the new title. "Winter lists may be our jam, Kay."

"It's surprising because we're summer people."

"You just never know," I tell her. "You never know."

Kaylan texts all the lunch table girls, and I finish typing up the list. We lie on our towels and stare at the ceiling as if we're really on a beach, soaking in the rays.

A few minutes later, there's a knock on my door. I say "Come in," completely forgetting that Kaylan and I are lying on the floor in bikinis with the thermostat turned up to eighty degrees.

"Ari!" my mom yelps. "What is going on in here? It's a thousand degrees. It's sweltering hot downstairs and I couldn't figure out why! Gemma is dripping wet!" She looks over at us. "And you're in bathing suits!"

"Beach-themed sleepover, Mom," I tell her. "Remember when you said I could order this floor mat?"

She groans. "Oh, right. This is too hot, though." She

walks over to the thermostat and turns it down. "Way, way, way too hot. I'm about to pass out, Ari!"

We laugh at my mom after she leaves the room.

"What if our daughters laugh at us the way we laugh at my mom?" I giggle.

"They won't." Kaylan's only half paying attention because she's texting all the lunch table girls at the same time. "We're literally the best people; we'll be the best moms, too. And our kids will be BFFs, no doubt."

"Oh, that can be on one of our later lists." I tap her knee. "Be amazing moms!"

She nods. "Mental note. Making a mental note."

I lean over and rest my head on her shoulder, trying to picture Kaylan and me as moms, filling out forms and driving our kids all around.

I crack up at the thought; it's just too ridiculous.

11

KAYLAN

AFTER OVER AN HOUR OF incessant Gemma annoyances and her begging over and over again to be part of our new list, we decide to go to my house for a change of scenery. We bring the sand floor mat and the bikinis, just in case we want to continue the beach-themed sleepover at my house, since Ari's mom didn't seem to be the hugest fan of the idea.

I check my email for the zillionth time, still waiting for a reply from my dad. I know he's always looking at his phone, so I'm completely confused about why it took him this long to respond.

Dear Kaylan,

I'm free any evening after seven. I have to update

you on some things as well. Looking forward to talking to you. Love, Dad

"Um, Ari." She's looking through my closet, trying to organize it by color. "Please look at this."

She hops up on my bed and reads the email on my phone.

"What do you think it means?" I ask her.

Ari pushes her lips out in a sort of thinking, sort of duck-like face. "Um. Could really be anything . . ."

"You think he's changed his mind? He's moving back home?" I ask her. "But then what happens to Robert Irwin Krieger and my mom? They're still really happy together, I think. They went together to see a show in the city a few weeks ago."

I think about how Ari and I wanted to find a nice guy for my mom, and how we put it on the last list, and we actually succeeded. Ari's Camp Silver BFF Zoe's dad and my mom are actually going out. It's funny when I think about it.

Ari laughs. "I love that they're, like, a couple and you're fine with it." She shakes her head. "So bizarrely great."

"Well, yeah, I want my mom to be happy. Duh. It's weird, though, but I think I'm fine with it." I stare at Ari, waiting for her to dissect my dad's email a little more. "So what do you think? About this email, I mean. Do you think he'll pay for comedy camp?"

She bites the inside of her lip. "I don't know, Kay. I wish I did."

I shove my phone back in my hoodie pocket and push all the swirling thoughts out of my head. "Okay, we'll put that issue on hold for now. We need to focus on the list."

Ari takes the paper out of her jeans pocket, and she shows me what we have so far:

13 Must-Dos to Keep Crushing It as 13-Year-Olds

1. Hula-hoop on a unicycle.
2. Start a movement.
3. Figure out how we feel about God.
4. Spend more time with Bubbie and Zeyda.
5. Perfect the art of persuasion, especially with Kaylan's mom.
6. Train for and run a race.
7. Come up with many fruit-infused water varieties.
8. Properly thank our teachers before the end of the year.

"It's really looking fab, Kay," Ari tells me. "And I kind of can't wait to see what the lunch table girls come up with."

"I know." My stomach rumbles again when I remember the email from my dad. "Can I text everyone to bring bathing suits and we can turn up the heat again and continue the beach theme for our meeting? Even though they're not sleeping over. I feel like I need more beach vibes, like, right now. It calms me."

Ari laughs and rolls her eyes at the same time. "Sure."

"K, let's go snack-up." I laugh at myself. "That can be one of our new words, okay?"

"Fab. Oh! And let's make a pitcher of fruit-infused water! Everyone can try it!" Ari wraps an arm around me. "How listy is that?"

"Super listy! And I love it!"

We get downstairs to the kitchen and my mom is cleaning out the cabinets. Like, full on. Taking out all of the plates and bowls and everything, stacking them on the table, and wiping and collecting crumbs. The whole thing.

"Mom." I have to say it three times to get her attention. "You know my friends are coming over in like ten minutes, right? It looks like we've been invaded by some kitchenware-obsessed robber or something. . . ."

"Okay, well, I need to clean out sometimes, Kaylan." She turns around, looking annoyed. "Hi, Ari."

"Hi," Ari replies, laughing a little.

"Go set up in the dining room," my mom instructs. "Take whatever snacks you want from the pantry. Or go in the den, but just make sure to be neat and clean up after. Whatever you girls want to do. I just need to get some cleaning in today. It's essential."

I bulge my eyes at Ari and she does the same right back at me.

"Speaking of cleaning and sprucing things up," I say, hopping up another step stool so I can be closer to my mom. "What do you think about Mrs. Etisof painting a mural in the basement?"

My mom turns around. "Huh?"

"It's really drab down there. Don't you agree, Ari?"

She giggles. "Um, yeah, it's basement-y."

My mom puts her hands on her hips. "If you finish cleaning out the basement, you can paint whatever you want." She turns back around. "Conversation over for now. Must clean."

The doorbell rings a few minutes later.

"OMG soooooo excited to be here for List-Making Day," Cami sings, hanging her puffer jacket on the coat tree. "Have you guys always had like an official day for the list making or it just happened or, um, what? I mean, tell me everything!"

"Come, I'm grabbing snacks." I crack up at Cami and pull a few things from the pantry. Once we're settled in the den, Ari and I start to explain.

"We never had an official day; did we, Ari?" I turn to face her and she's already snuggled under my favorite throw blanket.

"Um, no, we just made the lists. It was never this big of

an event. But this list is different in every possible way. Actually, for the first one we did have the sleepover and work on it outside by the fire pit. Remember?" she asks me.

Cami widens her eyes. "Ooh, that sounds ultra fab. Too bad it's winter. Love that we're trying to trick our minds that it's summer, though. When should I change into my bikini?" She grabs a mini doughnut out of the box. "Where's everyone else?"

"Coming," I tell her, wondering how many more questions she would ask if I didn't jump in. "So, any list ideas? You can get a head start."

"Ummmm." Cami stretches her legs out onto the coffee table. "Like my socks? They were on sale. I bought ten pairs."

"I love them," Ari adds, only a tiny bit sarcastic.

"I'm totally leaning into the unicorn fad, what can I say?" Cami giggles. "Oooh, that should be on the list! Find a unicorn!"

"What?" I gasp. "Cam, it needs to be, like, actual things we can do."

She shakes her head like we're not understanding her. "I know, I know. But I mean, a unicorn can mean different stuff. It could be like a mentor or a really unique thing or someone special or, I don't know. It just sounds so cool." She looks at us, waiting for a response. "Think about it."

Ari and I make eyes at each other.

"Pencil it in," Ari instructs. "The friends are allowed to add a maximum of five things; we already have the other eight. Just so you know. Setting up some ground rules."

Cami rolls her eyes and turns to me. "Since when has she become so serious?"

"Since she turned thirteen," I explain. "She's like this new, ultra-introspective teenager now. Chill Girl Ari is gone for good."

"No way. Stop." Ari throws a piece of popcorn at my head.

"Hey! You're going to need to clean that up," I tell her. "Remember what my mom said?"

"Yes. Don't worry. I always clean up."

Soon, June, M.W., Marie, and Amirah come traipsing in.

"The door was open," M.W. tells us. "We brought cake pops."

"Ooh." Ari sits up and peers into the box. "So fab, thank you."

After everyone changes into bathing suits and cover-ups, we all gather in the den. I sit up straight on the couch and tuck my feet under my legs. "So let's get this party started. Thank you all for coming. As you know, Ari and I are embarking on our third list and we're so grateful you're here. It's interesting to see how our lists have evolved. We started as wee ones about to enter sixth grade and here we are, in the middle of seventh grade. We're old now."

Everyone cracks up.

"Okay, get to the point, Kay." Ari nudges me with her toe and I pretend to fall over.

"That's my Ari, always guiding me. My north star. My comforting and trusty BFF, always making sure I'm on the right path."

"Stop!" Ari whines. "Come on, for real. I want to eat more doughnuts."

"You can eat while we work," I tell her. "Okay, but for real. This is gonna be fun. We think you guys should add a total of five list items; we already have eight. For example, fruit-infused water." I point to the table. "Please enjoy a pitcher of delicious, refreshing cucumber lemon." I move my hands in that direction like the pitcher is an intricate display. "Since Cami arrived first, she already came up with something on her own." I look over at her. "Cameron Josie, take it away."

Cami hops up and grabs a remote to use as a microphone. "Okay, so. My idea, and I know it's brilliant, so please hold applause . . ." She pauses, all dramatic-like. "Find a unicorn."

She bows, totally over the top, and I fall back laughing. Cami is literally the funniest but not because she's trying to be. She just is. "So, hear me out. I don't necessarily mean 'find a unicorn' like the real thing or even one of those giant pool floats. It could mean like something that brings good luck, or magic, or someone super unique in their lives . . . that's for Ari and Kaylan to figure out."

The rest of the group looks at us, I think expecting some kind of dramatic reaction. But we've already heard this so we just smile and raise our eyebrows at each other and then Ari says, "Sounds good to me. Kay?"

"Same." I grab the paper and jot it down. "Anyone else? Any other ideas?"

After a big gulp of cucumber-lemon water, M.W. raises her hand high in the air. "Ooooh, oooh. I have such a good one!"

Ari giggles. "Yes?"

"Okay." M.W. stands up, clasping her hands together high on her chest. "Go to Japan."

We all eye-bulge, waiting for her to say more.

"I mean, you both love sushi, and hello—a trip to Japan! How amazing would that be? That could incorporate the rest of the list items because it would be such an amazing experience."

"How are we going to afford a trip to Japan, M.W.?" I shriek. "For real. Obv it would be amazing, but I don't think that's really in the cards for us." I look over at Ari, waiting for her to weigh in.

"Yeah, unfortunately my bat mitzvah gifts wouldn't even cover a plane ticket . . . I don't think."

M.W. shakes her head. "Okay, don't give up yet. Wait for it." She pauses again, widening her eyes. "Win a trip to Japan!"

We look at each other, debating. I say, "Um, how, though? Explain, please."

June chimes in, "How about just win an online contest? My aunt enters them allllll the time and she's won a bunch of things—a barbecue, some skin products, even a slice of pizza pool float. But you never know. You gotta be in it to win it, right?"

"Yeah!" Ari exclaims. "That's a fab idea, guys! I'm writing it down."

For a second I can't tell if she's excited or faking it, but then I settle on real excitement.

She continues, "Even though I don't know if you can really control if you win or not. What do you think, Kay?"

"Add it. Some positive thinking will go a long way." I widen my eyes for emphasis and take another mini doughnut out of the box. "You never know."

"True," June replies. "I mean, my aunt really does win a lot of stuff."

I nod. "Okay, so what else?"

"How about get lives and stop making these dumb lists?" Ryan throws himself onto the recliner, bringing his smelly, dirty socks into the middle of the room. "And please pass me one of those doughnuts."

"Ry, get out of here. Now." I throw him one. "Leave."

"Fiiiiiiine," he groans. "But how many lists are you going to do? Will you do nineteen before twenty, thirty-nine before forty? If you live to be one hundred, you'll have to do ninety-nine things. . . ."

Everyone laughs even though he's not funny at all. I really don't like how so many girls feel a need to laugh at boys just because they're boys. And this boy isn't even like a real boy—he's my brother.

Marie adds, "Wait until they're turning one hundred and one and they need to do one hundred things . . . that'll take a while."

"Yeah, but it'll give us something to do when we're old," Ari says. "It's important to always keep busy."

"Hey, Ryan," Cami says, twirling a strand of hair around her finger. "Last year, did you have that two days of standardized testing in June? Like after finals. I heard they've gotten rid of it, but I'm not totally sure. I just, like, uh want to be prepared and stuff."

"Uh, yeah, I think we did," Ryan says, and then, thankfully, he leaves the room, not causing any more major damage, except stealing two more mini muffins on the way out.

After a little regrouping, I say, "Okay, so we have *find a unicorn* and *win an online contest*. It's a good start but I'm thinking we need to dig deeper. What are your thoughts, Ari?"

She thinks for a moment, readjusting herself on the couch. "I could see a little deeper digging." Everyone laughs. "Think about the two of us—what do you feel we need to accomplish? What can we do better? How about a little analysis, guys?"

"This is like some backward kind of therapy session," Marie adds. "Believe me, I snoop on my mom's appointments sometimes. She has a sound machine but I can still hear bits and pieces of what her patients are saying." She hesitates, suddenly nervous. "Wait, is that bad of me?"

"Kind of, yeah," I add. "It's like an invasion of privacy."

"True, hmm." She clenches her teeth. "Okay, forget I said that."

Amirah raises her hand. "Oooh, I just got a brainstorm! It's kind of along those lines, though. What about *Be Me*? Like, be whoever you want to be. And really focus on it. Be true to your authentic self, and concentrate on your strengths and stuff. . . ."

We think for a bit.

"I like it," I say, before anyone else adds a comment. "It can really tie into so many things, and also, like, we've realized how different we are, Ari. Ya know?"

She nods.

"So this can kind of highlight that, and we can keep exploring it throughout our listing adventures. . . ."

"Love," Ari says. "Add it!"

After a sip of iced tea, I say, "Okay, we only need two more list items from you guys and then we can chilllll and watch a movie or something. Of course if we change our minds and revise, we may come back to you for some new ideas."

"Okay, well, since I totally freaked you guys out with the eavesdropping on my mom's therapy sessions thing, I feel like I need to redeem myself," Marie says, looking down at her feet. "And I think after the whole bigness of the *Be Me*, you guys need to do something totally crazy and silly. Something to really push you out of your comfort zones a little."

"Oh, lord," I groan, rolling my eyes, and then squeezing closer to hug Marie. "I'm kidding. Okay, just tell us."

She sniffles, and I'm not sure if she has a cold or if she's faking crying or maybe even about to real cry. I hope not. "You know those YouTube videos with the spicy chips? And you have to order them months in advance and it's a whole big deal? You only get, like, one chip at a time?"

"Ummm." Ari looks confused. "I don't think I know about these chips." She pauses. "Are they legal?"

We all crack up. I wonder if Ari's really the funny one of the two of us, and we had it backward this whole time.

"Yes, they're legal!" Marie exclaims. "I'll send you a link later. But you should totally do that. And you could even have a chip-watching event and, like, invite people from school. It could be a whole thing. Maybe everyone contributes a dollar and then all the proceeds go to charity? Like how people do when someone is running a race and stuff. . . .”

“OMG, Marie,” Cami squeals. “You’re way into this. You’re not, like, doing the list with them. You know that, right?” She laughs. The air sort of stings a little after she says it.

“I know.” Marie rolls her eyes. “Whatever. They said they wanted ideas.” She pours herself a cup of cucumber-lemon water and drinks it down in one gulp.

“Whoa, this is getting to be so intense, but in a good way,” I say. “And we’re so grateful for everyone’s ideas, and they’re all great, and we do want to challenge ourselves. I love it. So basically we order the chips, and then they’re shipped to us, we invite everyone over to watch us eat spicy chips and people give a dollar and we donate the money?” I try to remember everything Marie just said.

“Yes, exactly. . . .” She smiles. “So. Yes or no?”

I look at Ari and she looks at me. “I think yes; what about you, Ar?”

“Definitely yes.” She glances over at Marie. “I’ve been wanting to expand my palate and eat more spicy stuff, actually.”

“See, I knew that,” Marie beams.

I laugh because Marie is still so hardcore about trying to be Ari’s BFF or best school friend, but I guess it just doesn’t bother me the way it used to. My friendship with

Ari is one hundred percent strong. Nothing will change that.

I look over the list again and realize M.W. hasn't suggested anything since the Japan thing. She's all cozy in a corner of the couch under a blanket, snacking on some chips, looking like she's about to fall asleep.

"M.W., any other ideas?" I ask her. "Are you awake?"

"I'm half-asleep, actually." She shakes her head. "I didn't tell you this yet because we're sort of in a trial period, but my mom decided that my brother and I need to show more responsibility so we're fostering a dog. . . ."

"A dog?" I yelp. "For real? What do you mean fostering?"

"Yeah, well, it's a dog that needs a home, but we may not be the ones to keep him permanently. We're just housing him until someone wants to adopt him," she explains. "But he doesn't sleep. He just barks all night. . . . I think he's scared." She makes a sad face. "So I'm super tired. I'm up all night, too! And I'm not sure I'm showing much responsibility."

We all nod, sympathetic.

Suddenly, M.W. perks up, throwing off the blanket and adjusting her posture on the couch. "Oh oh oh!" she yells. "That's it! Convince your parents you need to get a dog."

"Each of us?" Ari squeals.

She considers it, but then says, "No, that would be too much. Just one of you. But which one?"

I look at Ari and she looks at me.

"Well, Kay's already watching one of the school turtles so she really has a pet, at least for now . . ." Her voice trails off, and I roll my eyes at her. "It should be me. A dog would be a gift to our family! I mean, Gemma and I have always wanted one. And dogs are healing! Maybe it would be great for my bubbie, too. She'd have, like, a new grandchild. But a furry one!"

Everyone cheers, especially M.W.

"Yes! I am so happy I contributed something!" M.W. claps. "Oh, and add come up with a name for it. You need to think of an über fab name. We didn't get to do that, since we're fostering . . . and the dog's name is . . ." She pauses. "Dog."

We all crack up. Clearly this canine's original owners just didn't put any effort into him at all.

We look over the complete list.

13 Must-Dos to Keep Crushing It as 13-Year-Olds

1. Hula-hoop on a unicycle.
2. Start a movement.
3. Figure out how we feel about God.
4. Spend more time with Bubbie and Zeyda.
5. Perfect the art of persuasion, especially with Kaylan's mom.
6. Train for and run a race.

7. Come up with many varieties of fruit-infused water.
8. Properly thank our teachers before the end of the year.
9. Find a unicorn.
10. Win an online contest.
11. Be Me.
12. Eat one of those super-spicy chips.
13. Convince Ari's parents that they need a dog and come up with an awesome name for said dog.

We finish the brainstorm session, pleased with the breakdown and combination of our ideas and our friends' ideas.

When everyone is upstairs in my room, lying on towels in bikinis with the thermostat all the way up, our landline rings.

"Ryan! Kaylan!" my mom yells a few seconds later. "Dad's on the phone. He wants to talk to both of you."

Ari gives me a concerned look; only a true BFF would know to do this, would know that this is odd, and kind of a big deal.

I shrug it off, trying to stay calm, and leave my room.

"Kay." Cami grabs my arm when I'm almost out the door. "Don't go." She frowns and pretends to cry.

I laugh a little, and pick up the phone in my mom's room. Ryan picks up in the den.

"Hey," I say.

"What's up?" Ryan asks.

I can't see Ryan's face, but I imagine it's a combination of nervous and annoyed, and that he's probably playing a video game while he takes this call.

"How are you guys doin'?" my dad asks, trying to sound chummy.

"Fine," we both answer at the same time.

Truthfully, things were pretty okay with the three of us during our trip at the end of the summer, but after that, they sort of took a weird turn. Dad decided to tell us about his new girlfriend via text message, and then it was just mega awkward. He became super distant, and we haven't talked a ton. He hasn't been back to visit since.

"So, I mentioned this to Ryan in passing, but it's official now, and I just wanted you to know I'm coming to visit over February break. Looking forward to catching up on everything going on," he says. "So please save that week for me. We can spend a lot of time together."

Silence on our end. My heart pounds. He doesn't know about the Cami trip yet. I thought my mom would have told him.

"And Kaylan, I hope we can discuss the summer plans then? Mom says the camp forms don't need to be in until March."

"What do we need to discuss?" I ask, in the most polite

way I can. "I need to go. It's amazing I got in. Remember on the trip when you said to follow my dreams?"

"Um, okay," he says, not really answering the question. "There are just some logistics I want to go over. I think it's better if we discuss them in person."

My throat tightens. I get this feeling like someone is squeezing my throat, like I may pass out. He just talks in this cryptic, spooky way; it scares me. Like bad news is about to come from around the corner and gobble me up.

"I won't be here in February. I'm going on a trip with my friend Cami and her family. They already booked the plane tickets and everything." I hesitate. "I, um, have to go. My friends are all over right now."

"Oh, well, okay." He hesitates. "Have fun, then."

"Bye, Dad," Ryan says. "Keep it real."

I know Ryan says that to everyone about everything and anything, basically, and it pretty much has zero meaning, but when he says it to my dad, it really seems to apply. I feel like my dad is always hiding stuff, always telling half the story.

I really wish he would keep it real.

12

ARI

WHEN I GET HOME FROM Kaylan's the next day, I launch into a marathon texting session with the camp girls. Sometimes one person will write but then no one else will be free to respond and it will be silence for days. But then other times, we'll all be looking at our phones, texting like we're all sitting right next to each other. Those are the times I feel surrounded by love, so far away from loneliness.

Hana's bat mitzvah is coming up at the end of June, right after school ends, and we're using that as our countdown date now. It's before camp starts, but it's really the kickoff to summer.

Hana: So hard to figure out what to write in this speech though. Like how I feel about G-d and Judaism and stuff. Ugh.

Me: I know. Took me so long to figure it out, and now I realize I'm still figuring it out. It's a process.

Alice: so glad I have until September

Zoe: Same. Love u AlKal my bday twin

We text back and forth for at least an hour, covering every topic in the world, and then Golfy texts me.

Golfy: yo

Golfy: you've been so quiet

Me: hey

Golfy: what's going on? Fill me in

Me: not much

Me: just busy w/stuff

It's hard to switch back and forth between this conversation, and it still feels like too much to really fill him in on over text.

Me: too much 2 text

Me: let's talk later

Golfy: k

And then my phone rings, pausing all texting conversations.

"Ari," Kaylan says, all out of breath. "Did you check your email? I just sent you something."

"No," I reply. "What is it?"

"Just check. I'm hanging up."

I type out a quick text to the camp girls because I get a sense that whatever this Kaylan email is may take a while.

Me: g2g lovies. Talk later. mwaaaahhhhhhhh

I open up the mail app on my phone, grateful that my mom gave me her old iPhone and I don't have to go inside to check my email.

Dear Kaylan,

I'm disappointed I won't see you in February. I know you'll have a fun time with your friend and her family. I've left you three voicemails. You don't seem to be returning my calls, but I know you're busy.

My plan was to come to town in February and discuss summer plans with you. I have some big news that I wanted to share in person, but it seems that won't be possible.

I'm getting married.

I know this is a lot to take in. I hope you'll call me when you can. I didn't want to tell you this way.

I love you, Dad

I feel like someone took a sledgehammer to my heart. I hurt for Kaylan; anxious bubbles creep up my chest because I don't know how to help her.

I call her back.

"Kay," I say softly. "Wow. That's, um, that's a lot."

"My mom already knew," she explains. "Maybe that's why she was so crazy with all the cleaning."

"Yeah. Probably." We're quiet for a few seconds and then I say, "How do you feel about this?"

"Crummy. Annoyed. Glad I won't be here in February," she says. "Other than that, I don't know. And he still didn't answer about if he'll help with comedy camp or not."

"Yeah." I pause. "I don't know what to say about any of this either. Seems like all this big stuff is happening to us, all at once."

"Kinda does," she replies.

I look across the street because all I want right now is for Jason to come out of his house with a basketball and shoot hoops, and for him to see me, and then walk across the street to say hi.

"I'm sorry, Kay. This is sucky."

She answers, "It is so sucky. I mean, I know he left. But getting married? That's so official. Ya know?"

"Yeah, I know."

"It's weird that you can marry someone and plan for that to be it, forever, and then just, like, one day decide it's not forever and then end up marrying someone else," Kaylan muses. "I know we're thirteen and we're always having different crushes. But I thought that sort of ends at some point."

"I did too. I still do. I don't think your dad is, like, the way it is for everyone," I tell her. "He's just one guy, and maybe he's a little mixed up."

"That's one word, or I guess two words, for it," Kaylan says, laughing a bit. "Whatever."

"At least we have the list," I tell her, not sure if it'll really help at all. "We made it before any of the big things happened—with my bubbie and your dad and stuff. But aren't you glad we have it? To kind of guide us through?"

"Totally," she replies. "I guess it knew we needed it before we did."

13

KAYLAN

ARI AND I DECIDE TO walk to school on Monday so we can discuss fruit-infused water flavors and try and get in shape at the same time, a simple way to ease into the race training. Since she lives a tiny bit closer to school than I do, we plan to meet at her house and then walk together.

It's freezing today, but not super windy, so I think we'll be able to handle it.

When I get to Ari's house, she's sitting on her front porch, all bundled up, talking to Jason.

"Hey," I say, sort of out of breath. "So hot out today. Right, guys?"

They smile like my joke is only a little bit funny.

Even though we need to leave in two minutes, I sit down on one of the Adirondack chairs and pull my knees up to my chin, hoping that'll keep me a little warmer.

"What's up?" They're so quiet that I need to fill the air with words. Any words. I don't even know why Jason's here right now.

"Nothing much," Jason replies. He's still sort of icy to me, but not all the time. Things are fine with us, but they're not what they were when we were a couple (if we were ever really even a couple) or before when we were friends. I don't really even know what we are anymore.

But for Ari and Jason—they'll always be neighbors. They have a special thing that I'm not a part of, really. Just based on the fact that they live near one another. It's a fact of life.

"After school today, I'm going to shoot some hoops at that new indoor basketball place," he tells us. "So pumped it opened up since we're not allowed to go to the high school anymore."

Ari asks, "Why not? What happened?"

"Some kids totally vandalized it with spray paint or something," Jason explains. "Really weird. And so annoying because Cole, Judah, and I were getting really good. We're going to try out for the team next year."

"That's fab," Ari says, smiling at Jason.

I may be reading into things, but I'm sensing something going on here, an odd shift in the universe.

An Ari and Jason more-than-neighbors thing that was never there before.

"All right, I know you guys have your special list walk today or whatever." Jason laughs, and I look over at Ari, wondering what she told him, and when, and how much he knows. "I'm heading to the bus. Later."

"Later," Ari replies softly, sort of gazing at him, and I groan. "Bye, Jason."

When he's gone, Ari says, "Oh, sorry to spring this on you, but I have another thing we have to do this morning. My parents are in oddly good moods. My dad took the day off, and they're just spending the day together, trying to catch up on stuff." She pauses. "Let's go inside and talk to them about the dog thing."

"Now?" I gasp. "We need to get to school."

"I know," she replies. "And we will. But honestly—we can't pass up this moment."

We walk back inside with our coats on, and I really think this is a terrible plan. But somehow when Ari gets something in her head, there's no way to say no.

"Hey, guys, can we talk for a moment?" Ari asks, sitting on the edge of the recliner. She scootches over so I can sit, too.

"Uh, sure," Ari's mom replies, fumbling around for the remote in the couch cushions. She turns off the TV. "Don't you two need to get to school?"

We nod, and Ari says, "Yeah, this will be quick."

"What is it?" her dad asks, not exactly impatient sounding but not totally open to whatever we're about to say, either.

Ari looks from her mom to her dad and then back to her mom. She clears her throat. "So, I'm just going to cut right to the chase here." She pauses. "We should get a dog. I've printed out some materials about how good it is for all of our health. We can get a rescue dog so it won't be too expensive and we'll be doing a mitzvah giving the dog a home. I promise to assume all responsibility but I will let Gemma help me. We won't argue, I promise."

She stops talking; I think she's trying to gauge their reactions.

"It really is a mitzvah," I add. "And I feel cool that I know that now. Good deed, commandment, right? Or both?"

They laugh a little, but not as much as I expected them to.

"Well, winter isn't really the best time to get a dog," her dad says. "It'll be hard to train because it's so cold out. I'm just not sure this is right at the moment."

"Mom?" Ari asks.

"Well, I do love dogs." Her mom smiles. "And I've been wondering about the right time for this. The thing is, I'm kind of with Dad on this one. Plus there's really a lot going on right now; I'm not sure we can take on something else . . ." Her voice trails off. "Can we reevaluate in the spring?"

Ari looks at me. Technically we have until the end of the school year to finish this list. So I guess we don't need to have the dog right now. We do need to think of a name, though.

"Well, can we start looking for a rescue now?" Ari asks. "It can take a while to find one that is the right fit. We just want your blessing to start the process."

"Kaylan needs our blessing, too?" Mr. Nodberg laughs.

I crack up, and Ari giggles. "She does."

Her dad has one of those infectious laughs that makes everyone crack up along with him.

"Why?" Now Ari's mom is full-on cackling along with me, unable to get any more words out.

"The list," I say, not really thinking, and I turn to Ari. "Wait, do they know about the list? I forgot."

"Um." She scrunches up her nose. "I think so?"

"Another list?" Ari's mom screeches. "What's this one about?"

"We'll explain later." Ari clears her throat. "But can we just have your blessing to start searching for the rescue dog?"

Her parents look at each other. "You can start searching but we will need to clear any dog that you're considering and we are not signing off on this one hundred percent," her mom explains. "We're open to it, but we will need to reevaluate in the spring before we make it official. Does that make sense?"

"Yes, it does." I smile. "I know I don't live here, but I will be instrumental in this dog-searching process. And I will assume some of the responsibility as well. I'll basically be an honorary dog parent."

"Sounds good, Kaylan," Ari's dad says, smiling and looking at me sideways. "Also, Bubbie seems to be ready for visitors now. If you'd like to check in on her after school, that would be great since I have a late meeting tonight and Mom is taking Gemma to the dentist."

"Yes! We can totally do that," Ari says, looking at me.

We high-five and go back outside to walk to school.

"Success!" She fist-bumps me. "On the dog thing."

"On the path to success," I say. "But still a win. And also, amaze that your bubbie is ready for visitors! I can def go with you after school today."

"Fab." She looks at her watch. "All of this amazingness before eight in the morning. Now onto infused water. Ooh! We can make some for Bubbie today."

"Yes! By the way, I already have a page of notes in my phone with different varieties," I tell her. "I made this one the other night: kiwi, lemon, mango. What do you think?"

Ari nods. "Delish. And what do you think about strawberry, pineapple, lime?"

"Ooh, I can't wait to try that one."

We go back and forth, coming up with flavors the

whole walk to school. It goes so fast, and I don't even feel the cold.

I think that's the secret to getting through hard, freezing, less-than-ideal times: surround yourself with a BFF and come up with stuff to do.

You'll barely even notice the tough parts.

14

ARI

KAYLAN AND I TAKE THE bus home, and then we go over to Bubbie and Zeyda's. Their new apartment is so close that it feels like a dream. All those years with them living so far away—a plane flight and then a rental car—and now I can literally walk to their house.

"Did you know that turtles yawn?" Kaylan asks me, pulling her hood tighter around her head.

"No, I didn't." I laugh a little.

"The eighth-grade turtle loan thing is so cool. I hope I can do it next year, too."

I shake my head. "They yawn? For real? Is turtle existence so exhausting that they need to yawn? I mean, what do they even do all day?" What kind of meaning does a turtle have in its life—all day in a tank, alone. It fills me with gloom.

"They yawn. That's all I know so far."

We walk on a little farther and soon we're at their development.

"I love this place. It reminds me of a little village."

"Did you know they even have an ice cream parlor?" I ask her. "How cute is that?"

Kaylan thinks, almost lost in thought for a moment. "Let's live here when we're old, okay? We can have apartments right next door to each other and it'll be amazing." She takes her puffy-gloved hand and links with mine.

"Deal. But does Cami have to live here, too?" I roll my eyes, mostly joking.

She unclasps her hand and swats me. "Stop."

We run up to their front door, wipe our feet on the little lion doormat, and ring the doorbell.

"Hiiiii," I sing as we walk in. "Your favorite granddaughter is here."

Kaylan whispers, "What about Gemma?"

I roll my eyes. "What about her? I'm clearly the favorite."

Kaylan shrugs and whispers, "Whatever you say."

"We're in the den," Zeyda yells, but it wouldn't have been so hard for me to figure that one out. There are only three rooms—the living room, den, and bedroom. Plus the kitchen and two bathrooms.

We pass their blue velvety living room couch and I breathe in their soapy-soupy apartment smell. How is it possible that home smells transfer from one place to another? They're literally living in a different state now and yet their new place still smells like their old one—a combination of soup and soap.

We walk back to the den and find Bubbie in one burgundy recliner and Zeyda in the other burgundy recliner and it's the happiest thing I've ever seen—like a cookies-and-cream ice cream sundae with a trip to Disney World on top. That level of happiness. I pictured this so many times in my head—the two of them back at home together, side by side on their recliners.

The reality of it is even better than I imagined.

"Oh, I am so happy to see you at home, Bub." I run over and squeeze her tight, breathing in her laundry detergent Bubbie smell.

"You're happy. I'm happy. We're all happy." She smiles in a tired sort of way. "Hello, Kaylan. So nice of you to visit me again. How are you?"

"I'm good. I'm definitely on the path to becoming an honorary Nodberg granddaughter." Kaylan sits on the seat of one of the walkers and looks through the big sliding-door window. "It's so cloudy and gray out there."

I think people start to talk about the weather when they can't think of anything else to talk about. But I also think it's okay. The weather unites all of us. It's a subject on which we can all form an opinion. And people never really seem to get bored talking about it.

"And cold! Miserable," Zeyda says. "I'm a summer person."

I reply, "Me too."

"Me three." Kaylan laughs.

"I enjoy every season," Bubbie adds, her eyes closed, but clearly paying attention. "But when it's this cold, we don't stick our noses out!"

We sit there for a little while longer and I try to figure out how Bubbie seems. Normal, I think. Just a more tired version of her usual self. She's joking and laughing and she has color in her cheeks.

If I didn't know, I would never guess she just spent time in the hospital.

And the best thing of all: no more oxygen cords in her nose.

"So what can we do for you?" I ask. "Put us to work!"

"Yeah, can we get you anything to drink?" Kaylan asks. "I make a great instant hot chocolate."

"She does," I add.

"I think we're okay for now, dolls. You being here is all we need," Bubbie says.

Zeyda switches between the channels—watching news shows and a golf tournament and some football game, though I couldn't even tell you what teams are playing and I don't really care.

"You're all recovered from the bat mitzvah, Ari?"

Bubbie asks. She's asked me this so many times already and I'm not sure if she forgets that she's brought it up before, or that it was already a few months ago, or if she thinks there's more to the conversation. Either way, I don't mind. I just like hearing her voice and talking to her.

"I think so." I shrug. "I'm just so happy to be done with the thank-you notes. So there's that."

"I'm kind of glad I'm not Jewish," Kaylan adds. "I wouldn't be able to write that many thank-you notes. At least for my wedding, I'll have another person who will be able to help me do them."

"Very true," Bubbie replies. "Zeyda didn't help with thank-you notes, though. At least I don't think he did."

He shakes his head. "I don't know. Your handwriting is better than mine. But not by much."

"What about your sweet sixteen, Kay?" I ask. "I totally wanted to help you pick out a dress, and get our hair done together. I'd get a candle during the candle lighting. . . ."

"Nope. Skipping it. All to avoid the thank-you notes!" Bubbie and Zeyda start laughing and Kaylan pulls me into a sideways hug.

"She's funny," Bubbie adds.

I whisper to Kaylan that we should go make them the fruit water, and she hops up, and we walk into the kitchen.

"I don't know what fruit they have," I say, leaning into

the fridge. "Ooh, some apples . . . some blueberries . . . and I think that's it!"

"Perfect!" Kaylan reaches a high cabinet and grabs a pitcher, and I fill it with ice and filtered water. We cut up an apple and throw in some blueberries, and perfecto!

"Oh, cups." Kaylan raises a finger in the air. She grabs two tall glasses from the cabinet and we bring everything back to the den.

"What is this?" Bubbie asks. "Are we at a spa?" She widens her eyes, a crooked smile forming on her lips.

"You are, dahling," I say.

"What treatment!" Zeyda pours Bubbie a cup of apple-blueberry water and then pours one for himself.

"You guys want to move in?" he asks after a sip. "This is delicious!"

We all start laughing and Kaylan leans over toward me and whispers in my ear, "They're the coolest."

Somewhere along the way, Kaylan switched from friend BFF to sister BFF.

Maybe we *will* end up in side-by-side apartments in Woodbury Cove one day.

15

KAYLAN

"VACATION, ALL I'VE EVER WANTED . . . ," Cami sings into the phone the following week. It's early morning, before school starts, and I'm a little freaked that she called me this early. "Wooooooo-hooooo!"

"This is for real happening, so soon," I reply, stating the obvious.

"I know," she squeals. "Aren't you so happy that my parents said that since Jane and Lou brought friends last year, I could bring one this year, and I picked you?" She talks super speedily. "I could've picked June but she's been such a downer lately. Hasn't she?"

I pause to think. Cami seems to find fault with everyone at the lunch table; I'm not sure why. "Um, I don't think so. But I'm so glad you picked me."

So glad is an understatement. I'm picturing white sand beaches, fancy dinners with sparkling water in wine-glasses, amazing sunsets. Quality time with Cami and her family, and a chance to really be on my own.

Ari got to go to camp and be her own, different, exciting self there. I never got that.

This is my time. I need to seize the moment.

Plus I need to practice being away from home, before I really *am* away for a while, all on my own, for comedy camp.

"Kaylan, for real, we are going to have the best time ever." She pauses for emphasis. "This one time when my other cousin, Tara, on my mom's side, anyway, she brought her BFF Amelia on vacation and they literally had the sickest time. They were out until like two a.m. every night, and it was fine, and they could just do whatever they wanted." She pauses again. "That will be us!"

"Two a.m.? Really?"

"Yes! We can go out wherever, because we're, like, on a resort and it's totally safe but they still have all these restaurants and clubs and stuff. I mean, it'll be like spring break like for college students but for us!"

I start to wonder how Cami knows so much about all of this—spring break and clubs and everything. She does have older sisters but it's still odd; they're only in high school.

She's always dreaming about being older.

Cami groans in her annoyed way. "Hello! Are you there?"

"Yes, hi. Totally here. Just freaking out about the awesomeness, Cam," I reassure her. "I feel like my mom needs to know more about the logistics. She keeps asking me questions, and I don't know the answers. Ack! Tell me what to do next. I'm feeling overwhelmed with excitement."

I don't want to admit that agita levels are pretty high about the dad visit happening at the same time.

My first instinct is to call Ari and talk through all of it with her and make a game plan and everything, but that feels like old Kaylan business and I truly feel like I'm more evolved now. I can do this on my own.

"Okay, so my mom and I are having a sushi date tonight—just the two of us. Why don't you and your mom come, too, and we can discuss all the deets," Cami suggests. "It'll be fab. Plus everything is better over sushi. Don't you agree?"

I laugh a little. Cami is so over the top she almost doesn't feel like a real person sometimes, but I guess that's one of the things I love about her. "I agree. Yes."

"It's a date, then. Hibino at seven?"

"Let's say six thirty, if that's okay. My mom likes to eat early."

"Fine. Done. I'll alert the mothership." She laughs at

herself. "See you later, dahling."

"Later, Cams."

I hang up the phone and wonder what I've gotten myself into. It's a good thing—an all-expenses-paid trip to this fancy resort. And everyone knows Cami's like a billionaire so it's not like I need to feel bad about them spending the money. But missing this weird dad visit? I have a little slimy guilt slithering around in my chest. Ryan dealing with it alone? My mom having to shoulder whatever happens? That feels depressing.

It's impossible to know the right thing to do in these situations. Because even if you're doing something super fun for yourself—you're picturing others feeling depressed and lonely because of your decision. I wonder if that ultimately makes it the wrong thing to do. I wonder if there's ever a set of rules for deciding when to think about yourself and when to think about others. Like maybe I could find a checklist online or something.

I flop back onto my bed and look at the clock on my night table to see how much time I have before I need to head to school. Exactly seven minutes. Good. I need to brush my hair, get dressed, grab a granola bar, and tell my mom about the sushi date.

I guess that means I need to get out of bed.

Like, now.

I brush my teeth and throw on my comfiest pair of jeans and my gray crewneck. I'm brushing my hair when my mom yells from the bottom of the staircase. "Kaylan, come down now if you want a ride. Otherwise you're on the bus. Chip chop . . . What's going on up there?"

I take one final look in the mirror and smooth the sides of my hair. "Coming!"

When I get to the kitchen, my mom hands me a breakfast bar and my coat and tells me to hurry. Sometimes I wonder if it's really such a great thing to get a ride to school. I'm rushing either way, but when I take the bus, there's no one telling me to hustle. It's all on me.

"So this vacation with Cami is coming up really soon," I start as soon as we're in the car with buckled seat belts. "You never said how you really feel about it."

"It sounds fun," she replies, like there's more behind that thought.

"And?" I ask, trying to pull it out of her.

"It's a bit complicated with your father visiting, but nothing we can't work through," she replies. "What are your thoughts?"

"I sort of feel bad about missing Dad's visit, but to be honest it kind of sounds like an awesome experience and it would be dumb to pass it up," I say.

"True."

"But part of me feels like I shouldn't go and leave you and Ryan when Dad comes, but I really, really want to go." I clench my teeth. "Is that bad?"

"It's not bad," she says softly. "Also, Cami's parents

already paid for this trip. It wouldn't be right to back out now, anyway."

I look over at her, and wonder if I should bring up the wedding. I know she knows, and she knows that I know, but we haven't talked about it.

Maybe now isn't the right time.

"Anyway, I told Cami we'd go out for sushi with her and her mom tonight and we can discuss all the details. So, cool?"

My mom hesitates. "Sure."

We pull into the circular driveway by the main doors. "Have a great day," my mom says. "I should be home pretty soon after you this afternoon."

"Cool. Thanks for the ride."

I walk inside and find all the girls at our lockers. Ari is writing in this marble journal notebook she got a few weeks ago at the pharmacy in town. She's never been much of a journal keeper, but all of sudden she's really into it. We always said we'd be the kind of BFFs that read each other's journals but she hasn't suggested I read hers and I haven't asked. So I'm not sure what to make of that.

She looks up from the notebook. "Hey." She caps her pen and puts everything away, safely, in her backpack.

I'm about to ask her if she wants to go have a quick heart-to-heart in the third-floor bathroom when she announces that she's going to pop in for a little math extra help.

"K, see ya."

She blows me a kiss and adjusts her backpack straps and walks on ahead, and even though I feel like things are great between us, it seems like she's keeping something from me. And I know I kept the Cami trip from her at first, and I was nervous to tell her about it.

I start to wonder if a friendship can be real and true if secrets are kept between one BFF and the other?

16

ARI

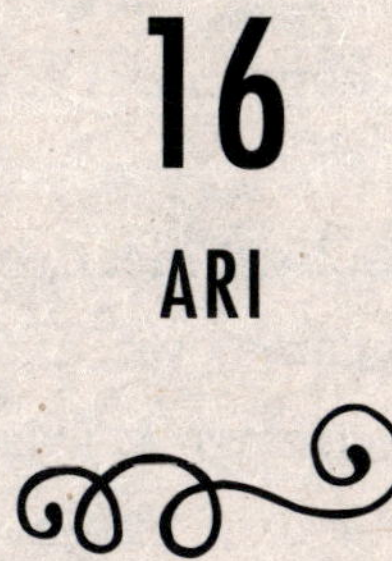

I SPEND ALL OF STUDY hall researching stuff on the list. It helps keep my mind off of other things.

Cough, cough, Jason, Cough, cough.

I'd heard about things like this happening. Someone who's always been around and then that person suddenly becomes someone else. I mean, not literally becomes someone else. But becomes someone else in your mind.

That's what's happened here.

The main question is this, though: Have I become someone else in his mind? I'm not sure.

That day that Kaylan, Jason, and I were all on my front porch together, before school, I just felt so lost. Something shifted and I've been ignoring it. I haven't told anyone. I haven't even really told myself. But it's there and it's happening and I'm going to have to face it one way or another.

I like Jason.

I didn't expect it to happen, not at all. It seriously came out of nowhere.

I thought I loved Golfy. I mean, maybe I do still love Golfy. But then Jason came over, and we were sitting on the front porch even though it was freezing, and then he looked at me and I looked at him and it felt like there were those little sparklers around us, like the ones from the Fourth of July.

I couldn't believe it. But it was there. It happened.

And now it's like we can't go back.

But what about Golfy? And what about Kaylan? Jason was hers, in that way, at least. He was her first kiss. That's huge.

But he was mine, too. Neighbor-wise. And friend-wise.

I don't know.

It's too much to deal with on top of everything else.

So right now, in Ms. Lincoln's study hall, I'm on my laptop, following all school regulations—not playing video games, not chatting with friends, not shopping online—and researching list items we need to complete. Kaylan's already ordered the world's spiciest chip but she keeps getting emails that the delivery is delayed. We're not sure when it'll actually come.

I already found the 5K for us, but we haven't started

training at all. We've already started on the fruit-infused waters, and we've laid the groundwork for the dog thing.

So. Where does that leave me?

Online contests! That's totally a school-appropriate study hall thing to do, and even though Kaylan's already entered some, the more we enter, the better chance we have of winning. I can pass the time during this period and work on the list at the same time.

We decided to make up a fake name and fake email address to use for all of them, so we're not giving out our real information. After Kaylan saw some news segment on identity theft, she got super freaked out.

The only issue is that I have no idea where to start. June's aunt is obsessed with online contests and that's one reason we put it on the list. Well, that and the whole win a trip to Japan thing from when we had our friends involved in suggesting stuff to do. But seriously, Theresa (June's mom's sister) spends an hour every morning entering online contests. And she's actually won stuff, too. Some smaller things like a duffel bag and a set of face lotions. But she also won a free cruise to Bermuda! And a dining room table. I mean, come on. That's big.

I do a quick search for online contests and a million different sites pop up. Contest Wiz, Contest Maven, Contest Bug, Sweepstakes Craze, and on and on and on. So I just start with the first one and I keep entering one after another, all the contests I can find that don't have an age requirement. I put my fake name and fake my email and it's super easy. But what's even easier is imagining all the stuff we could win! A trip to Disney World for Kaylan and me! A whole new wardrobe from Abercrombie!

I'm going to leave Kaylan a locker note right after this period so I can tell her about my brilliant idea. Maybe we can make a pact to spend all of our study halls this way from now until we finish the list.

"Arianna?" Ms. Lincoln is suddenly standing over me. The powerful stench of her fruity perfume seems to be taking over the whole room. "May I ask what you're doing?"

"Uh." Hmm. So how to explain this? It would be awkward to tell a teacher that I'm entering online contests. I'm not quite sure I can do that. But I can't lie either. I'm faced with a conundrum here. I wish I could quickly close the computer window, but I think it's too late for that. Actually, I know it's too late for that. My heart is pounding.

I offer Ms. Lincoln a half smile and hope that something else in the classroom will distract her and take her away from this situation.

"Arianna, please explain. Or you'll be explaining in the main office very shortly."

"Um, well, I'm trying to win a vacation for my family," I explain, not totally sure where these words are coming from. "My dad lost his job earlier this year, and he got a new one, but money is still really tight, and so I finished all my homework and I just wondered if I could take this time to try and win us a trip somewhere. Ya know, like, a memorable family vacation?"

I look up at her and offer my saddest eyes. I can't tell if I'm being convincing or not.

"Arianna, it appears you're on a page to win Welch's Fruit Snacks for a year." She puts her hands on her hips. "I'm concerned. You're not in trouble, but I'd like to speak with you about this after class."

I nod and she walks away and then I just sit there, staring at the screen.

So much for my brilliant idea.

I close the windows and open up a new document and pretend to type something. At least we only have ten minutes left in this period.

I look around to see if anyone else noticed what just happened, but the rest of the students actually appear to be studying. None of my friends are in this section because of the whole honors block system, and even though it's nearly February I still don't really know any of these kids. Might be time to make some friends in this study hall. To prevent another incident like this one from happening.

Finally, the bell rings, and Ms. Lincoln says, loud enough for all the students to hear, "Arianna, please come up to my desk."

I pack up all my stuff and walk over there, prepared (sort of) for whatever is about to happen.

"So, talk to me," she says, reaching to pull over a chair. "Take a seat."

"I'm worried I'm going to be late for my next class," I say, as respectfully as I possibly can.

"It'll just be a minute," she starts. "But I'm concerned. Is there anything you'd like to talk about? And if you're not comfortable talking to me, maybe someone in guidance? Or the administration?"

"Um, I'm really okay." I smile. "It's just that it's so cold and I figured I could maybe win a warm weather vacation somewhere."

She sighs. "I know it's hard here. Where everyone goes on vacation for every break. And they come back tan, despite all the warnings about sun exposure." She pauses. "I digress. I know this is a tough community to be in when things aren't going your way."

I crinkle my eyebrows a little. I wonder if Ms. Lincoln is the one who needs to talk to someone. Maybe that someone is me.

"It's not so bad, really." I laugh for a second. "I'm totally fine. But thanks for your concern."

She nods like she doesn't believe me. "I'm going to alert Ms. Min in guidance, not that you're in trouble, but it's my duty to share things that concern me. And you can go talk to her if you need to." She scribbles something down on a piece of lined paper. "Do you know her? She's a doll."

I shake my head. "No. I've never gone to guidance."

"She's really lovely, Arianna."

"Um, okay, well, thanks. I should really be getting to class, though." I shift my weight from foot to foot. "Thanks, Ms. Lincoln."

"You're welcome." She puts a hand awkwardly on my arm and then removes it. "And remember, study hall is for schoolwork. Right?"

"Right." I walk out of the classroom, finally able to breathe again, but I get the sense that this little episode isn't over yet. For some reason, it seems like there may be more to come. Either with Ms. Lincoln or Ms. Min.

I can't wait to tell Kaylan about this. How some innocent little list work turned into a full-on therapy session with Ms. Lincoln.

Maybe Ms. Min will forget about it. I just can't see myself in her office explaining this. It's way too complicated. And I wonder if the fact that Kaylan and I make lists like this will concern her even more. I don't know.

I'm at my locker cramming for the science quiz, switching my books for my next class, and hoping to find Kaylan here. But there's no sign of her. Someone comes up behind me and drapes an arm over my shoulder.

I'd know that arm anywhere.

For one simple reason.

The watch.

It's Jason.

I whip around and my insides turn glittery. I don't know how this happened so quickly or where it even came from.

Most of all, I don't know what I'm going to tell Golfy.

"Hey." I smile.

"Hey," he replies, moving his arm away. "Want to walk together?"

I nod. "Totally."

"Oh, and I have the craziest story to tell you," he starts, but then I sort of stop listening.

All I can think about is this sudden new Jason feeling. I don't know where it came from or how long it'll last or anything at all, really.

And the biggest problem is that I have no idea what I'm going to do about it.

17

KAYLAN

I MISS LUNCH BECAUSE I have to finish a science test, so I don't have any time to tell Ari about the Cami and moms sushi date. And she's not on the bus home because she's going right to a youth group event at her temple.

But after school, when I'm obsessively studying the Laurel Lake website, I get a text from her.

Craziest thing with Ms. Lincoln in study hall today. Call me later. Xx

I write back okay, and then plan to call her after sushi.

My mom and I get to the restaurant before Cami and her mom, so we sit at our favorite table in the big bay window and order edamame to munch on before they arrive.

"You sure you're okay with all of this, Mom?" I ask, just as our waitress, Meg, brings over our waters. We've known Meg forever, and in a way, she's kind of part of the family. My mom and I always go to Hibino when we need a mother-daughter heart-to-heart, and Meg senses just the right time to join in the conversation and also to leave us alone when necessary.

"Hi, Meg."

"How are things, ladies?" she asks, setting the waters down on the table. "Winter going well so far? Pretty cold out there."

"Yeah, so so so cold. But we're good," I tell her.

She side-eyes me like she knows something's up. Probably because this is the place we always come when we have something serious to discuss.

"Sure?" she asks.

I crack up. "Yes, Meggy Meg."

"Going to check on your edamame." She nods and walks away.

Maybe Meg's my unicorn. That steady, reliable outsider who feels like an insider, who makes me feel at home when we're here. She gets me somehow, without even knowing me that well. She's kind of like a kindred spirit in a way.

Feels a little too easy, though. And now's probably not the time to be working on the list.

Mom sips her water and looks at me. "I think I'm okay with this. I think your father is disappointed, but that's not a reason not to go. He understands what a unique experience it'll be."

"Yeah." I pause. "Mom, are you okay, though? I mean, about the wedding and, like, life. We haven't talked about any of it."

"I'm sorry we haven't talked about it. Maybe we should have." She looks down at the table. "Um, am I okay? To be perfectly honest, I'm not sure."

I nod, waiting for her to elaborate. I want to ask her about Robert Irwin Krieger. As far as I know she's still happy with him. They don't see each other a ton, but they talk all the time. And when they do see each other, she always comes home smiling.

My mom sort of stares at me for a minute in that awkward mom way where you can tell she wants to say something else but isn't sure if she should or not. And this kind of thing is usually followed with a "you're so beautiful" or an "I can't believe how grown-up you are."

I wait for it to come, but she just sits there sort of half smiling at me, like maybe she's not even thinking about the wedding anymore. I pray for Meg to bring the edamame or Cami and her mom to get here. I'm not sure what's taking them so long.

I slyly take my phone out of my sweatshirt pocket to see if she texted me.

Nothing.

"So what else is going on, Mom?" I ask her. "Anything new at work? Seems like Ryan's in a good place these days."

"Yup." She smiles.

"Have you given any more thought to Mrs. Etisof painting the mural in the basement?"

It's like no matter what I'm doing, the list finds a way to creep in. Now that we're on our third list, it seems like it's just part of my life now. Something I'm always working on. Even when I'm not even really working on it. That's one of the things I love most about it—that it really ties into everyday life.

"I think we can do it, if Mrs. Etisof wants to, but I want you and Ryan to finish cleaning out the basement first. You started the process but there's more work to do." She smiles. "So get on that, and then we can discuss the mural. Sound good?"

I nod, and see Cami and her mom coming in. I wave to them and they hurry over to the table.

"So sorry we're late," Cami's mom says. "The phone rang and I got stuck on a call with this friend who goes on and on. You know how it is."

My mom chuckles. "I do."

"Eeeeep," Cami says, sitting down, already at freak-out levels of excitement. Not sure if it's about this sushi dinner or the trip or both or everything. Probably everything.

She grabs my hand. "Lannie! I am so excited that this is actually happening."

"Lannie?" I laugh.

She lifts her shoulders. "Well, Ari calls you Kay and I realized I need my own nickname for you. Does Lannie work?"

"Um . . . I'm not sure."

"Okay, well, TBD. Anyway. I am just so beyond excited."

"So am I!"

I wonder why she chose me. Out of all the people at the lunch table, she chose me to come on this fancy trip. Why, though? I don't really get it. It's nagging at me, but it's not the kind of thing I can ask her. At least not right now. Maybe on the trip, I'll ask. As we're watching the sunset and sipping fruity drinks with mini umbrellas and we get all soul-searchy and introspective. That's what I'll do.

Our moms start talking about something with the parents' association and Cami launches into a whole explanation about the resort. "It has the sickest water-slides. Like literally the best ever. I mean, you know how the indoor one we went to is fine but not great. Well, this place is the best in the world. And get this, you can order lunch on this app on our phones. It's all-inclusive, too, so don't even worry. Get like three thousand Cokes if you want!"

I burst out laughing. "Three thousand Cokes, Cam?"

"Well, you know what I mean." She pauses. "Anyway, it's amazing. We'll definitely have a balcony and the sunsets are beyond. They have a teen lounge with an arcade where we can hang out and meet other kids, but we can always just totally lounge by the pool or the ocean and tan and whatever. And I'm bringing like a zillion magazines. I always do."

"Sounds amazing," I reply. "How many years have you guys been going?" I ask, but then Meg comes over to take our order.

"This is Meg," I introduce her. "She's our fave."

"Of course we know Meg!" Cami's mom smiles.

I get a little pang of jealousy—that other people are as close to Meg as I am.

We order our sushi, hopefully enough for all of us, but with sushi it never seems like enough. And then the moms go back to discussing whatever mom stuff they have to talk about and Cami goes on and on about the resort. I don't mind it, though. It sounds so fabulous and perfect and I'm just so excited that I get to go.

There's a break in the conversation and then Cami's mom clears her throat and says, "So should we talk about the trip?"

I'm embarrassed that I can't remember Cami's mom's name and I think it's too awkward to ask now. I make a mental note that I'll have to ask my mom after dinner.

Cami nods, all-enthusiastic.

Her mom smiles. “I want to answer any questions you may have and, you know, just discuss it. We’re very excited that you’re coming, Kaylan.”

I smile. “Oh, I am so excited, too. I was just asking Cami how many years you’ve been going. And do you always go February break?”

“Oh, we’ve been going forever, since Cam was a baby,” her mom explains. “We love it, and the people at the resort really roll out the red carpet for us, if you know what I mean. It’s just heaven on earth, basically. We can’t wait to share it with you.”

I look over at my mom, suddenly feeling a twinge of guilt that I’m going on this fancy trip and she’s not. I don’t know if she feels bad about it. And I’m not really sure why I do, either. It’s not like I begged to go. They asked me. That was it.

“Sounds like a dream,” I say.

Our sushi boat comes a minute later and I’m grateful for the break in this discussion. I could listen to them go on and on about this fancy resort forever but I don’t want my mom to start to feel bad that we never went on these kinds of vacations, even when my dad was around.

“This looks amazing!” Cami says. “There’s a fab sushi place at the resort, too. But Hibino is probably better, I think.” She looks at her mom for confirmation.

“Yeah, Hibino is the best sushi I’ve ever had,” her mom replies.

After that the conversation turns to other things—how Cami's grandma joined a tap-dancing group and they're trying to arrange a cross-country tour. We all crack up at that one. We discuss the Harvey Deli, of course, because the owners live across the street from Cami's family and they're basically Brookside celebrities. And then Cami's struggles in math and if the school chorus is going to sing the national anthem at a baseball game again this summer.

It feels like it's only been a few minutes, but when I look down at my phone to check the time, I see that close to two hours have passed.

With Cami and her mom, the conversation just flows so easily. I'm not sure if it's because they talk a ton or if it's because they're easy to talk to. Maybe it's both.

I wonder if by the end of the trip I'll be an honorary member of Cami's family, like I'm an honorary Nodberg granddaughter.

A speck of guilt appears on my brain when I realize how much I enjoy other people's families. Maybe deep down there's a part of me that wishes I enjoyed my own a little bit more.

18

ARI

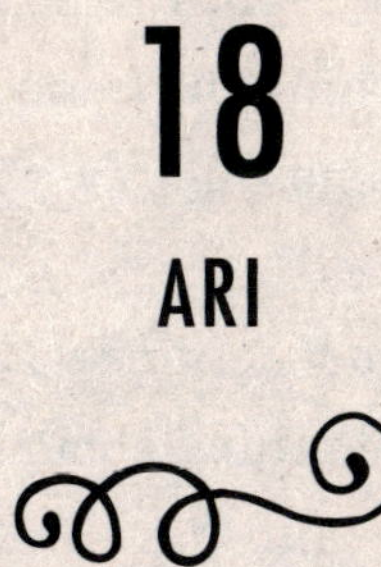

"SO WHAT ARE YOU GOING to do?" Alice asks me over the phone after I tell her about my change in feelings. "I know you haven't seen Golfy since your bat mitzvah. And you kind of won't see him for a while, probably. Right?"

"Yeah, that's the thing. He just seems so far away." I sigh.

I hear a crash and then Alice's faraway voice say, "Oops, dropped you on the floor. Sorry!" She picks up the phone and her voice is normal again. "He kind of is. I know what you mean. It's like we want the year to fly by so we can be back at camp, but it's kind of a long time between summers."

"I know. It's just, one day, I looked at Jason and he looked at me and I had the craziest urge to smooch him. And it hasn't died down."

"Smooch. That's such a silly word."

"It is. But do you know what I mean?"

"Yeah, I guess," she replies. "I don't know what to tell you, Noddie. Do you think the Jason thing will pass? Are you sure you want to end things with Golfy before Valentine's Day?" She laughs.

"I don't care about Valentine's Day. We never really celebrate it—the whole thing about it not really being a Jewish holiday," I explain. "I mean, who even knows if Jason likes me like that? But I think he does."

I wait for Alice to say something encouraging or helpful, but she doesn't. She listens, which is good, but I need advice. Real, solid advice. And I obviously can't ask Kaylan because she liked Jason first. Maybe on some level she still likes him. Hard to say for sure.

"Maybe just sort of tell a little bit of a white lie," Alice suggests finally. "Tell Golfy it's hard because you don't live near each other, but you'll see what happens when we're all back at camp.

"Yeah, I could say that." I lean back against my pillows. "Thanks, AlKal."

"I don't think I did anything, but you're welcome."

We hang up a few minutes later and Kaylan calls, interrupting my train of thought.

"Hey," I answer.

"So this trip." Kaylan launches right into a monologue and it takes me a few seconds to even figure out what she's talking about. "I'm so excited. But I need to know if you hate me."

I scoff. "Why would I hate you?"

"Because it's Cami and I'm leaving over break and the list and everything, and I know how you get, Ar."

"How I get?" I squeak. "Hello? I'm the one who left *you* for camp last summer. Remember?"

She laughs. "Oh yeah. True."

"It's no big deal, Kay," I reply because it seems like the right thing to say. "You'll have a fab time."

Truth is, I'm kind of jealous. If for no other reason than that she gets to escape these frigid temperatures. Plus anything Cami does is amazing and fabulous. I bet it's the kind of resort where they have super-plush robes you can borrow and fluffy slippers and massages on the beach and stuff.

"What will you do without me over break? I mean, we can divide up stuff on the list and keep working on everything, duh."

I pause to think about what I'll do without her. And then it occurs to me, this is kind of a blessing.

I can figure out this Jason thing without Kaylan around. Not in a mean way, like I don't want her here. Of course I do. But it's hard because of her old feelings about Jason. This way I can actually figure things out.

"Um, I'll hang with my grandparents, of course. Maybe see movies. Hang with my camp girls. Read. I dunno," I say. "I'll find stuff to do. I gotta work on the list; there are tons more fruit-water varieties I can make."

"That's true. Are you gonna see Golfy?" she asks. "You haven't mentioned him in a while."

I feel frozen. "Um, well, I mean, he lives kind of far away, but I don't know . . . maybe."

"Yeah." She pauses. "So did I tell you about the suite Cami's family gets?"

I start to tune out the vacation talk just because there's so much of it, and the more she talks, the more I feel disconnected and scratchy about her having this experience without me. I look over the list while Kaylan talks, and then my phone beeps, alerting me that I have another call. I never talk on the phone this much in one night.

It's Golfy.

Did Kaylan mentioning him send a signal to the universe that he should call me or something?

I let it go to voicemail.

I don't understand how feelings change so quickly. How I thought Golfy was the best boy ever.

Truth is, I still kind of think that on a factual level, but don't have that lovey-dovey feeling toward him anymore.

Nothing even happened between us. But something changed.

Kay's still going on and on about the resort while I ponder all of this.

"You're going to have the best time," I tell her again

even though I'm not entirely sure what she just said. "What day do you leave again?"

"Right at the beginning of February break, I don't know the exact day. And I don't get back until the day before we go back to school." She sniffles.

"Oh. Well, if you miss me, we can FaceTime," I suggest.

"Definitely. Oh, did I tell you my mom says Mrs. Etisof can do the mural once Ryan and I finish cleaning out the basement?" she asks. "You can help, too. It might make the process a little speedier."

"Okay, sure." I'm trying to think of a way to end this call so I can listen to Golfy's voicemail and figure out what I'm going to do. "Kay, I need to finish some homework. See you at the bus?"

"Um, I may get a ride. Not sure. I'll text you."

Kaylan never offers me a ride, and I'm okay with it. She's always running late so there's never really time to pick me up. And I don't like to stress about it. The bus may be annoying but at least I know I'll get to school on time.

And Jason takes the bus.

So there's that, too.

"Oh! I forgot! Another reason why I called," Kaylan says.

"What?"

"The unicycle! Let's ask the PE department if we can use the gym to practice before school some days. Maybe the gym teachers can help us learn," she says. "And who knows? Maybe they'll love it so much they put unicycling into the curriculum."

I crack up. "Really? You think they would?"

"You never know, but it ties into our art of persuasion thing," she says. "Anyway, maybe I'll email Mr. Kohnmi and see if we can meet with him? And then you can bring the unicycle to school?"

I laugh. I truly don't know where Kaylan gets these ideas, but it's just so fun to see where they end up.

"Sure, email him." I laugh again. "But I really need to get back to homework. Nighty-night, Kay."

"Nighty-night, Arianna Simone Nodberg, BFFFFFFF."

19

KAYLAN

"THANK YOU, THANK YOU, THANK you," I say a thousand times to Mr. Kohnmi, after he finds me at my locker a few days later. "This is really nice of you."

He lowers an eyebrow, looking confused. "I had no idea you were this, uh, interested in unicycling. Are you considering a career in the circus?"

I laugh. "Maybe!"

"Well, I'm happy to help. I was going to email you back but this was such an unusual thing, I figured it was easier to talk in person. The thing is, I'm not sure we'll be able to add this to the curriculum." He shakes his head, laughing a little bit. "I've never had that kind of request before, and I can look into it, but in the meantime, if you want to come and practice in the gym, you may. But one of the PE teachers must be here."

"Of course. Thank you, Mr. Kohnmi!"

Ari comes in a few minutes later, and as she's hanging up her coat, I say, "Ar, I have a major announcement: we can unicycle in the gym!"

"For real?" Ari jumps up. "Exciting!"

"Persuasion, baby!" I yell, a little too loud. "Working on it! Perfecting it!"

"Oh yeahhhhh." Ari laughs.

We hug and sway in the hallway and we probably look super loony, but who cares? This feels like a big victory. We have a designated unicycle practice space, at least dedicated to us when no one else is there.

"You are certified wacky-pants, Kaylan Terrel and Arianna Nodberg," Marie says, walking up to the lockers, shaking her head. "We love you guys, but you're wacky. Do you know that?"

"I gotta be me. Ya know?" I shrug. "You be you. We be we. I be me."

Ari and I look at each other, our eyes wide.

That saying is everything.

It applies to so much.

At lunch, Cami is going on and on about the resort and I kind of wish she wouldn't. I was the only one invited and of course it would make sense for her to only bring one person, but I still don't want the others (especially Ari) to feel bad. Not that Cami would have ever invited Ari. The thought of it makes me chuckle, actually. I picture Ari being so annoyed with Cami that as soon as she arrives, she begs her mom to find her a flight home. But still. I just don't want anyone to feel bad.

"And there's this swim-up bar. That we're, like, allowed to go to! I mean, they won't serve us alcohol, but we can still sit on bar stools in a pool!" Cami yelps. "It's amazing. And the lazy river—don't even get me started. The literal best."

I look around the table and all the girls are nodding and smiling, but in that teeth-clenched sort of way like they just can't wait for her to stop talking. And we still have a few weeks before break. We can't do this every day. We just can't.

"So anyway," I say. "All sounds super fab, Cam. Did I tell you they may integrate a unicycle component into the gym curriculum?"

Okay, that's stretching it a bit, but I needed something to break up her monologue.

I look at Ari with a head tilt because it was really all I could think to say.

"Um, no," June replies. "I can barely ride a bike! How can I unicycle?"

"Same. For real." Amirah rolls her eyes. "Where do they even come up with this stuff? When do we work on running the mile? I mean, I know I can do it, but I want to practice because I want to try out for track in eighth grade and I need to be ready."

"Well, Kay and I are training for a race," Ari jumps in. "Remember we put that on the list?"

Amirah shakes her head.

How quickly they forget . . . I guess it's kind of a lot for them to remember, though.

"Yeah, for stroke awareness. It's the day school ends. We're raising money and everything," Ari announces, all proud. "You can train with us, Amirah."

I think back to last year, our first list, and our falling out when Ari invited Marie to do the list with us. We've come so far. I almost can't believe it.

"Um, maybe," Amirah says. "Sounds cool. Give me all the details. For the record, I've never really run like an actual real race before. I just run for fun, and, like, I want to be a runner." She pauses, like she's about to get all philosophical. "I see myself as a runner. Does that make sense? And since Kariman Abuljadayel wore a hijab running the Olympics, I feel pretty confident that I can, too."

"Oh, def. This is totally you, Amirah," Ari reassures her. "Join the team!"

Amirah nods, all excited, and I feel pretty good about all of this.

After that, the conversation turns to whether there will ever be a Valentine's Day dance again. They cancelled it a few years ago after some eighth graders got super rowdy and turned on all the sprinklers and flooded the building.

Cami adds, “My sisters both had the best time ever when they went, but I guess that was a bunch of years ago, before the incident.” She shrugs. “What does Ryan say about it?” Cami asks me. She does this pretty often—whenever we don’t know anything. Since Ryan’s only one year older than me, Cami assumes I know everything because he’s been through it recently.

“I don’t think he cares about a Valentine’s Day dance,” I tell them. “And last year he was in that weird friend zone with Tyler and stuff so I def don’t think he wanted to go to that kind of thing.”

“Oh yeah,” Ari says. “OMG, remember when you loved Tyler?”

Everyone starts laughing and I join with them because they’re not really laughing *at* me. That was a crazy, obsessive crush that sort of took over my life for a few months. “What was I thinking? For real.”

They all shake their heads.

“Did you hear he got in trouble last week for skateboarding in the hallway?” M.W. tells us. “He tried to, like, skateboard up a locker.”

“What a doofus,” Cami adds. “Seriously. But, Kay, you have weird taste.”

“Yeah, Jason Klee. Hello?” June pops a few pretzels in her mouth. “I never thought he was cute.”

My cheeks turn fiery. It was one thing to make fun of Tyler. But Jason, no. Jason’s like in his own special category. He was a friend first. I think that's why I think of him differently. Even if I don't *like him* like him anymore, I still don't want them to be mean about him.

I look over at Ari and her cheeks are bright red, and she's staring down at the remnants of her chicken salad sandwich. I wait for her to say something, but she doesn't. I'm not sure if I want her to. Or if I don't want her to.

It doesn't matter, though. She's silent.

"Oh, come on, Jason is very cute," Marie interjects. "Seriously, June. That's weird. Everyone thinks Jason is cute."

"Agree," M.W. says. "I think he's the cutest kid in our school, no question."

"Guys, sssh. He sits right behind us."

They all roll their eyes and the table goes silent.

"Are you and Golfy going on, like, a Valentine's Day date?" Marie asks Ari in a whisper, but everyone can hear her.

"Um, I don't know." She laughs. "That sounds kind of cheesy, no offense. Plus he doesn't live near me." She looks down at the table. Her face is still bright red.

"No way," M.W. says, no longer whispering. "That's like the most amazing thing about having a boyfriend, I think. I mean a whole day where everyone's thinking about love, and you have someone who loves you. A boy, I mean."

I tilt my head and look at her a little crooked. Is she for real?

"Yeah, but it's just kind of a made-up holiday. I don't believe in it," Ari debates. "I mean, shouldn't we love each other every day?"

M.W. rolls her eyes. "You sound like my mom, Ari. Whatever."

Ari shrugs. "Your mom's smart."

She looks over at me and I nod, agreeing with her.

"Can we go back to talking about my vacation now?" Cami scoffs. "For real. We spent this whole lunch arguing about Jason Klee and Valentine's Day. Puh-lease."

I start to wonder about Jason and Valentine's Day, actually. He probably doesn't even know it exists. He'd never do anything for it, even if he did have a girlfriend. He's just not that kind of kid.

Ari shakes her head, like she can't deal with Cami or any of the other girls for one more second, and she pulls together her lunch remnants in the brown paper bag and gets up to throw everything away. We all turn to look at her as she walks away and then Marie whispers, "What's up with her? She's been kind of ignoring my texts and stuff. Sort of out of the blue."

"What? Nothing. She's fine." I run my words together and start collecting my lunch remnants, too. "I'm going to see if there are any apples left."

I find Ari by the garbage can. "I hate Valentine's Day discussions, don't you?"

"Yeah, so dumb." She doesn't look at me. "I honestly

don't celebrate it. You know that."

"I know. But it's cool about Amirah joining the race training with us."

She mumbles, "Yeah, I think so, too."

We stand there awkwardly for a minute until I explain I'm going to see what fruit they have on the salad bar counter.

"Cool. Grab me a banana if they have."

She walks back to the table and I can tell her thoughts are somewhere else. I know something's going on with Jason but I don't know what it is. I wish she'd just tell me. Be honest. Even if it's just a little bit honest. Over the summer we had that whole thing about Total Honesty Friends and Protecting Feelings friends. I wonder if Ari forgot all about it.

That's part of *Be Me*, too, I think.

Plus when she keeps these secrets, it makes her feel far away even when she's standing right next to me.

I guess I could be wrong, that I'm making this whole Ari/Jason thing up. It was only that one incident on the porch, and then her being quiet at the lunch table just now.

Maybe I'm totally reading into this.

Or maybe my gut is a hundred percent right.

20

ARI

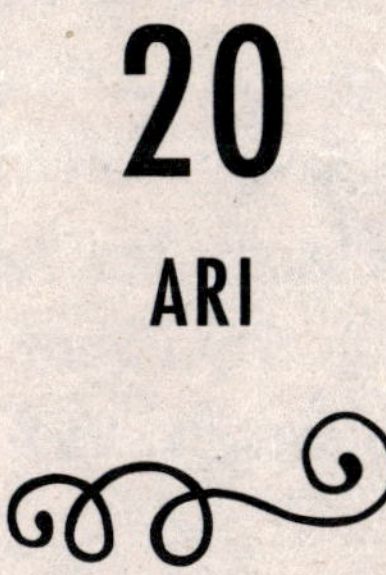

"I'M TELLING GOLFY TONIGHT," I announce to Alice over the phone a few days later. "I haven't called him back and we haven't texted either. He has to know something's up. I mean, his voicemail was literally two seconds and all he said was *hi* and hung up. But I get an eerie feeling like he knows things are off."

At lunch it's been nonstop talk about Cami and Kaylan's trip, with occasional discussions about Amirah training for the race with us, and the others debating if they want to as well. And of course the Jason cuteness discussion, which seems to find its way in every day for some reason, and sporadic Valentine's Day talks.

It's cold and I have tons of homework and Bubbie is better but not quite herself yet and the whole world feels gloomy and gray. I can't have this Golfy thing hanging over my head anymore.

"I just need it to be done," I explain.

She sighs. "I really thought you were going to be one of those camp romances."

"For life?" I gasp. "Like get married?"

"Kinda, yeah." She laughs too. "Like when they have the couples who met at camp come back every summer for a blessing or whatever. It's weird, but that's what I thought."

"Okay, Al. But you know we're thirteen, right?"

"Yes," she says, still laughing. "Okay, good luck with the call."

"Thanks."

I hang up and wait a few seconds, staring at the snow falling outside my bedroom window.

"Hey, hey." Golfy answers the phone on the second ring. He's told me so many times how much he hates talking on the phone, but he'll always talk to me. That's something, and when I think about it, I feel instantly guilt-ridden. He's so good. Too good, maybe. I wish I still liked him as much as he liked me. "Where have you been?"

"Hey," I say, and then wonder if I should make small talk first or not. "Listen, Golfy, I don't know how to say this, but I think we should just be friends, um, like for now, until camp starts and we see each other again and then, um, we can see . . ." My voice trails off, and I kind of wish he'd interjected but he just let me talk and talk.

"Huh?" He cracks up. "Is this some kind of prank?"

I hesitate. "Um, unfortunately, no. You're so great and everything but the thing is, we don't see each other that much, or like at all, and I have a lot going on and, um, my bubbie is not doing so well and I have a lot of stress and it's just too much right now."

He doesn't say anything right away.

"I'm sorry about your bubbie," he says, after a long time of silence. "You never really told me much about what was going on. You just said stuff in passing. I wish you'd, like, told me for real."

"She'll be okay," I explain. "It's a long recovery but I think she'll bounce back. Actually, I know she will."

"Good to hear." He pauses. "I'm sorry to hear this, Ari. About, um, us. But you do whatever you need to do. I'm not going anywhere." He laughs. "Well, I mean, I am. My grandparents are taking our whole fam on a cruise pretty soon. But you know what I mean."

"Yeah, I do." I laugh a little. "Thanks for understanding, Golfy."

"You bet. I gotta run, though. So, uh, keep rockin' or whatever."

"You too."

I hang up the phone, expecting to feel all sorts of relieved but I don't, really. I have a sticky-stomach feeling from lying. I mean, it wasn't totally a lie—all of the things are true. But I didn't mention the Jason part.

I had planned to call Jason right away and ask if I could come over and we'd sit in his sunroom in our pajamas and I'd tell him I loved him all along even though I didn't realize it and how amazing is it that we're across-the-street neighbors and on and on and on.

But I don't feel like calling him. Or doing any of that.

I put on my pajamas and crawl under my covers and fall asleep with the lights on.

At midnight my phone buzzes with a text from Alice asking how the call went, but I don't reply. I get out of bed and turn out the lights and fall back to sleep immediately.

All of this drama can really make a girl tired.

Then at three in the morning, I'm up, wide awake, as if it's eleven a.m. and I've slept twelve hours and I'm totally refreshed. I check my email. Nothing. I take out all of the clothes in my drawers and refold them and put everything away. I sort through my closet and make a pile on my beanbag chair of stuff to donate. I test all my pens to see which ones work and I throw away the ones that don't.

It's amazing how much you can accomplish at three a.m.

And then I read over the list.

Be Me.

I kind of feel like I can check that one off. I've been doing a pretty good job at *being me.* I didn't go to the water park that day when I didn't want to, I told Golfy how I feel, and I'm working on pursuing my sudden feelings-about-Jason thing.

Be Me.

I feel like I did this one without even really trying. But maybe that's the way it's supposed to be. I look over the list again, stopping on the *start a movement* thing.

Maybe *Be Me* is the movement. The opportunity for everyone to feel okay, that they have permission to just be themselves.

Like how Kaylan applied to comedy camp all on her own. That's a *Be Me* kind of thing. And Amirah training for the race with us, wearing her hijab with pride while running. That's totally *Be Me*.

And Cami, um, hello. Cami is *Be Me* all the time. One hundred percent. Cami could basically lead the *Be Me* movement.

I start to type out a text to Kaylan and I'm about to hit send when I realize it's only three thirty in the morning and I would completely wake her up. And then I realize I can't tell her the Jason part. Not yet, anyway.

So is that really *Be Me*? If I'm keeping it from my BFF.

My head starts to spin and I start to feel tired again, which makes sense since it is the middle of the night. I crawl back under the covers and when my alarm goes off at six thirty I am awakened out of the deepest sleep imaginable.

21

KAYLAN

"HULA-HOOPING IS REALLY MORE OF a side-to-side thing than a swishy, circle-y movement," M.W. explains at our lockers. Marie is with her, trying to help, too. "You're overthinking it."

I clench my teeth. I remember being good at hula-hooping a few years ago, but now it seems like I've never done it in my whole life.

"Kaylan, honey, hula-hooping in the hallway isn't the best idea," Ms. Phipps says. People always use the word *honey* when they want to make whatever they're saying seem nicer. It doesn't work.

"But no one's even here yet," I tell her. "That's why I came to school early."

"To practice hula-hooping?" She tilts her head to the side, laughing a little.

Forcefully, but still respectfully, I say, "Yes, exactly. It's like a New Year's resolution kind of thing and Marie and M.W. are helping me."

I look over at M.W. and Marie and they half nod and half shrug. I wish they'd lean in to this a little more. It'd help, but oh well.

"Okay, but when the rest of the students start arriving, please stop. And where are you planning to store these Hula-Hoops all day?" she asks, looking up at the clock above the closest row of beige lockers.

"I asked the gym department and they said we could store them in the big equipment closet for the day. Thanks for understanding, Ms. Phipps. I know it's a little, uh, out of the ordinary."

"Okay, Kaylan." She sighs and walks away, shaking her head.

I put my hands on my hips and watch M.W. show me again how to do it. "See?" she asks. "Side to side. Side to side. Super-gentle movements."

I pull the Hula-Hoop up to my waist and try to do what M.W. says. "Like this?" I ask.

She stands back with a hand on her hip, her head tilted to the side, and she watches me hula-hoop. "Better," she says. "Definitely better. But doing that on a unicycle—that's going to be tough."

"I can do it. It'll take work, but I can do it."

"I love your dedication," she replies, laughing.

The rest of the girls arrive and as soon as I see Ari walk in, I know something's up. Her eyes are all red and puffy and she looks like she didn't sleep a single minute last night.

She goes straight to her locker and hangs up her coat and then turns to me. "I need to go to the library and cram for my history test. I'll see you guys later, K?"

I nod. "You all right, Ar?"

"Yeah, why?"

I shrug. "You just look, um, kind of tired."

"I'm fine," she says.

But when she walks away, the rest of the girls just look at me, and we all sort of shrug at each other, and then Cami says, "Something is totally up with her. We need to find out."

My stomach sinks because when Cami comes up with stuff like this, she follows through. Like last spring, when she was convinced our teacher Ms. Vicks was in a relationship with our other teacher Mr. Nitel and she started following them around to get all the information. She even spied on them at their cars at the end of the day, and kept a daily log of their habits.

She just gets these things in her head and then has to see them through to completion. But the thing about Ari is it kind of takes her a while to sort out what she's feeling and then to tell people. Like with her dad's job—we all didn't know right away.

"Cam," I warn. "She'll tell us when she wants to tell us." But what I really mean is that she'll tell *me* when she wants to tell *me*.

"Kaylan, come with me." Cami grabs my backpack, puts it on my shoulders, and then takes my hand. "I need to talk to you. About the trip."

I see all the others roll their eyes, laughing at her a little bit, and I wonder if this is when and how things change. Cami slowly distancing herself from everyone else so she can be BFF with me. She loses her status as ruler of the group, or whatever it is. I don't even know. And then what becomes of me? I'm just torn between Cami and Ari. But I like the other girls, too. I want to be friends with everyone.

People always wonder when and how friendships change because they can't pinpoint the moment. But right now, I can pinpoint it. Maybe not the exact minute but the time frame, the period when things went from one thing to another thing.

I didn't choose this, though; I don't think I like it.

Cami and I walk down the B wing and she doesn't say anything for a few seconds, until she stops in the middle of the hallway and says, "We need to follow her, Kay. I think something's really going on with Ari and I'm concerned."

"Cam, honestly, I talk to her every day. She's going through a lot, but she's okay. We need to give her space."

"No. It's more than that. There's something you need to see."

I get a rumbly feeling in my stomach. People always say "something you need to see" but it's never "something you want to see."

We continue walking. Past the main office, past the cafeteria, past the music wing and the science labs and around the corner to the library. We look through the big glass windows with the pretty display from the recent author visit.

And we see them.

Ari and Jason at one of the tables, talking with heads close, while Mr. Singer the librarian is behind the desk, taking books from the basket and scanning them.

They're the only ones in the library.

They look up and they see us, and I smile, and they half smile, and then Cami says, "See, this has been going on for weeks. I just didn't know how to tell you. But we're almost at February break and I needed you to know before the trip."

"Cam." I take a deep breath and then exhale. "I already knew."

"You did?"

"Well, kind of. I had a feeling. A BFF intuition kind of thing."

"And you're okay with it?" she hisses. "I mean, Jason

was your boyfriend. And not even that long ago. I mean, all I'm saying . . ."

"Cam, stop." I clear my throat. "We can't talk about this here. And we can't talk about it right now."

The bell rings and we have to separate and go to our first-period classes.

She shakes her head again. "I'm just saying, I can't believe you're okay with it."

I laugh, trying to make Cami realize she's taking this too seriously, but she doesn't laugh along with me. And I love Cami, but it seems like she's trying to create drama right now, when there really isn't any. I don't even like Jason anymore. And he was Ari's neighbor first. And it's just, like, one of those things.

"I'll walk with you," she says. "I have study hall, anyway. And a study hall first period is literally the dumbest."

"Okay." I don't say anything for a while because I'm still processing this situation. I mean, it shouldn't bother me. And I don't think it does. Everyone can choose who they like and just because I liked Jason at one time doesn't mean he's mine forever, or off-limits.

"It's not okay for your best friend to take your boyfriend," she goes on. "Really, it's not. My sisters would totally say the same thing, by the way."

"She's not taking my boyfriend. He's not even my boyfriend."

"Well, he was," she scoffs. "I think you're playing this down because you don't want to make drama, Kay, but for real, this isn't cool."

"Okay, Cam." I laugh again. "I get your point of view, but can we just chill for a second? This feels like a lot."

She yelps, "Because it is a lot!" She shakes her head. "Okay, here's my study hall room. We'll talk more later. I hope it's not weird at lunch."

I keep walking down the hall to get to the science labs and I think about what Cami said. She's creating drama and I'm not sure if it's because she likes drama or if it's because she wants complete best friend status.

I sit down in science and take out my notebooks and try to focus on something else, anything else.

I look over the list and the first thing that catches my eye is *Be Me*.

What does that even mean right now? In this situation. I don't know why it's so confusing for me to figure out my own feelings here. Am I really okay with it? Or am I pushing them away because I don't want to create drama?

I'm not really sure.

I kind of want to ask others, but I think that would be a bad idea. I don't want to bring other people into this.

And when I consider *Be Me*, I think this is the kind of thing I might need to sort out on my own. I don't know how long that will take, though, or what will happen in the meantime.

Keeping our friendship strong is still the number one priority in all of this, really, even though it's not on the new list. I know that, of course. And Ari does, too. At least I think she does.

22

ARI

"I KIND OF FEEL LIKE we're a little bit of a cliché, though," I tell Jason after school. We're sitting on his front porch. His mom is inside making us peanut butter and jelly sandwiches for a snack and she thinks that everything is normal and we're just friends hanging out and it's so funny when someone thinks one thing because there's no reason for them not to, or for them to think anything else. But you know it's something totally different. "Like across-the-street neighbors. My best friend's ex-boyfriend. These are like every movie stereotype ever created."

He laughs. "So what?"

"Yeah. I guess."

"I've liked you for a really long time, Ari," he says. "But then you came back from camp and you loved Golfy, and that was that."

"Yeah," I say. "And hello—Kaylan."

"Of course, Kaylan. I liked her, too, but she didn't like me like that. I don't think she ever really did. It was more of a just-getting-her-mind-away-from-Tyler thing."

"I don't think so." I shake my head. "She did like you. Honestly. A lot."

He shrugs. "Well, whatever. It is what it is. Do you ever notice how people just say that to get out of discussing something? It doesn't really say much. But at the same time, it says everything." He bulges his eyes at me.

I laugh. "Very true."

We sit there quietly for a moment and then I say, "So what should we tell Kaylan? Or what should *I* tell Kaylan? She knows what's up. It's awkward not to have it out in the open."

He pauses to think a minute. "Um . . ." Then he starts laughing and I realize he's still a seventh-grade boy and goofy and silly and really doesn't give much thought to these kinds of situations.

"Never mind," I say. "I'll figure it out."

In that moment, I start to question everything: Why are boys so dumb? Why am I in this situation? Do I even like Jason? Will there ever be a time when boys aren't dumb? Should I ask my parents about going to boarding school?

I don't really know why, in stressful situations, I start to question literally everything in life instead of just focusing on one issue at a time.

We look at each other for a few minutes, not saying anything, and then we burst into laughter. Unstoppable, belly-pain-inducing laughter. And all of the stress just fades away.

This is proof that a human's mood can change literally thirteen times in a matter of minutes. That's not really a bad thing.

Later that night, I'm up in my room doing homework when I hear the doorbell ring.

My heart thuds immediately.

I imagine the worst.

The police are here and something happened to Bubbie and all of that. My mind wanders with all of the terrible possibilities.

But then I hear the unmistakable stomping up the stairs and I know it's not that kind of emergency.

Three knocks on my door.

It's Kaylan.

"Hey, Ar," she says, flopping back onto my bed and then sitting up. "What's up?"

I giggle. "You tell me. You're here at nine at night."

"Right. I am." She giggles too. "Can you just tell me what's going on with you. And Jason. And everything. Just tell me. Give it to me straight. Enough is enough. I'm not holding stuff back anymore, like when I was sad that you were BFF with the camp girls. This is new and improved

Kaylan. *Be Me.* I'm being me, maybe a new me—open, honest, straightforward."

"Nothing's really going on," I start, because it's kind of true. We haven't kissed or anything. We've just hung out and laughed and admitted we like each other. That's not really a ton going on.

"Come on, Ar." She smiles. "It's totally fine. Just tell me. I feel like you're distant and I don't know what's going on. And we still have tons to do on the list. So this is really for the sake of the list. Ya know?"

I nod. "I like Jason. I don't know how it happened."

Kaylan bursts out laughing right then and repeats, "I don't know how it happened."

"What?" I ask. "It's true."

Kaylan shrugs. "I'm okay with this. Honestly. I'm totally over Jason."

"You sure?" I ask. "I mean, not about the being over him part but about the being okay with it part."

She nods. "Yes. Totally. I spent an hour hula-hooping to sort out my feelings. It was a great use of time because I worked on the list, figured stuff out . . . and it'll be great for my comedy routine." She looks at me, and I laugh. "I just don't want you to be so distant. That's the only thing I'm not okay with."

"*Be Me*," I tell her. "That whole thing. I think I am being me. I think this is who I am. I think I'm sort of a distant loner in many ways."

Kaylan crinkles her face. "What? Being distant? That's who you are?"

I sit back in my desk chair. "I don't know, kind of. I feel like I've become this private person all of a sudden. I can't even explain it."

Kaylan looks at me, and sadness spreads over her face like some kind of allergic reaction. Maybe she was fine with all of the Jason stuff, but this distant thing is really bugging her. She looks concerned like she's heard someone got a bad medical diagnosis.

She sits there, quiet, taking that in. "That's hard to hear, Ari. It's okay to want to do your own thing sometimes, but we're BFFs. We're a team. A duo. Ya know?"

"I know," I say quietly. And the thing is, I still want to be all of that. Just in a different way. And I'm not even sure what that means.

"Are you saying we're not that way anymore? At all?" she asks, and I start to wonder why this feels like a breakup all of a sudden. It's not a breakup. We didn't even have a fight. We're not even angry.

"No, we are," I reassure her. "I don't know. It's just . . . Things are changing whether we want them to or not. It's not a bad thing. It's just a reality. So if everything is changing around us, our friendship is changing, too."

"But what does that mean?" Kaylan asks, all forceful. "I want to know what it's going to be."

"I don't know what it's going to be," I say quietly. "I'm

just in a weird place right now."

"I want to help, though," she replies. "Even if you did steal my ex-boyfriend."

I sit up, laughing. "See! You're not okay with it!"

"I am." She rolls her eyes. "I'm kidding."

I half shrug. "Fine."

"Okay, I'm going home," Kaylan says, but after she says that, she stays on my bed and doesn't get up to leave.

"Night-night," I tell her. "See you at the bus?"

"I think my mom is going to drive me again," she replies. "That way I can sleep an extra three minutes. It's worth it."

"I totally get it."

Kaylan gets up to leave, finally, and I watch her walk out of my room and hear her thump down the stairs and everything feels so slimy and strange. I don't know what's going on with me, or what's going on with us.

The thing is, I don't feel like we're in a fight. We're not mad at one another. It's nothing that needs to be fixed. We're just being honest about our feelings and our differences, and I think all of these talks actually bond us closer together.

23

KAYLAN

MRS. ETISOF WAS OUT OF town for a few days but now she's back and I'm ready for some real talk with the best next-door neighbor in the history of the world.

"Kaylan, my love," she says with outstretched arms as I run up the few stairs to her front porch. "How are you, my dearie?"

I sit down on the rocking chair next to her even though it's snowing and pretty cold. I zip my coat up tight and pull my hood over my head.

"Well, I've been great, except for a few things. But we'll get to that in a minute. I actually have something important to ask you."

"Yes?" she sings.

"Well, my mom agreed to this already, so don't worry about that, but I want you to paint a mural in our basement." I lift my eyebrows. "It's not going to be right away because Ryan and I still need to do some cleaning. But my mom says when we finish cleaning it out, you can paint. And I think it would be so super awesome."

"I see," she says, smiling. "Certainly a very exciting proposal."

"I know!"

"What would you like me to paint?" she asks. "And would you want to help, too?"

I pause to think a minute. "Umm. I could maybe help, but I'm not the best painter. I'm thinking something cool. Maybe like squiggles and designs and stuff. Or maybe our street. Or maybe the Brookside Pool. Who knows? Something fab, though."

"Oh, it will be fab." Mrs. Etisof laughs. "You'll let me know if you think of any other ideas, okay?"

"Totally." I smile.

"So what else can I do for you, my dear?" She picks up her mug of tea and takes a sip. I don't know how she's still sitting out here. I am freezing down to my bones. My teeth are chattering.

"I think Ari loves Jason now," I tell her. "What should I do? I don't think I love Jason. I don't even think I care that much. But Cami keeps making it seem like it's such a big deal, like I'm supposed to be upset, so I don't really know."

Mrs. Etisof slow-nods like she's thinking everything over. "I see."

We sit there quietly for a while and the only thing on my mind is when I can suggest that we go inside.

"Kaylan, may I offer some advice?" Mrs. Etisof asks finally.

I nod. My teeth chatter but I try to quiet them.

"Trust your feelings. If you're not bothered by it, that's okay. It seems to me that some people, like your friend Cami, maybe, like to make trouble. Which is okay. But you don't need to make trouble, too."

I giggle. "Yeah. Very true."

"You know what people mean when they say 'trust your gut'?"

I wobble my head from side to side. "I think so."

"So that's just it," she tells me. "Trust your gut."

"Got it." I smile. "I have to go, Mrs. Etisof. You're not freezing out here?"

"Not a bit. But go. Let's talk soon about the mural."

I nod. "Thank you so much."

I run down the steps and back to my house and sigh with relief when I'm back in the warmth. I have no idea how Mrs. Etisof sits outside in this frigid air. Was she raised in an igloo or something? I don't get it.

"How's Mrs. Etisof?" my mom asks when I'm in the kitchen, scanning the pantry for a snack. "I think it's so lovely that you two are friends. Were you telling her about the mural?"

"Yeah. She's excited. We still need to decide what it's going to be, though."

"Do I get any say in the matter?" My mom looks up from her magazine. "Also, the basement doesn't appear to be cleaned out yet. . . ."

"I know. Working on it." I shrug. "Okay, I'm going to study."

"Good."

When I'm back up in my room, I see that I have a string of texts from Ari. I didn't even realize I'd left my phone at home. That's how involved I was in the Mrs. Etisof conversation. Actually, that's how cold I was. Too cold to take my fingers out of my gloves to try and find my phone.

Ari: Want to go see my grandparents?

Ari: My mom can drive us.

Ari: For the list, I mean.

Ari: And for fun.

Ari: LOL

These texts came in twenty minutes ago. I wonder if she already went over there.

Me: Was talking to Mrs. E about the mural.

Me: Are you still home?

Me: I'll come visit them!

Me: LMK

No response from Ari. I guess she's already over there. I hate to miss a list opportunity, especially since I'm going to miss a big chunk of time over break.

I run back down the stairs. “Mom, can you drive me to Woodbury Cove?”

“You have a friend who lives here now?” my mom asks, confused. It’s a sixty-and-over retirement community and everyone knows that.

I crack up, imagining all those people in my classes and the cafeteria. It could be kind of fun, actually.

“No, Ari’s grandparents. We said we were going to hang with them more since they live close by now and I think Ari already went over there.”

My mom still looks very confused. “Um, okay. You’re already done studying?”

“Yeah, I’m going to crush this history test,” I reassure her.

My mom sighs. “Well, I can’t say no to visiting grandparents. Let me get my stuff together. Give me five minutes.”

We drive over there and every few seconds, my mom looks at me sideways like she’s about to say something but then decides not to. This seems to be happening a lot lately.

“Okay, so you’ll call me when you’re ready to be picked up? Or you’ll get a ride with Ari?” she asks as we pull up in front of their condo. “They really do live close by now. How wonderful.”

"Yup. And yup." I lean over and kiss her on the cheek. "Thanks for the ride."

"Kay, can I ask you something?" she says as I'm almost out of the car, doing that classic mom thing where they start conversations at the absolute worst times.

"Yes." I try not to groan.

"Never mind, I'll ask later." She looks away.

"What is it, Mom?"

She smiles. "Nothing. Seriously. Talk later. Love you. Bye." She runs all of her words together, trying to be funny. I close the car door and walk up the path to Ari's grandparents' house.

No one answers. For like ten minutes. I don't know if I should keep ringing the doorbell. Maybe they're sleeping. Or maybe they can't hear the doorbell. Or maybe they've fallen and they're on the floor. My heart starts to pound. This was a mistake. I shouldn't have come here alone. I don't even know if Ari's visiting them right now. And they don't know me *that* well. I have no clue what I was thinking. Sometimes I do the absolute dumbest stuff. I mean, *Loyal to the List*, to a point. I take it too far.

I'm about to walk away and sit on the bench in front of their building even though it's three degrees outside, when someone answers the door. Someone I don't know.

"Hi, um, I'm Kaylan. I came to visit, uh—" I hesitate because I suddenly can't remember their names. I don't even know what's happening right now.

"Come in, come in," the lady at the door says.

I walk down the hallway of their apartment and all of the art is hung on the walls. There are a zillion pictures of Ari and Gemma through the years. With teeth, without teeth, eating ice cream, awkward school photos, even some from Ari's bat mitzvah already framed.

"Who's there?" Ari's bubbie asks, sounding like we're in the middle of a knock-knock joke.

"Oh, um." I laugh. "It's Kaylan. Hi!" I keep walking and when I get back to the den, I notice that Ari's not here. It's just Bubbie in one recliner and Zeyda in another watching an episode of *Judge Judy*.

"Kaylan, what a surprise," Bubbie says, all cheerful. "Come sit. Pull over a walker." She laughs at herself.

I pull over the blue one with the fluffy seat and sit down, facing the TV because it's hard to turn away from Judge Judy. She kind of has a commanding presence.

"How are you guys doing?" I ask, my voice catching a little. It's awkward to be here and talk to them without Ari. I mean, I know them. But not that well. They always lived far away. Maybe she's in the bathroom?

"Eh, we're doing." Bubbie smiles. "We're walking; well, he is." She points to Zeyda. "We're both talking and squawking."

I crack up.

"I don't know how well we're doing any of it. But we're doing it." She sighs. "And how are you?"

"Um, I'm good." I laugh for no real reason other than my awkward levels being at an all-time high. "School is school. And it's freezing. But ya know? It's good."

"Oh, it's so cold," Bubbie says. "We're not sticking our noses out there."

"You're lucky," I say. "I wouldn't either. But I'm forced to go to school. By, like, the government, I guess."

Zeyda laughs a deep, throaty laugh.

"You're funny," Bubbie adds.

"Actually, I have some good news," I say, sensing that they could use some cheering up. "I got accepted to this comedy camp for the summer. I applied totally secretly, I didn't even tell my parents or Ari or anyone, but I got in!"

"How wonderful!" Bubbie exclaims, her voice rising at the end.

"Yeah, it's at this camp called Laurel Lake." I pause. "I honestly can't wait."

Bubbie sits there smiling as I go on and on about the program.

"I loved camp," Bubbie adds. "It was my favorite time of the year! It meant I could get away from everyone at home, really be myself." She laughs.

"I think that's how Ari felt, too, when she went to camp last summer." I pause. "Maybe we all have our home selves and our camp selves."

She nods. "Maybe. I think you're onto something, Kaylan."

It's quiet after that, but I kind of want to keep talking. They're such great listeners—they sit quietly and smile and laugh at all the right spots. It's something I never realized before—how good it feels to share your good news with someone. It's like a built-in way to make someone happy.

"So is Ari here? Or was she here today?" I ask, when all we've heard is Judge Judy for what feels like way too long.

"She was going to come," Bubbie says, "but then I think her mother got involved in something and it was too cold to walk."

I nod. "Oh, okay."

I start to wonder how long I should stay or if I should text Ari that I'm here, but maybe they'd see that as rude. I stare at the cordless phone, praying that Ari calls or her mom or Gemma or someone, so they can know I'm here and maybe join me. The clock on the wall chirps—some kind of bird sound that I can't identify. Each hour is a different bird.

"So lovely of you to come see us," Bubbie adds. "And thank you for sharing your good news! I hope you don't mind if we fall asleep. Don't take it personally. We don't sleep at night, so sometimes we doze off."

“No problem. I totally get it.” I laugh.

“I still can’t get over everything you did for Ari’s bat mitzvah,” she continues. “It was really remarkable.”

“Oh, it wasn’t that much.”

“No, I mean it. It was very special. There aren’t many people who would go to that effort for a friend.” She nods for emphasis. “You’re something special, Kaylan.”

All of a sudden, I’m choked up. I’m about to get up out of this walker and lean down and hug her in the recliner, but maybe that would be too much. It’s so important to be seen. I don’t think we even realize it all the time, or even realize it until it happens, but then when we are recognized and appreciated, we realize how much we’ve needed it all along.

My friendship with Ari is literally the most special thing in the world to me; it just feels so good for someone else to see that, too.

“Thank you so much for saying that, um, Helen.” I remembered her name. Finally! It feels like a major victory.

“Oh, call me Bubbie. You’re a granddaughter to me like Ari and Gemma. I only have two so I’m happy to have one more.”

“You can call me whatever you want,” Zeyda adds. “Just don’t call me late for breakfast.”

I burst out laughing. I’m not sure if he means call him

by the name “late for breakfast” or call him too late to come to breakfast.

But either way, it’s the funniest thing I’ve heard in forever.

24

ARI

"WAIT, WHAT?" I ASK KAYLAN over the phone.

"I went to visit Bub and Zeyda," she says, laughing. "I thought you were there because you said you were going but then I didn't hear from you, so I went anyway because Loyal to the List, ya know? And then you weren't there. But I hung out for a while, anyway."

I crack up. "For real?"

"Yes! And it was awesome," she says. "They're the best. I even told them about comedy camp, and they were so psyched! I'm jealous that I don't have grandparents."

"They are the best. But you have Mrs. Etisof," I remind her.

"That's true."

I ask, "How did Bubbie seem today? My mom was going to take me over but then she got busy with this planning meeting for the parents' association and we never made it."

"Oh." I pause and flip my hair over to pull it up into a bun. "Honestly, it was kind of fun to be there on my own. I mean, it was super awkward at first but then it was fun."

"Love it," I reply. "So you're all ready for the trip? It's so soon."

"Yeah," she says. "I started packing. But can you come over one day soon and help me decide on bathing suits? I don't think I need fifteen for an eight-day trip."

"I still can't believe you own fifteen bathing suits and still borrow mine sometimes."

She laughs again.

"I'll help." I pause. "So you're okay about this Jason thing?"

"I think so," she says. "Is it weird that I'm so fine with it?"

"Not really," I add. "I think part of being thirteen is changing our minds a ton. Like I just thought I was in love with Golfy and now I'm totally not. And you liked Jason and now you don't at all. It's just the way life goes these days."

"You're right. Well, I'm glad we're on the same page."

"I think we're really on our way with *Be Me*, and we're pretty good with the infused water. We have like a zillion varieties. I'll email you the list." I take a sip. "I'm drinking some raspberry lemon right now. And we're getting to school early tomorrow to practice with the unicycle and the Hula-Hoop right?"

"Right. My mom will pick you up. And when we're back from February break, we'll keep doing our unicycle practice in the gym, so that will help."

"Fab," I tell her. "I snuggle up under my covers and look out the window, across the street to Jason's house. From this angle, I have a perfect view of him, in his room, sitting at his desk playing some kind of handheld video game.

It's the easiest thing in the world to have a crush on the boy across the street. It's so easy to just do a quick snoop here and there, to know what he's up to, without even really trying.

I keep watching him across the street while Kaylan goes on and on about the unicycle and then about Cami and the resort and her family.

"I can't believe I won't be there when my dad comes to visit," she says, and I refocus. "I wish I could send you over to my house for some reason, so you can snoop and tell me what's happening."

"I'll go." I pause. "Oh, wait! I can bring over some fruit water. For them to sample? Would that be weird?"

"Um, kinda? Maybe. Maybe not?" She laughs. "I'm not sure. We might need a better reason. Maybe you forgot something and need to pick it up."

"That could work."

She sighs. "Ugh, it's like I don't really want to be there for it, but I also don't want to not be there for it."

"Yeah. I know what you mean," I reply. "Well, I'll go over there if you want. Or at the very least spy on them from your back deck." I look over at Jason's house again. "I'm very good at spying. Do you think that means I should become a private eye when I get older?"

"Definitely a possibility." She laughs. "Okay, I gotta go finish homework since I spent so long at your grandparents' house. We'll be over to get you around seven fifteen so we have lots of time to practice unicycling."

"Great. Nighty-night."

"Nighty-night."

I stay on my bed for a while after that, watching Jason across the street and thinking about Kaylan and her dad and her Cami trip.

I send Kaylan an email with the waters we've come up with so far:

Ari and Kaylan's Fruit-Infused Water Varieties:
Raspberry lemon
Kiwi strawberry
Pear apple peach
Cucumber mint
Cucumber lemon
Strawberry peach

Orange

Lemon lime

My phone buzzes a few minutes later, an ongoing group text chain with my camp girls.

Zoe: so golfy and ari are no more? Officially?

Alice: Ari?

Me: It's true. Don't hate.

Hana: why would we hate?

Me: IDK

Zoe: only love from us to you

Alice: obvvvvvvvv

Me: LOL. Ok.

We text on and on for hours about nothing, but I laugh out loud a zillion times and it feels like I'm with them. Like we're all sitting on the bunk floor eating snacks and cracking up and talking about nothing and everything all at once.

I glance over the list.

Find a unicorn.

I think about it for a minute, but no.

The Camp Silver girls are special; they're magic, really. But a unicorn is something even more than that.

25

KAYLAN

WE PICK ARI UP AND she runs out to the car the fastest I've ever seen her run in the whole time I've known her. Maybe she will really be amazing at the race we're doing.

"So cold. So cold," she says over and over again. "Thank you for picking me up."

"Of course," my mom replies. "I'll put on your seat warmer. That was one of the most exciting things when I first got this car. To discover we have seat warmers in the front and the back! Incredible!"

"You'll be warm and toasty in no time, Ar," I reassure her.

My mom asks, "How are your grandparents doing? I haven't gotten an update from your mom in a few weeks. Must be so nice to have them close by."

"It is," Ari says. "But my bubbie's not one hundred

percent right. Did you hear she had a stroke?"

"I did."

"It seems like it's taking longer than normal for her to be walking around and stuff like she usually does."

"It takes time," my mom reassures her. "But having you all close will be healing for sure."

I peek at Ari in the backseat, kind of wishing we weren't in this conversation. I don't want Ari to get upset in the car.

She smiles and says, "I think so, too."

We get to school and hop out of the car and run inside as quickly as possible. "It's seriously colder than I can even really comprehend," Ari says. "Like we don't live in Alaska. How is it honestly this cold?"

"You need to move to a warm climate when you're older," I tell her. "Maybe for our fifty-nine before sixty list." I burst out laughing. "OMG, that one will be 'sit on rocking chairs every day,' 'drink tea.'" I fall on the floor laughing and Ari does too.

She says, "For our eighty-nine before ninety list, we can add: walker races!"

We crack up, unable to control ourselves, and when we finally do, Ari says, "Our next list should have a thing on it that says 'make another list' and on and on and on." She bursts out laughing again.

"I think so, too!" My cheeks hurt from laughing so much. "Okay, let's go to the gym. We lost a good five minutes with that laugh-fest."

"But it was worth it," Ari replies.

We walk over to the gym with our arms around each other, but I stop in the middle of the hallway because I realize something I forgot to tell her. "Mrs. Etisof. I think she may be my unicorn."

"Really?" Ari asks.

"Yeah, that one person who's not related to you and doesn't have to love you but gives you advice when you need it and helps and is always there for you." I pause. "What do you think?"

She thinks for a second. "Could be. I don't know. Don't just be grasping at stuff because you feel like you need to fulfill this list thing. We have time. We can wait it out until we know for sure about the unicorn." She hesitates like something just dawned on her. "Wait, do we need to have the same unicorn?"

"Um. I don't think so."

"Me neither."

"Want to hear a joke?" I ask her.

She nods.

I crack up before I even start the joke. "What's the difference between a well-dressed man on a unicycle and a poorly dressed man on a bike?"

"What?" Ari asks

"Attire!" I burst out laughing again.

"Oh, Kaylan." Ari shakes her head. "That wasn't one of

your best, but definitely fitting for the situation."

"I thought it was so funny! It popped up when I was searching for unicycles online."

We get to the gym and the new student teacher, Ms. Gidlitz, is there, filling in for Mr. Kohnmi today.

"Hi, girls," she says, all cheerful.

"Hi!" Ari and I say at the same time.

"Do you have any unicycling experience?" she asks us.

"Not yet," Ari replies. "But we're ready to become experts. Do you have unicycling experience?"

"No." She laughs. "But I'm here to help."

"And this is actually just step one of our mission," I explain. "We really want to learn how to hula-hoop on a unicycle."

"Interesting. Well, let's get started."

She grabs our unicycle from the closet, and I'm grateful she's letting us store it here. And then she hands us a printout from the International Unicycling Federation. That's really a thing that exists.

"Read this first," she tells us. "You have to be prepared to fall at first. That's basically the gist of it."

"That's the basic gist of life, too," Ari adds, completely serious. "Don't you think?"

Ms. Gidlitz thinks about it. "I do. I agree with that."

I try to get on first, and Ms. Gidlitz shows me how to get on from the side, the way you would with a bicycle, and where to put my feet on the pedals.

Ms. Gidlitz explains, "From what I know about unicycling, which isn't much, I'll admit, is that it's going to feel weird at first but eventually you will get the hang of it. Stick with it."

"That metaphor applies to life, too," Ari adds.

"You're a deep thinker," Ms. Gidlitz says.

"She is," I add. "Very deep."

"Lean forward. Start pedaling! Go with it," Ms. Gidlitz instructs.

"Don't look at me," I tell Ari through my teeth. "Ar, if you look at me I will fall."

"I'm not looking at you," she yelps.

I stay up for a good minute and a half, I think. It felt like a really long time, but based on when I looked at the gym clock before and when I'm looking at it now, I realize it was only a minute and a half.

After that, Ari goes, and I have to say—I think she learned from watching me go first. She's not as wobbly getting on, and she's able to stay up for over two minutes.

"Ari!" I yelp. "You're practically a pro."

"Yeah, right." She cracks up.

"Great start, girls," Ms. Gidlitz says. "Really great!"

"Thanks for your support," I tell her. "We're going to try and come a lot in the mornings if we can, and then we'll resume after break, for sure."

"Sounds good. It would be cool if we end up offering this as a PE elective. This school is open to ideas and suggestions, which is rare and very wonderful, but it's not a guarantee." She looks at us, all serious. "You know that, right?"

"Yeah. Okay, bye; thanks, Ms. Gidlitz," Ari adds as we pick up our backpacks and leave the gym.

"That went well," I say to Ari. "Maybe Ms. Gidlitz is our unicorn."

She shakes her head. "Okay, we're pausing the unicorn thing for now, because I think we're just grasping at straws. No?"

"Maybe," I admit.

At lunch, Ari's telling everyone about our fab unicycling experience. "I mean, it was our first try and we honestly did amazing. Didn't we, Kay?"

"We did." I nod. "We completely crushed it."

"Tell them your joke." Ari taps my knee. "The more I think about it, the more I realize how funny it was."

"You guys want to hear a joke?" I ask them.

It feels good when a friend is into something you did, but when it's your BFF—it's the literal best.

"A unicycle joke?" Amirah asks.

"Uh-huh."

Everyone sort of groans but says sure, and listens while they eat their lunch.

"Attire! Get it!" I crack up again, and this time Ari really laughs.

The rest of the girls fully laugh but Cami just sits there.

"Oh, because it's only one wheel?" she asks.

We all stare at her.

"No, but also because, like, attire meaning clothing. So, it's a double meaning." I pause. "Never mind, it's no good if you have to explain the joke."

"Ohhhhh," Cami sings. "OMG, Kaylan. Where did you even hear that?"

"I found it online." I laugh again.

There's an awkwardness at the table after that and I'm not sure what it is or what's causing it. It seems Cami's confusion sucked all of the happy air away from our table. At least lunch is over soon.

Ari leaves a few minutes early but doesn't say why. "See you guys later."

We watch her walk out of the cafeteria and down the hall and then Cami cranes her head around to see what's happening.

"She's with Jason," Cami declares like we were all waiting to know. To be honest, I wasn't even concerned.

"Okay." I shrug. "Whatever."

"Don't you think it's weird that Kaylan doesn't even care that Ari is with Jason now?" Cami asks the table like she's taking a poll for a very important scientific study.

June rolls her eyes. "Who cares, Cam? If Kaylan's okay with it, why are you so obsessed? Maybe *you* like Jason."

"What? Um, no. June, come on. You know that's not

the case here." Cami rolls her eyes right back. "Whatever, you guys never really see what's going on in a situation. I like to analyze stuff so I think about everything a little more deeply. It's just a difference in personality."

It's right then that something dawns on me.

Something kind of serious.

Something not so great.

I think the rest of the lunch table girls have lost patience with Cami and I was the only one left who still thought she was great. Maybe she asked everyone else to go on the trip but no one else wanted to.

I like her, though. Despite what the others think. Yeah, she can be a little annoying and obnoxious and know-it-all-y. But she's still fun.

I look at her across the table, seeming all gloomy that no one's chiming in about her analyzing and stuff. I have a crazy urge to just get up and leave the table because it feels like all of this awkwardness is swallowing me whole.

But then I decide to do something else. I offer Cami a relaxed smile.

It's all going to be okay. Even though the relationships between the lunch table girls seem to change on an hourly basis, it's all going to be all right.

I know it is.

As we walk to class, an unexpected sense of pride washes over me.

We unicycled today.

And we were pretty good at it.

That's a huge thing and I'm not going to let any lunch table awkwardness get in the way of that.

26

ARI

TIME STARTS TO FLY BY. That always happens right before break.

It's like the break actually starts before it officially does. Teachers let us watch more movies in class. We don't have any tests. Even homework gets lighter. Everyone's off in another world thinking about vacation even if they're not really going anywhere. The ones who are staying home are imagining cozy mornings, sleeping late, staying in pajamas and watching movies. And the ones who are going away are thinking of beach time and pool time or ski time or whatever.

No one's really here anymore even though we're all still here, in the same school building, doing the same things we always do.

And when Valentine's Day is one of the last days

before break—well, that's a whole other thing. It zaps some energy into the overall sense of sleepiness.

"I brought you gals some chocolate hearts," Cami sings as she walks into school. "You're all my loves."

She hands them out to us, and then pulls me over. "Are you and Jason doing something special?"

I laugh, trying to pretend I'm not annoyed. "No, we didn't even discuss it. Honestly, I've said this a hundred times. I don't really celebrate Valentine's Day."

"Whatever. I don't believe that." Cami rolls her eyes. "Everyone celebrates it."

The rest of the girls bring in candy and pass it out to whoever wants a piece, and there's a bake sale in the lobby and we all buy powdered doughnuts. The teachers wear red to get into the spirit but Ms. Phipps takes it a step further—she has a headband on with light-up hearts.

We're at lunch when Ms. O'Leary comes to our table and taps me on the shoulder.

"Ari?" she asks, all tentative.

My throat tightens; my heart thrashes in my chest like a fish dying to get back into water. "Yes?"

The whole lunch table stares at me; I know they're thinking what I'm thinking.

Something with Bubbie.

Something terrible.

I imagine it all day, every day, pretty much. There's

just no way to picture this world without her, and so I worry about it constantly. Because how will I know what to do when she's gone?

"You, um, have a delivery. In the main office." Ms. O'Leary smiles, and it eases my mind a little. So maybe it isn't something terrible. "Come with me."

I look at everyone at the table, and then turn around and see Jason sitting behind us, clueless as ever, trying to eat the cafeteria corn on the cob as if he's in some kind of contest.

"Kay." I nudge my head in her direction. "Come with me."

She doesn't hesitate at all; she just gets up, and we walk with Ms. O'Leary.

When we get to the main office, we see a giant teddy bear sitting on one of the chairs, with a red bow around its neck.

"This, um, arrived for you, Arianna," Ms. O'Leary tells us, with a crinkle of a smile.

I walk over and read the card.

To keep you company until we're back at camp.
Love, Golfy

My insides turn to slush.

"Wow." Kaylan laughs, reading over my shoulder. "That is literally gigantic. And why did he send it to school? And wow. Just wow." She sits down in the chair next to the bear, puts an arm around it, and leans over as if they're going to take a photo together.

"Kaylan, stop." I burst out laughing. It's just too much to see her sitting there like that.

"You can come pick this up at the end of the day," Ms. O'Leary says, "but you should probably get back to lunch now. Happy Valentine's Day, girls."

Kaylan and I walk back to the cafeteria, and she puts an arm over my shoulder. "Well, this is certainly a Valentine's Day to remember."

"Yeah." I sniffle. "I guess it was too late for him to cancel the order?"

"Probably." Kaylan shrugs. "You never told him you don't celebrate Valentine's Day?"

"Um." I think about it. "I guess it didn't come up? I can't remember."

Back at the lunch table, Kaylan tells everyone about the big bear.

"That is the most romantic thing I've ever heard," M.W. says. "For real. Ditch Jason and marry Golf Guy or whatever."

"It's Golfy, for the zillionth time." Kaylan shakes her head.

"Okay, guys, enough." I smile. "Honestly, this is crazy. I don't even know how I'm going to get it home."

* * *

After school, Jason finds me at my locker and asks if I'm taking the bus.

"I can't," I tell him. "I need to, uh, bring something big home, so my mom is coming to get me."

"Huh?" he asks. "Did we need to do a major locker cleanout before break? No one told me."

"No, it's hard to explain." I look away, praying he'll leave soon for the bus. I don't want to tell him about the bear. I don't want to alert him to the fact that he missed Valentine's Day, even if I don't really celebrate it.

"All right, well, good luck." He smiles, touching my shoulder for a moment and then pulling his hand away. "I'll come say hey later."

"Cool. Sounds good."

My mom comes to get me, and thankfully she doesn't ask too many questions about the big bear.

"That may need to go down to the basement eventually," she says. "But keep it in your room for now."

"Okay." I pray she stops talking and I can hide the bear from Gemma and my dad and pretty much the rest of the world.

When I get up to my room, I type out a quick text to Golfy

Me: Thnx 4 the bear

Golfy: Ur welcome. It was 2 late 2 cancel. Kinda funny, no?

Me: Kinda

Before I shove it into the back of my closet, I snap a picture of the bear and send it to the camp girls.

Me: Look what showed up at school today . . .

Alice: Ummm??? What??

Zoe: #soconfused

Hana: who sent that?

Me: Golfy. Dying.

Alice: OMGGGGGGGGGG

Hana: sooooo crazy

Zoe: Seriously. WHOA.

Me: soooooooo excited about our sleepover lovies

Alice: sammeeeeeeeeeeeeeeeeeee

Zoe: ditto

Hana: +1

Finally, we reach the last day before vacation.

It seems like I never needed a break more than I need this one.

Jason finds me at my locker between classes and does that thing where he leans up against it like a boy in a teen movie, all over-the-top and silly, and I crack up so loud half the hallway turns around to look at me.

"There's a watch thing over break," he explains. "It's at the coliseum and it's supposed to be really cool. Do you want to come?"

"Um." I grab my math book off the top shelf. "Like we just walk around and look at watches? Or what?"

"Or what," he repeats, and laughs. "No, I mean, I don't know exactly what it is. But it'll be different watches and designers and stuff and I think it'll be awesome, plus it's so close to us. I mean, how could I miss it?"

"You couldn't miss it." I shake my head, trying as hard as I can to take him seriously. "Sure, I'll come."

"You're the best," he says. "See you later. I'll come over tonight and we can have a bonfire in your backyard and burn last semester's papers?"

"Cool. Perfect." I crack up, but it actually sounds delightful.

I'm collecting a few other things from my locker and putting them in my backpack and then throwing out some other stuff when Kaylan runs up to me, all out of breath.

"Oh my gosh, you're never going to believe this." She pants. "Cami's mom mixed up the flights. We're actually leaving today, not tomorrow, in like two hours. I'm leaving school right now to go home and pack and head to the airport. I won't even have time for the pedicure I wanted. I'm freaking out right now!" She shakes her head, still out of breath. "And you never helped me with the bathing suits!"

"That's crazy! How did she mix the flights up?" I ask, trying not to laugh at this madness.

"I don't know, but I have to go. I love you. Have an amazing break. Text me every day and keep me updated on Bubbie and all of that. And I love you." She stands up on her tiptoes to kiss me on the forehead, like she's my mom, but it's actually pretty sweet.

"I love you, too, Kay. Have so much fun." I kiss her back and she starts to walk away. "Please text me funny stories. Or jokes. Even the unicycle one," I yell out to her, hoping she can still hear me.

"Arianna. Please. Quiet in the hallway," Ms. Phipps says, shaking her head like I've just tried to declaw a cat right here. It's the last day before break; you think she'd chill out a little bit.

"Sorry." I roll my eyes to my locker so she's not able to see me.

I spend the rest of the day imagining where Kaylan is on her journey. I miss her already and she's not even really gone yet. She's only at the airport now.

I miss you, I text her after school when I'm sitting in my den under a blanket feeling that oh so wonderful all-of-break-stretched-out-in-front-of-me feeling.

I miss you, too, she writes back. *Now you know how I felt when you were at camp. But you didn't even have your phone. Hahahahahaha (evil laugh LOL)*

Ari: Ew. ☹

Kaylan: Smooches forever Ari

Ari: Smooches right back Kay-kay

Kaylan: Don't forget to snoop on my dad when he visits!

Ari: Ok!

"Ari," my mom calls, coming into the house from the garage. I know she's probably carrying five bags of groceries all on her own but I really don't want to get up and help her. I'm just so cozy. I wonder if that makes me a bad person. "Ari, are you home?"

"In the den," I call back.

"Come help me with the groceries, please. And then we need to get over to Bubbie and Zeyda's. Get your shoes on. And please make sure the water is turned off for the washing machine. Oh, and grab that bag of clothing donations, too."

How many instructions can one mom give one daughter in a three-second period? I'll never know the answer. It seems to grow and grow with each passing day.

"Ari, now. Please. We need to get going."

Well, my cozy-under-a-blanket, all-of-break-stretched-out-in-front-of-me feeling only lasted for fifteen minutes. But it was a good fifteen minutes.

"Coming," I yell back.

I help her put the groceries away and I do all of the other stuff and then I sit down at the kitchen table and take a sip of seltzer.

"Ari, I need to tell you something before we go over to Bubbie and Zeyda's."

My heart speeds up like I was running a marathon even though all I was doing was sitting right here, doing nothing.

"What?" I ask, praying that it's nothing bad or that it's only something a little bad.

I need to update Kaylan on the God thing. I know I believe in God. It's not even a debate. But I still want to have some more soul-searchy talks about it. Not only for the list, but because I really do like talking about it.

"Bubbie's on oxygen permanently now. It's not a big deal. It's going to help her feel more awake and alert and make her more comfortable, but I wanted to warn you." She pauses, adjusting her glasses on her nose. "It's alarming when you first see the tubes in her nose. I know you saw her with it in the hospital, but it feels different at home, somehow. At least that's what I think."

I nod. "I read an article online about how some people in the city go to these oxygen bars, for fun, even if they don't really need it. So, like, how big of a deal can it be?" I ask, telling myself it's nothing and that we could all be walking around with oxygen if we wanted to.

"Interesting. Okay. Well. We can see for ourselves when we get there." She looks down at my feet. "Okay, your boots are on. Come on. Let's go."

We drive silently to Bubbie and Zeyda's and it takes forever for the heat to come on in the car. It's still freezing when we arrive.

We get inside the apartment and take off our boots and hang our coats on their coat tree and then we find Bubbie and Zeyda back in the den in their recliners.

Bubbie has an aqua-greenish-bluish oxygen cord thing in her nose and the big metal tank makes a whirring sound that seems louder than it needs to be.

Mom was right. It is alarming.

Maybe if she had a clear cord, it wouldn't be so frightening. But this aqua-blue-green thing doesn't work for me.

I sit down on the walker next to the recliner.

"You like my new look?" Bubbie's words come out slurred but her sense of humor is still there. It's like the whole "laughter is the best medicine" thing. Since her sense of humor is so awesome, she's pretty much giving herself her own medicine. That's gotta work.

"You look fab, Bub." I smile and kiss her on the cheek. "How can we help?"

Zeyda gives us a half-shrug, half-head-tilt thing that seems to say everything and nothing all at the same time. But I know what he means.

My mom is busy in their kitchen, organizing things and throwing things away and moving stuff around, and it's hard to say if she's really getting anything accomplished. She looks busy, though, and she feels busy, and sometimes I wonder if that's the most important thing to some people.

"I'm just happy you're here," Bub mumbles. I make a note in my head to ask someone about this later.

We sit there quietly for a while after that and Bubbie

grabs my hand. Her skin is wrinkly and tired-looking and her nails are painted a pale purple.

She's still Bubbie, though. Just a more tired, more worn-out version of herself.

I start to realize that we're always the same selves we've been—just different versions. I expected that as soon as I turned thirteen I would change into a different person—this teenage person who went out on dates and was way more serious and busy and important.

I don't know why I thought that; I just did.

But we don't become different. We change, that's true. But deep down, we're still the same people we've always been.

"Do you feel like you're seventy-five?" I ask Bubbie.

She shakes her head. "I still feel nineteen. In my mind. My body—that's another story. But deep down, nineteen. I think I'll feel nineteen forever."

I think about that for a second. "Why nineteen?"

"It was a good age," she tells me. "But I did cry on my nineteenth birthday. I was sad to be leaving my teens, my last birthday as a teen . . . you know."

"And I just had my first birthday as a teen," I say, even though she clearly knows that. Sometimes it's hard to talk to sick people. You say things that are obvious because you're scared of the quiet. This is Bubbie, the easiest person in the world to talk to, and yet I feel a little shaky talking to her right now.

"You need to stretch it," she says. "Just stretch it all. Make it last."

"You always tell me that." I smile.

"I know. Because I'm right." She nod-smiles at me. "I'm always right."

She laughs, and I laugh, and that's when I know that even though she's hooked up to oxygen and her words are slurred and mumbled—she's still Bubbie.

My main goal for now, and the future, and for however long I can keep it up, is to make sure she's still Bubbie. I don't know if it's in my control, but I'll do whatever I can, whatever it takes to make that happen.

27

KAYLAN

Dear Ari, I'm writing you on the back of this airplane napkin to solidify our thing about God on the list. I don't know if you'll ever see this note. I may die. This plane is so shaky and so turbulent and it feels like we may almost flip over. You know that thing about looking at the flight attendants on a plane to know if you're in danger? Well, I've been doing that and for real, they look scared. I may die. And if you find this note and I'm dead, know that I love you beyond words. And know that I believe in God, 100%, so you can check that off the list. Okay?

ARIIIIIIIII I'm so freaked out.

I wish I'd bought the wifi on the plane so I could be texting you instead of writing you a note you may never see.

Xoxooxxoxoxoxoxo your bffffffffffff Kaylan

“Holy cannoli, that was insane,” I tell Cami when we’re on a turbulence break. I’m not convinced we’re out of the woods yet with the bumpiness but at least it’s stopped for a bit. “For real, do you think we’re going to die?”

She shakes her head, sort of laughing. “Kaylan, come on! I fly all the time. On my flight to Paris two summers ago, I honestly thought we were going to die. We had to make an emergency landing somewhere I’d never even heard of. But then we were back up in the air and everything was fine. Honestly, I think you’re just a nervous flier because you don’t fly as often as I do.”

I’m not sure if her words are comforting or reassuring or condescending or what. Probably a combination of all of those things. I sip my soda and push my seat back a little and close my eyes and pray. How did we ever even debate the belief in God thing? I mean, I’m totally, completely in the believe category and there’s no doubt about it.

Cami’s still going on and on about all the flights she’s taken, including the time she took a helicopter from the city to the Hamptons for some kind of event and it was just so amazing and worth it and there was no traffic and on and on and on.

“Do you believe in God?” I ask her, because I’m genuinely curious but I also really want to change the topic and talk about something else. Cami’s the kind of girl who doesn't get offended when you change the topic mid-conversation. I think it's because she can truly talk about anything at all.

"Yes, totally," she replies. "I mean, how did all of us just get here? And the world and stuff? I believe in science, of course, but there has to be more than science. There has to be some, like, big, magnetic, incredible force guiding us and helping us and overseeing everything. Don't you think?"

I nod. "Yeah, I do. I am entirely in the believe category but I was just curious about what you were thinking on the subject."

"I try really hard to understand people who don't believe in God," Cami goes on. "I want to hear them out because I want to get everyone's beliefs, so I listen to them, but the thing is, I don't honestly get it. Ya know?"

"Yeah, it's like, how can you not believe in something bigger? Doesn't that feel so scary? You're just out there, floating, all on your own? Who do they turn to when they're freaked out from major turbulence?" I crack up.

"Or when someone is sick and all they want is for that person to get better?" Cami says softly, and I start to see this other side of her. This deeper, more sensitive side that I've honestly never seen before. This whole other Cami is surfacing on this plane and I'm not even sure who she'll be by the time we land.

Maybe all it takes is being seventy thousand feet in

the air (or whatever we are right now) to be your true, ultimate self. The definition of *Be Me*.

"Totally. Or what about on a roller coaster when you're so freaked out and you just pray and pray you'll survive?" I bulge my eyes. "Roller coasters are seriously the best and the worst all at the same time."

"Roller coasters don't scare me," Cami says, all matter-of-fact. "But can I admit something to you?"

I nod.

"Sometimes I'm still afraid of the dark. And sometimes I'll pray to God when things are really dark."

"Like at night, you mean? Or dark times? In life?"

"Both. Definitely both."

We're quiet after that, even sleeping a little bit, probably because we're so exhausted from all the turbulence stress. The plane finally lands and we make it to Turks and Caicos in one piece.

"How come you got to bring a friend but your sisters didn't?" I whisper as we're standing in the aisle of the plane, ready to get off.

"They got to last year," she explains. "We're supposed to alternate, but I've never brought a friend before."

I nod and think back to our recent lunch table conversations. I want to ask if she's asked other people to come in the past or this year, but I decide not to. What difference does it make, anyway?

When we're all in the black SUV taking us to the resort,

Cami talks nonstop. "Okay, Kaylan, first thing we do is go to the room, unpack, and then get right into our bathing suits so we can go to the pool and do all the waterslides. Got it?"

"Got it," I reply.

"Cam, you're so mega controlling. Chill out a bit," her sister Jane says. "You need to seriously calm down. You're already making me crazy and we're not even at the resort yet."

"Jane," their dad warns. "Watch your tone. Please."

I can tell Jane's rolling her eyes even though I can't see them. She has a certain head tilt she does when she rolls her eyes. I guess it runs in the family.

Jane turns and whispers something to the middle sister, Louisa. They all call her Lou. And then Lou cackles into hysterics. I look over at Cami, who's staring out the window, acting like she's not hearing any of this, but I know she is. I start to feel bad for her. This isn't the Cami I know from school. With her family, she's a completely different Cami.

We're all quiet the rest of the ride, except for the occasional whispers between Jane and Lou. They're only two years apart and then Lou and Cami are four. So it's like the two of them have teamed up and Cami's on her own team. When I think about it, Cami should really be able to bring a friend every year. Since Lou and Jane have each other.

Cami's parents got a gigantic suite with three bedrooms

and three bathrooms and a living and dining room that's bigger than my living and dining room at home. It also has two balconies and a fireplace, though I'm not sure if it's a real working fireplace.

Cami and I have our own room with two queen beds, and Jane and Lou have one just like ours, and then Cami's parents have a gigantic room with a jacuzzi tub in their bathroom.

"Do you always get this suite?" I ask her as we're unpacking everything and putting our clothing in the drawers.

She nods. "Yup. Did you see the sign welcoming us on the door? They don't do that for everyone."

"Oh. Okay."

As I'm unpacking and putting all of my clothes away, I start to get a sinking kind of sadness that seems to move from my throat to my stomach and even drips a little to my toes. Here I am at this fancy resort with a view of the ocean and an amazing pool and we can get as much room service as we want and I feel so sad. Even though all of this is amazing and great, I don't want any of it. I feel a deep desire to just leave right now, call my mom, and get a flight home.

"You okay?" Cami asks. "We'll go to the pool really soon. I just like to get all set up first. And my parents don't care if we go off on our own and do whatever we want. We won't have to see my sisters at all, I promise.

This is gonna be so fun, Kaylan."

"Oh, it's okay. I'm fine." I force a laugh. "Plus, I always wanted a sister."

"Not one like the two I have. For real." She shakes her head. "I can't wait until Jane goes to college."

I nod.

Cami takes a while longer to unpack so I lie down on the hotel bed and close my eyes for a second. Traveling is exhausting, I guess. I text my mom to let her know we landed and we're safe at the resort and then I text Ari to see what's up.

I think about how different this trip would be if it were me with Ari's family. I wouldn't have this awkward, sad sliminess, that's for sure. I'd paint Gemma's nails on the balcony and then we'd all go down to the pool together and it would feel relaxed and peaceful and safe.

Me: Hey Ar, miss you

She writes back a second later.

Ari: Miss you so much too. Think I've maxed out on the fruit-water thing. Can we JHH that even though we're not JHHing? My favorite is def the strawberry peach.

Me: Yes. Def. What else is up?

Ari: Nada really. Freezing. Jelly you're in the sun

Me: Yeah.

Ari: How's Cami?

Me: She's good. Still unpacking.

Ari: LOL. Love ya

Me: Love ya too.

When we get down the pool, my icky sad feeling fades away a bit. We order piña coladas and they come with giant pieces of pineapple and pink umbrellas and it's really impossible to feel sad when you're drinking something with an umbrella. I think that's pretty much an undeniable fact of life. And then we go on the lazy river three times and down the waterslides six times.

"That jump in your stomach when we take that second turn, isn't that the best?" Cami asks. "And even though you're expecting it, it's still kind of surprising, right?"

"Yeah, totally. It's like I hate it but love it at the same time."

"That's how I felt when I kissed Everett Kramer for the first time," Cami explains as we're holding our floats, waiting to go on the lazy river again. "I totally hated it, waiting for it to happen, and I wanted to back out a thousand times, but then we kissed and I loved it."

"How many times have you kissed Everett? I didn't even know this. I don't think I did, anyway." I shake my flip-flop to get a pebble out.

"Six times. Maybe seven." Cami tilts her head like she's calculating. "I dunno. We haven't kissed since sixth grade. He's in love with Grace now. Do you see how he stares at her in math?"

"Grace Chu?" I ask. "Or Grace Shickman?"

"Chu. He's obsessed. I mean, she's so pretty. But, still. It's still upsetting." She crinkles her nose and looks away and I can't tell if she's about to cry or just trying to shield herself from the sun. It's so strange to be somewhere so sunny when it's freezing back at home. It's like my brain knows it's true, but still can't totally understand it.

"She is pretty," I admit. "But Everett's kind of lame, Cam. I wouldn't stress it."

"I'm not stressing it. I was just saying how it felt to kiss him. Sheesh." She turns away even further and crosses her arms across her chest. And then we just stand there silently for what feels like three thousand years. I see Jane and Lou walk past us with a group of other teenagers—three more girls and four guys—and I want to ask Cami if they're kids they see every year. But I don't because it'll probably just annoy her.

We finally get to the front of the line for the lazy river and the guy says to us, "You can hop in the river anytime, you don't have to be at the starting point. Just so you know."

Cami and I look at each other.

"But we like to start at the beginning," she explains, and I nod like I agree with her even though I don't really care at all.

The mood lightens a little when we're floating along on the lazy river. We go under a waterfall and get completely drenched but it feels refreshing and amazing.

"Want to go lounge for a while?" Cami asks me as we put our floats down.

"Yes, def," I reply. I hope to take a short nap or maybe read. Anything to sort of mentally check out for a little bit. I'm not usually this one-on-one with Cami and I think that's the difference. We're usually in a big group together so her intensity doesn't feel this intense.

We get to our lounge chairs and Cami orders two plates of fries and two Cokes. "We can get whatever we want," she explains. "Don't worry. It's all-inclusive."

She's already told me this at least twelve times, but I still try to act surprised and pleased about it.

"That's the best," I say, adjusting my chair and a rolled-up towel behind my head.

"I'm so glad we've become so close," Cami says, turning to face me. "Do you feel as close to Ari as you always did now or is it different since you and I are so close? Or, like, because of other stuff, too? I don't know. Has your friendship changed?"

Cami's one of these people who will literally say whatever's on her mind, and ask anyone any question. She walks through life carrying a hot poker like you'd use in a fireplace and then just jabs it into your side from time to time.

"Um, I think we're still just as close as we've always been." I shut my eyes, feeling the hot sun on my face, anticipating extra freckles along my nose.

"What do you mean you think?" She props herself up on her elbow and stares at me.

"I think friendships are always changing. And Ari and I are literal BFFs. In the forever part. But, like, it's not always the same friendship it was. And it probably won't stay the way it is now, forever, either. She's really more of a sister than a friend. It's on another level."

"Yeah. But you might think your friendship is forever and then it ends up not being totally that way. It was like that with June and me, but now I think she just finds me so annoying," Cami admits. "Do you ever see that?"

I hesitate and think about it for a second. "I'm always a little zoned out at lunch. So I don't really know. I think things will be different after break. We all needed some time apart."

"Even you and Ari?" she asks.

I shrug, trying to appear patient. "Kinda, yeah." I look right at her and say, "Listen, Cam, let's make a pact. This has to be a fun week. No drama, no stressing, just fun. Okay?"

"But you're the queen of stressing! Agita girl, remember?" She cracks up.

"I do remember." I laugh. "But this is a vacation. Let's have fun! Woo!"

"Woo!" she yells back.

Right then, Jane and Lou pass us and look a little

confused, but that only makes us laugh more.

"Woo!" I yell again.

A little while later, my phone dings and I see that I have an email from my dad.

Dear Kaylan,

I hope you're enjoying the trip. I've given some thought to comedy camp. I'll cover some of the cost, and your mother will cover some, but you're going to need to use some of your birthday savings as well. And next time, you must be honest when you apply for something like this. I'd still like for you to give some thought to my wedding. I know it will mean missing a few days of the program, but I really want you to be there. Please think about it.

Love, Dad

This email from my dad could force me to bang my head against the wall or scream at the top of my lungs or maybe both at the exact same time.

Cami's intensity could suck me in and make this whole time away a swirling mess of drama.

But I'm not going to let any of those things happen.

At least he's paying for part of it. That means I can go.

And this is a vacation.

I'm going to have fun.

28

ARI

ALICE, ZOE, AND HANA ARE sleeping over tomorrow, so I spend a good chunk of my break texting with them and planning out what we're going to do. So far all we've come up with is: watch all the old camp videos we can find online and eat as much as humanly possible.

We decide we'll go out for Chinese food and see a movie and try to stay up all night.

All of that sounds good to me.

Most of all, I am just so excited to have them here.

I haven't heard from Golfy at all, which isn't surprising really. But I do miss him. I miss his stories the most.

My parents agreed to move their cars to the driveway so I can practice unicycling in the garage. It didn't make sense to leave it at school over break, since I'd miss out on so much good practice time.

"You're doing great," Jason says, sitting on a milk crate in the corner of my garage watching me try to unicycle.

"How long was I up that time?" I ask him.

He looks at the stopwatch. "Forty-seven seconds."

"That's it?" I squeak. "I did over two minutes once in school."

"Are you sure the clock was working?" He looks at me sideways, laughing.

I roll my eyes. "I'll kick you out if you're not helpful!"

"Try it again," he says. "You'll do better with each time you try it."

"But how am I ever going to get to the point where I'll be able to hula-hoop while on this thing?" I ask, feeling slumpy and depressed.

"You'll get there." He cracks up. "Why do you guys torture yourselves like this, anyway?"

"We don't torture ourselves. We like *challenging* ourselves."

He shakes his head, not convinced.

"So your camp friends are coming tomorrow?" he asks me.

I don't respond. I can't talk while unicycling, which isn't a very good sign. If I can't talk while doing it, how can I expect to hula-hoop while doing it?

I lose my balance and say, "Sorry, it's hard for me to talk and stay up at the same time. Yeah, they're coming tomorrow."

"Are you excited?" he asks.

"Yup. They want to meet you."

"Oooh." He laughs. "So they can compare me to the Golfster?"

I slap his arm. "Don't call him the Golfster. His name is Golfy."

"Whatever." He laughs. "Okay, try again. I'll time you."

I smile. Jason is pretty much my coach right now and it feels good. I have a new sense of confidence on this unicycle—I don't think it has anything to do with Jason specifically, but having someone here, timing me, is helpful.

My butt is starting to hurt from the unicycle seat, though, and I wonder if I should research comfier seats or cushions or something.

"Yes!" he yells. "That was close to two minutes. Amazing job!"

"For real?" I ask, pulling over a milk crate and sitting down next to him.

"Yes, for real." He laughs and moves his milk crate closer to me. "You're doing great."

I look up at him right then and he looks at me and even though it's only about seven degrees outside, it's warm in my garage, even with the door open. I guess some of the heat from the house seeps in through the walls and keeps it sorta toasty in here. I'm not sure.

Before I know what's happening, Jason kisses me. A

quick peck on the lips, by the side of my garage, under the faded poster from when my mom ran for the school board.

"There," he says. "I just had to. Was that okay?"

"It was okay." I laugh. "Maybe a little better than okay."

"You know what I mean." He flicks my knee. "Okay, only a three-second break and then back to unicycling. You're doing well, you can't lose your momentum now."

"Okay." I pick up my phone and see five texts from Kaylan updating me on this sushi dinner they had last night and that Cami's sister Jane made out with some random guy on the beach.

Kaylan: I think they actually met last year. So maybe it's not that random.

Me: Oh. Interesting. Practicing my unicycling rn btw. Going to do some more online contests later.

Kaylan: Fab. On my 4th pina colada btw. Have been asking for fruit in my water all day

Me: Jelllllllll

I catch Jason reading over my shoulder.

"Hey! Stop!" I swat his hand away. "You can't read my texts."

"Why not?" he laughs. "They're interesting."

I shake my head. "Jason, for real. No. You can't do that."

He slumps down on the milk crate like a toddler who just got in trouble. He sits there sulking for a few minutes.

"Are you going to tell Kaylan we kissed?" he asks.

"I don't know. Maybe. Probably. Not over text, though. Not while she's away. I don't know."

He laughs. "You just said like six different answers."

"I know." I pause. "Because I don't know yet."

"Are you listening to yourself? You're so funny but I don't even think you're trying to be funny right now. Which makes it even funnier."

"You're pretty funny yourself." I take off his baseball cap and swat his face with it.

"Funny, funny, funny."

We keep saying the word over and over again until we're laughing so much we can't stop, and we completely forget what was even so funny in the first place.

We're back up in my room after all the unicycling practice and it's kind of strange to have him here now, since things have changed between us.

"Let me see the list," he says.

"What? No!" I yell from across the room. I'm searching through my drawers to find my comfiest pajamas for the camp friends sleepover.

"Why not?" he asks. "I saw all the other lists."

"That was different. For the first one you were just our friend. And for the second one you were half Kaylan's boyfriend and half my friend. And for this one you're, well, I don't know what you are."

He sits back on my beanbag chair with his arms behind his head. "Well, what am I? Tell me, Arianna Simone Nodberg."

"You tell me, Jason Samuel Klee," I say right back to him.

We're quiet then, both of us with smug expressions on our faces.

"Well, I'm still a friend to both of you. Maybe more. I don't know. Anyway, show me the list," he demands. "I want to help. And you're gonna want my help, especially with the fruit-infused-water thing. My mom has like a million varieties. She has a special recipe book just for that!"

"She does?"

"Yes. So seriously, you're only hurting yourself by not letting me help you."

I consider it for a moment, and then I reason that it's actually fine to show him the list. He's seen the others. He's still my neighbor and friend and obviously more than a friend, but whatever—we have history with him. Both of us do.

I grab a copy from the top drawer of my desk and show it to him.

He looks it over for what feels like an extra-long time. Like he shouldn't really need this long to read over a list of thirteen things.

"Interesting," he says finally. "Lots to discuss."

"Jason, you know you're not, like, doing the list with us, right? Haven't we had to tell you this every time?"

He nods. "Yes. And I know I'm not doing it with you. But I can help. I can be, like, a list coach. A resource. Some of this stuff is hard, obviously."

"Actually . . ." I look it over. "I think this is our easiest one yet."

13 Must-Dos to Keep Crushing It as 13-Year-Olds

1. Hula-hoop on a unicycle. (in process)
2. Start a movement. (trying)
3. Figure out how we feel about God. (on the path)
4. Spend more time with Bubbie and Zeyda. (doing this)
5. Perfect the art of persuasion, especially with Kaylan's mom. (on it)
6. Train for and run a race. (not yet)
7. Come up with many varieties of fruit-infused water. (yum. doing this)
8. Properly thank our teachers before the end of the year.
9. Find a unicorn. (hmm)
10. Win an online contest. (TBD)
11. Be Me. (crushing this)
12. Eat one of those super-spicy chips. (on order)
13. Convince Ari's parents that they need a dog and come up

with an awesome name for said dog. (working on it, on hold until spring)

"You do?" he asks. "How?"

"Well, we've started each thing already, and are well on our way with all of it," I explain. "And we have way more time with this one."

"Yeah, but win an online contest? How can you control if you're going to win? If it said enter online contests, I'd understand. But win? No way. You can't demand that of yourselves."

"Well, we're obviously going to try."

He shakes his head defiantly. "And figure out how you feel about God? People spend their whole lives on that. I mean, you can't have that done by the end of the school year."

"True."

"Plus, wasn't that what your bat mitzvah was about? You kind of have an advantage over Kaylan."

I shake my head at him, realizing that he can actually be quite frustrating, but that may be one of the things I like about him. "Yes, it was partly what my bat mitzvah was about and I loved thinking about all that stuff. But I don't have an advantage. We're both working on it."

"I just don't think you can have a deadline for that." He sighs. "I'm sorry."

“Jason.” I sit down next to him on the beanbag chair. We’re sitting so close, the string of his hoodie tickles my arm. “We’re not saying we’ll have it figured out or we’ll never debate it for the rest of our lives. We’re just saying we’ll come to some kind of conclusion.”

He nods like he’s listening but isn’t convinced. “Okay. Well, good luck. And remember I’m here to help.”

He looks over at my door and then leans over a little like he’s about to kiss me again. My stomach flips over three times the way I usually do in the pool, and then my phone rings.

It’s a FaceTime call.

It’s Kaylan.

29

KAYLAN

"SHE'S PROBABLY HAVING DINNER RIGHT now," Cami says over my shoulder. So far Ari hasn't answered the FaceTime call. It's not like I have anything that mega important to tell her, but I wanted to show her our room and the balcony and the view of the ocean. There's gonna be fireworks tomorrow so maybe I will FaceTime her in for that, too. I don't want to tell her about the email from my dad since I'm trying as hard as I can to push it away from my thoughts. I guess it's not going that well.

"Hiiii," Ari sings, answering the call, her face appearing in the little box.

"Ari, my love!" I yelp, and Cami swats my arm.

"Hey, I thought I was your love." She laughs like she's kidding but I don't think she's really kidding.

"You are too," I mouth.

"OMG, it looks so amazing there," Ari says. "Even the little of what I can see of the room looks so über fab. Give me a tour! Give me a tour!"

I get up from the chair and start walking around.

"Hey!" Cami hits my arm again. "I want to say hi, too!"

"Hi, Cami," Ari yells out, and then Cami moves the phone a little so she can say hi.

"Ari, your room is fab. I've never seen it," Cami says.

"Oh," Ari replies. "Um, thanks."

"Hey, whose shoes are those in the corner, by the door?" Cami asks. "Those blue Nikes."

It's quiet for a minute and then another head pops into view on the phone.

Jason.

Guess he got new shoes. Guess he's over at Ari's.

My stomach drops.

I'm suddenly regretting this call.

"Hey," Jason says. "I was just, uh, making a photocopy of the break math packet."

Sure he was. I don't know why he has to lie. I know what's up. Lying only makes it worse.

"Cool," Cami replies, and then glares at me like *puh-lease*.

I ignore her. "Hey hey. So what's—"

Ari interrupts, "So can I please have a tour of the room and stuff? And can you bring me down to the pool? Show me everything. It's one degree here but with the wind chill it feels like negative twenty."

"Ouch," Cami says. "That's torture."

No one says anything for a few minutes after that.

It's basically just Ari and me staring at each other, with Jason popping his head in every other second.

This is more awkward than I expected and I kind of want to say that we have a bad connection and hang up.

"Come on. Tour! Tour!" Ari yells. Is she not sensing this awkwardness? I don't think she is.

I take her around the room and show her everything and she oohs and aahs and I take her out to the balcony.

"Wowie, amazing view," she says.

Jason adds, "Cami, invite me next year!"

And she laughs like it's the funniest thing ever that would never in the world happen.

After that, my enthusiasm for this tour and FaceTime fades. The whole interaction is just weird and awkward and I'm not even getting any time to really talk to Ari. I just want to hang up.

"Okay, guys, we're going back down to the pool and I need to charge my phone. Talk later. Bye!" I don't even give Ari a chance to respond, which is probably rude. I'll text her later and clear the air and catch up on all the important stuff.

As we're walking down the hallway with towels over our necks, heading to the elevator, Cami says, "See, that was super weird."

I don't answer.

I agree with her, but I don't want to discuss it.

"They were probably making out like right before we FaceTimed." She stops walking. "Don't you think?"

"I don't know," I say quietly; my stomach is feeling queasy and unsettled. I thought I didn't care about this Ari/Jason thing. But maybe I do care. Or maybe Cami is making me care.

Is it possible for another person to make you care about something? In a bad way? I don't know.

"He's not that great," Cami continues. "I saw his feet through the screen and his toenails looked really long."

"He was wearing socks!" I yell louder than I meant to, and the other people waiting for the elevator with us look very confused.

"Oh, he was? Hmm. I imagined it then, I guess."

We're quiet for a while after that, and even at the pool, I take out my magazines and read on the lounge while Cami plays a game on her phone. I kind of wish Lou or Jane would walk by, or even her parents. I think I need to interact with some other people. Maybe we could make other friends here or something.

All I know is this—I'm starting to feel like this is going to be a very long week.

At dinner that night, we're all showered and our cheeks are red and we're sitting around the table talking about the day. Cami's parents order cocktails and Lou and Jane order mocktails of the fancy drinks they have on the menu—they have giant pieces of kiwi and strawberries on skewers. Cami and I order Shirley Temples.

I try to tell myself that this is great and I'm having fun and we're sitting by the ocean eating dinner and I'm wearing a new sundress my mom ordered online for me. I tell myself all the happy, great things, but inside I feel like I'm slowly being buried under the sand and I can't breathe.

I don't think I want to be here.

I feel awkward with Cami's family, and Cami's really annoying me. That FaceTime call was so strange and I haven't even had a moment of privacy to talk to Ari about it.

I miss my mom. I miss Ryan's annoying video game sounds.

I tell myself it's great that Dad's helping to pay for comedy camp and that I'm going! But that doesn't really help, either. It just feels icky. And missing my dad's visit only makes me more nervous about it for some reason.

Why in the world did I think this was a good idea? I feel like I didn't think it through. All I thought about was sunshine and warmth and fanciness but I didn't consider the rest of it.

"Kaylan, you okay?" Cami's mom asks, taking an olive out of her drink.

I nod. "Yeah, fine." I force a smile.

"Okay. Just checking." She smiles back at me.

"After dinner, we'll go make s'mores," Cami whispers. "They have it every night here. But get this—they help you assemble it. So you don't even need to get your hands sticky!"

"Wow." I force another smile. "That's great."

30

ARI

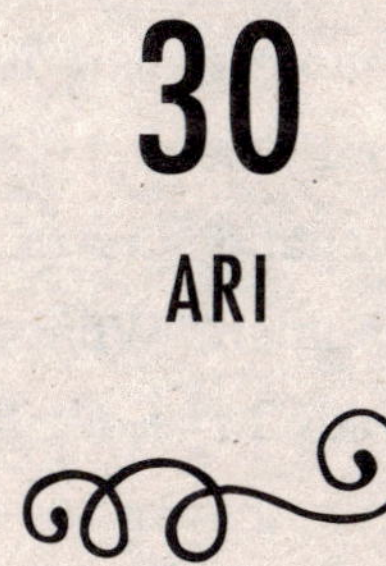

"YOU'RE GOING TO KAYLAN'S EVEN though she's not there?" my mom asks me. She's scrambling some eggs for Gemma, my dad, and me. "And what time are your camp friends coming over? I'm so confused about the plans. Please explain, Ari."

"I forgot my favorite cardigan there, and I really want it." I pause, peeling apart a biscuit and popping the pieces into my mouth. "My camp friends are coming later this afternoon and we're going to the movies and then dinner at Hunan Balcony."

"You're going to walk over there right after the movie?" my dad chimes in.

My mom adds, "Call and make a reservation; they've been so busy lately, and you're a big group."

"Um, okay."

My dad says, "I'm going to be over at my parents' this afternoon going through some paperwork."

"Mom and I are cleaning out my room," Gemma tells us. "I need to have a more grown-up room. I mean, I'm almost ten. It's essential. Ooooh, I just had a brainstorm! Ari, you should've put that on one of your lists!"

I consider it for a moment. What a good idea. But it's too late now. We already have our list and my room is already pretty grown-up anyway.

"Oooh," I mock her in a loving way. "Gem! You could make a list! And put that on it."

My dad looks from Gemma to me and then back to Gemma. "I have no idea what we're talking about," he admits.

"Don't worry about it." My mom takes another biscuit off the plate. "Okay, seems like we all have a lot to do today."

I spend the rest of the morning making piles of books and old toys I want to donate. Around lunchtime, I get to Kaylan's house and Ryan answers the door.

"Hey," he grumbles. "Kaylan's not here."

"Hi. I know that. Duh." I smile and take off my boots and leave them by the door. "I came over because I left my cardigan in her room."

He shrugs.

"Ari!" Kaylan's mom comes to greet me, wearing her personalized apron. "Everything okay?"

"Yeah, I just forgot my cardigan," I tell her.

"Oh, you sure it's here? I was just organizing Kaylan's room, and I didn't see it."

I feel my cheeks flash red. "I'll go check."

She smiles. "It's great to see you, though."

I ask, "Are you missing Kay?" and laugh a little.

"Of course," she says. "But we'll manage. You think she's having fun?"

I nod, and think back to the FaceTime call. "Yeah, I'm sure. I mean, it's a super-fab resort. How could she not have fun?"

"Well, yeah. You're probably right. Okay, well, go look. We're eating lunch in about fifteen minutes. Would you like to stay?"

"Um." I think for a minute, realizing this is exactly what I'd hoped to happen. I hear TV sounds coming from the den, and I assume Kaylan's dad is in there. "Sure! Can I test out something for you guys? Do you have any fruit in the fridge?"

Kaylan's mom crinkles her eyebrows together. "I think we have a few plums, some blueberries . . . maybe a lime? I'm not sure."

"That's perfect." I run up the stairs. "Be back in a few."

I get back downstairs and pop my head into the den. Kaylan's dad and Ryan are in there watching some game and not talking at all. Every few seconds, Mr. Terrel takes out his phone and types furiously and then puts it down.

Ryan doesn't seem to notice. It's awkward to sit here like this, in total silence, so I decide to text Kaylan.

Me: Hey. At your house. Gonna test a fruit water out on your fam!

She writes back a second later.

Kaylan: Oh! What am I missing there?

Me: Not much. Ryan and your dad are in the den not talking and your mom's making lunch.

Kaylan: Sounds about right. LOL.

Kaylan: Tell me if you notice anything out of the ordinary. K? Maybe my dad canceled his wedding and he wants to get back together with my mom?

Ari: Um. Okay.

"Is it okay to borrow this pitcher?" I ask Kaylan's mom once I'm in the kitchen.

"Sure," she says, looking at me, confused. I can't remember if we told her about the new list or not, so I decide not to mention it.

"I'm just really into fruit water," I tell her. "And I'm trying to come up with as many varieties as I can. Kaylan is, too, ever since the hibachi place. Has she tried any out on you?"

She nods. "Oh, yes! The fruit water. She made an outstanding cucumber pineapple before she left."

"Delish! This is going to be a plum blueberry," I tell her, cutting up the fruit and putting them in the pitcher.

"We'll let it sit in the fridge a few minutes before lunch, okay?"

She smiles. "Okay, Ari."

When we sit down for lunch, I pay attention as best I can, but so far there's nothing to notice at all. Kaylan's dad doesn't even offer to help bring anything out. He's quiet most of the time, except for asking to have things passed. Like, "pass the chicken salad," "pass the chips" and stuff like that.

I'm starting to wish I hadn't done this. It's mega awkward to be here without Kaylan, even if it was just her mom and Ryan. But with her dad here, too—it seems like everyone is sitting on a painting, trying as hard as they can not to smudge it.

"So how's everyone?" Kaylan's mom asks. "Isn't it lovely to have Ari with us? What a special surprise."

Ryan head-tilts, not as enthusiastic as a nod, and takes another roll out of the basket.

"It's great," Kaylan's dad says. "I'm happy to be here, even if it is freezing."

He looks pretty much the opposite of happy.

"Well, lucky Kaylan got to escape this cold," I say, when I can't think of anything else.

"That's true," Kaylan's mom says. "I'm going to refill the salad and bring out your water, Ari. Be right back."

Again, no one offers to help, so I get up to follow her

into the kitchen. On my way in, I notice Kaylan's dad texting under the table. I try as hard as I can not to snoop but it's weird when you see a dad doing something a teenager would do. It feels so funny and out of place, like when you see a little kid dressed up like an elderly person on Halloween.

I can't read any of his texts but whatever he's discussing seems tense and angry.

We come back with the refilled salad bowl and the water and we all eat, occasionally discussing sports and random TV shows, but nothing exciting or important. Ryan talks a little bit about his band and that they're trying to get some local gigs for summer.

"What is this water?" Ryan makes a face.

"It's fruit-infused," I explain. "Blueberry plum."

"Uh, okay."

"I think it's delicious," Kaylan's mom adds. Her dad takes a sip and nods, seemingly unsure of what to say.

I want to have something great to tell Kaylan later. Some out-of-the-blue love connection between her parents, even though that would be sort of sad for Robert Irwin Krieger and Zoe. But people's parents are people's parents. I think no matter what age someone is, they'll still deep-down hope that their parents get back together. Even if it wasn't a great marriage or anything.

People want their parents to love each other.

It's a basic fact of human existence.

The thing is, though, there's nothing good to tell her. Her dad is checked out, more interested in his phone than anything else. He hasn't said anything of importance. He hasn't even mentioned the wedding, not that I'd really want him to. Her mom is doing all the work here, trying to make everything amazing. She's cheery, carrying this whole lunch on her shoulders.

I have no idea what I'll tell Kaylan later, when she asks about it. I guess I can say that the fruit-infused water reactions were mixed, but her mom really seemed to like it. That's something.

I debate this the rest of the afternoon, until my friends arrive. When they do, we hug and squee in the driveway even though it's frigid outside and then we run up to my room so they can all settle in. It's cheesy to say but just having them here makes everything feel warmer.

"This is literally the best ever," Alice says, plopping down on my beanbag chair.

"The beanbag?" I ask, laughing.

"No, just being here. All together. Can we stay up all night?" she asks. "Can we squeeze amazingness out of every second?"

"Of course," I tell her. "All I have planned so far is going for Chinese and seeing a movie, okay? And Jason wants to come over and hang later."

"Ooh, Jason." Zoe shakes her head. "I still can't believe you're totally over Golfy after all that."

“I can’t either,” Hana adds. “Super crazy.”

“Can we see the bear?” Alice asks, squeezing her face tight.

I shake my head. “Um, no. After hiding it in my closet for a bit, I decided to just give it to Gemma. It’s hers now and it lives in her room, and if we go in there, she’ll never leave us alone . . . I mean, never.”

Everyone laughs.

“It’s a little romantic that he sent it to you,” Hana says. “I mean, that he sent it to you at school. It’s pretty cool.”

Alice raises her eyebrows. “I know . . . who knew Golfy had this super-sweet side to him?”

Zoe shrugs. “We underestimated the boy, I guess. And Ari broke his heart. . . .”

I sigh. “Guys, I thought you were all supposed to be my friends. And be supportive. You said you still loved me when we texted about it. Remember?”

“We are, we are,” Alice says defensively. “It’s just, like, awkward a bit. And Golfy is our friend, too, and so, ya know.”

I nod.

They’re all quiet after that, looking at each other like they’re thinking something they don’t want to say out loud.

I say, “Okay, let’s talk about something else.”

We stay up until three in the morning watching old camp videos and fast-forwarding and rewinding and then fast-forwarding again.

"OMG, look at Golfy there," Zoe squeals. "The summer we were nine. He was so little!"

Hana agrees, "He really was."

"Look at me, guys," Alice says a second later when she comes on the video. "Oh, remember that girl Hope who was in our bunk that summer? She never came back."

They go on and on like this, and I realize it's possible to feel left out at a sleepover at your own home with girls who are your BFFs. There will always be camp memories I'm not part of; there will always be summers they had without me. There's no way to turn back time and for me to be there when I wasn't.

I sit quietly while they yelp every few minutes when someone they know comes on, or when they're reliving a memory.

There are only so many *remember whens* you can hear about before you start to tune them out, before you wish you hadn't suggested this activity.

"Okay, this is the last old one, guys," I tell everyone. "Then we're watching the one from this past summer? Okay?"

Alice answers *sure*, not really paying attention, and I go to my window and look over at Jason's room with the light on. I can see him sitting with his feet up on his desk, playing a handheld video game.

I feel torn between two worlds, in a way. Not exactly sure where I want to be.

31

KAYLAN

CAMI AND I FIND A few new friends on this trip. They're from Massachusetts, a town called Gloucester, and live right on the ocean.

"We need warmth in the winter, though," one of them tells us. Her name is Ali.

The other one is named Eliza. They're best friends and their parents are best friends and they always vacation together in the winter, but they go somewhere different every year.

Ali's like Ari and Eliza's like me and I start to imagine our families going on vacation together. It makes me feel lonely in a way, and I'm not sure why.

I've settled into a groove with Cami, though. We're by the pool all day, every day doing the waterslides and the lazy river and everything, but when we want time to chill and lounge, she gets it. It took all week—and I'm not even sure how we did it—but we finally got there.

And we have fun, we really do.

It's just that she's not Ari. And even though Ari and I have our ups and downs, she's the one friend I never really get sick of, the friend who truly gets me.

At the end of the trip, when we're on the plane home, Cami starts crying. "I'm so sad it's over. I really wanted us to bond and stuff, and be like official BFFs by the time we came home, but I don't think that happened, do you?"

"I mean, we're really close friends," I reassure her, a sense of agita creeping in.

"But BFF? Like hardcore? Like you and Ari? Like soulmate best friends?"

"Cam, come on." I pause, really wishing we weren't having this conversation. "Everyone's friendships are different. You and June have been best friends since preschool, and Ari and I have only known each other since fourth grade. No friendship is exactly like any other friendship."

She rolls her eyes. "That feels lame, no offense."

I look over at Jane and Lou across the aisle and I know they're listening and whispering to each other about us like they've done the whole trip. But I don't even care. Maybe if they were nicer sisters to Cami she wouldn't be so needy. Maybe she wouldn't have to act like such a know-it-all at the lunch table. Maybe I wouldn't even be on this trip because she would have been happy to hang out with her sisters and she wouldn't need me as much.

"It's not lame. It's the truth." I hesitate before saying anything else. "But don't stress it so much. I think you're always worried about who's BFF with who and the drama and the whole Jason and Ari thing with the whole Jason and me thing. But it's taking you out of the moment. You spent most of the time on this trip convincing me I should be annoyed about Jason and Ari."

"Well, you should. That's not what a real best friend would do, Kaylan. I think you know that deep down." She rolls her eyes at the seat in front of her. "I'm listening to music now and hopefully falling asleep. See you when we land."

"Sweet dreams," I say.

I close my eyes and lean my head back and think about this trip and whatever happened at home while I was away.

On some level, I can't wait to be home and have this whole experience behind me. But on another level, I feel like so many things have changed and it's going to be even weirder to go back to normal life.

Bubbly, funny Cami doesn't seem quite so bubbly and funny anymore.

I guess I was the last one to realize that.

* * *

As soon as I walk in the house after getting back from the airport, I run upstairs and collapse on my bed, sighing the hugest sigh of relief I've ever sighed.

I'm home.

I didn't realize this about myself, but I like home. I like my bed and my window seat and my desk and my curtains and even the creaky floorboards. I like that when I walk into the house it always smells like a mixture of Mom's Christmas candles and folded laundry.

I like the way our landline rings.

I like the way our dishwasher sings when it's done running.

I like home.

I hear my mom coming up the stairs, and I lie back on my bed. I sniff my sheets—fresh and clean from the dryer. If this is what it's like to be away for a week, how am I going to survive one session at comedy camp? What if it's a whole place full of people like Cami?

I wonder if it's too late to convert to Judaism and go to Camp Silver with Ari.

"So happy you're home, Kay." My mom smiles, lying down next to me. "We missed you."

"I missed you so much, Mom. I don't think I'm going to go away for college, okay? I may just live here forever." I laugh. "Not even kidding."

"Kaylan, come on. I'm not that exciting." I lean my head on her shoulder and breathe in her fruity perfume.

My mom is magic. I don't know why it took me so long to realize that. I never want to leave her again. I reach over and wrap my arms around her back.

"I love you, Mommy."

She pulls back after a minute. "I love you, too, but what's happening? Are you okay? Where is this coming from?"

I try as hard as I can to swallow back tears but eventually I can't do it anymore.

"Kaylan. What happened?" She looks at me, eyes wide, all serious. "Tell me. Now. Did someone hurt you?"

She truly looks petrified.

"No, Mom." I laugh and cry at the same time. "Nothing like that. Come on."

"Well, talk to me. Please."

I sit up and inch back against my pillows. "I don't know. It was just so awkward. And Cami got really annoying," I start. "I just felt so out of place. Like I could never really get comfortable there."

My mom nods. "I see."

I think about telling her the other stuff—about Ari and Jason—but truthfully I don't know if it's really even bothering me. How is it possible to not know your own feelings?

We should have put that on the list: figure out our own feelings.

"So that was it? I'm not saying that's not a bad feeling.

But I just want to make sure you're not leaving anything out." She looks at me in that mom way where it seems like she's actually seeing some inner crevices of my soul and can tell exactly what I'm thinking without me even saying anything.

I nod. "That was it."

"I'm always here if you want to talk. You know that. Yes?"

"Yes," I reply. "Thank you."

32

ARI

AFTER BREAK, TIME SORT OF goes in slow motion. It's like there's really nothing to look forward to and the weeks just sort of melt away.

Kaylan and I keep busy with lots of Bubbie and Zeyda visits. We try out more fruit-water varieties on them—Bubbie's favorite is the pineapple peach. I think that may be mine, too.

Pretty soon we find ourselves in the doldrums of March, and each day bleeds into the next. It's cold and gray and no one really wants to do anything.

Even the lunch table conversations are sort of slow and boring.

Something changed on that trip that Cami and Kaylan went on and I don't know what it is.

It's like all the air was sucked out of Cami. She's a deflated balloon now. A soda without the fizz.

I can't figure it out.

After school, I meet Kaylan at the lockers. We sit down, our knees pulled up to our chests so we don't accidentally trip anyone walking by, and we look over the list.

13 Must-Dos to Keep Crushing It as 13-Year-Olds

1. Hula-hoop on a unicycle. (in process)
2. Start a movement. (trying)
3. Figure out how we feel about God. (on the path)
4. Spend more time with Bubbie and Zeyda. (doing this)
5. Perfect the art of persuasion, especially with Kaylan's mom. (on it)
6. Train for and run a race. (not yet)
7. Come up with many varieties of fruit-infused water. (yum. doing this)
8. Properly thank our teachers before the end of the year. (on hold)
9. Find a unicorn. (hmm)
10. Win an online contest. (TBD)
11. Be Me. (crushing this)
12. Eat one of those super-spicy chips. (on order)

13. Convince Ari's parents that they need a dog and come up with an awesome name for said dog. (working on it, on hold until spring)

"Well, we start training for the race next week," Kaylan reminds me. "It should be warmer by then. Almost April, ya know. But we can't thank the teachers yet. It would be mega weird to do that before the end of the year."

I nod. "And we're working on the unicycle thing, obv." I look over at her. "I think we need a sleepover to tackle the God thing, and the Movement thing. We can also enter a ton of online contests and search Pet Finder for the dog. We'll get a ton done in a short time."

"Good plan," Kaylan replies, scrolling through her phone. "Oh! I meant to tell you! Our chip delivery just got moved up! It'll be here this weekend."

"Oh, yay!" I pause to think about what I'm going to say next. I decide not to say it; I can save it for when the chip actually arrives. "By the way, I'm so glad we're not JHH-ing this list. It's so many works in progress."

Kaylan pauses a minute. "Yeah, you're totally right. This list pretty much is us. We are works in progress, too. Duh."

I nod, sort of zoning out.

She continues, "That's why it's okay if we make dumb decisions because we're still figuring stuff out."

I look at Kaylan out of one eye, not totally sure what she means. I wait for her to elaborate.

She doesn't, though. She's just quiet, looking at the list.

Then she says, "Parents don't have an excuse to make dumb decisions, though. They're supposed to know better."

I nod. When Kaylan gets like this, all philosophical and rant-y, I know it's best to just let her go. Let her talk. Free her mind and her feelings.

I don't think I know anyone better than I know Kaylan.

Even Gemma, even Alice and the camp girls.

Kaylan's more of a sister to me than Gemma is, I think. But I'd feel pretty bad saying that out loud.

"Parents aren't supposed to be so dumb," Kaylan says. "They're not supposed to only think about themselves."

"That's true. It's like you lose your time to be selfish when you have kids. It's over. And people should know that," I say softly, not really knowing exactly what she's talking about, but trying to offer something helpful.

"I hate everyone." Kaylan buries her head in her knees and doesn't look up. I stare at the list because I don't know what else to do. Taking out my phone would be rude. But I also don't want to interrogate Kaylan and ask her what's up. Then I start to wonder if she means me, too. That she hates me. And I start to think about my decisions and if they've been dumb.

Maybe she's talking about the Jason thing.

I look at the clock above one of the classrooms and we have five minutes to get to the gym. I need to reel her back in, get us on track to move forward with this unicycle thing.

"What do you mean you hate everyone?" I ask finally, almost in a whisper.

She doesn't pick her head up and she doesn't say anything for a few moments. But then finally she does.

"The thing with my dad getting remarried. It's all hitting me. I'm so mad about it."

"Yeah." I put an arm around her. "I get that."

"Why is he literally the dumbest human ever to live? Why does he want to marry someone else, anyway? I mean, my mom is the best ever. And so am I. And Ryan's, like, fine. Not amazing, but fine."

I laugh, even though I shouldn't.

Kaylan's funny even when she's at her saddest. I guess that means she's really, truly a funny person. Destined to be a comedian. I'm so glad she's going to comedy camp.

"Oh, what did he say about camp?" I ask her. "Don't tell me he said no, and that's another reason you're mad. . . ."

She replies, "He finally said I can go to comedy camp. He emailed me when I was on the trip and said he'll help pay for some of it, but I have to use some of my birthday savings, too. I was so mixed up about his email that I couldn't even talk about it out loud." I pause.

I lean in closer to her and she keeps talking. "And he wants me leave for part of comedy camp so I can go to the wedding. How crazy is that? Like we're just going to be fine and happy at this thing? Celebrating this new stupid life he has with this stupid lady in Arizona. I mean, come on. Why would we want to see that? No one even wants to see their own parents kiss, but to see one parent kiss another adult, a stranger? I mean, ew. Grossest thing ever. Right?"

I try to put myself in her position right now, and I can't even imagine it. "Yeah, super gross."

We're quiet after that and I want to tell her it's time to go to the gym but I also think this conversation is important and we should keep talking.

"I just hate everyone," she continues. "I mean, I love you, but I also hate you right now. This Jason thing is super awk, Ari."

My skin prickles a little and my instant reaction is to just get up and run away and cry in the bathroom.

She goes on, "I mean, I liked him, and even though I sort of stopped liking him, I didn't totally stop. And you knew that. And it's like a violation of some kind of ethical code to start going out with someone your best friend used to go out with. Ya know?"

"I'm not familiar with that code," I say quietly. "I honestly thought you were totally over Jason, and also I thought you didn't even care. So where is this coming from now?"

"I thought I didn't care, but then I realized I do care." She puts her head back down on her knees. "Can you go tell the PE teachers that we're not coming today? I'm not in the mood to unicycle."

"But the list, Kay. Come on, we have tons to do." I put an arm around her. "Loyal to the List."

"I know. But not today," she replies without picking her head up again.

I sit there for a minute, wondering if I can just email the PE department because I really don't feel like getting up.

"You're the only one I told about my dad, by the way," she mumbles. "Not even Cami when we were on the trip, and I was so miserable. And I haven't told anyone about comedy camp since I wasn't even sure my dad would help pay for it so I could go!" She huffs. "So even though I hate you, I obviously love you, too. Just FYI. We're obviously on another level."

My mind flashes to the unicorn thing.

"Good to know." I lean my head on my palm and close my eyes for a minute. I try to find the energy to get up and walk all the way to the gym to tell them about our change in plans.

And when I finally do, I walk over there, and I think about what Kaylan was saying about decisions and selfishness and all that stuff.

I think about what my camp friends said during the sleepover about Golfy being their friend, too.

I don't know how all of this got so complicated.

I kind of wish I had one of those thick white erasers that I use for math, but a giant one, life-sized, really. And I could just erase all the stuff I didn't like, and start over, and then I'd do it differently.

Is there a way to buy something like that?

A restart button maybe.

An eraser that helps fix bad decisions.

It wouldn't need to erase all of it. Just a few things.

33

KAYLAN

Ari: is it okay if we just do the spicy chip just us

Ari: I know we said we'd invite all the lunch table girls but I don't feel like having a whole party 4 it

Ari: is that ok

Me: um, I guess

Ari: r u mad

Me: no

I spend the rest of the school week having an internal debate about if I'm starting to take my frustrations about my dad getting married out on Ari with the Jason thing. I think I may be a little bit, but not entirely.

I still think it's weird that she'd want to go out with him, given my history with the boy. To be honest, I thought they'd be over by now. But it's spring and they're still going strong.

It seems like I'm never totally feeling one way about anything. I'm always half and half—like swirl soft serve, but in this case an unappealing variety. I'm basically half pickle, half smoked-salmon soft serve right now.

Also, I'm kind of surprised Ari doesn't want to invite the lunch table girls to come over when we eat the spicy chip like we'd planned on. It's totally a the-more-the-merrier kind of thing. But I guess she never really wants to do anything with them, except eat lunch at school.

Cami never calls me to hang out one-on-one anymore. We see each other at lunch, and the whole group of us has hung out a few times since the trip, but that's it. Something happened between us at that fancy resort and I don't think it'll ever go back to the way it was. I'm okay with that, though.

The silver lining to all of this is that my forms are in for Laurel Lake. And each week they send a different video highlighting stuff that happens during the summer. This week's was when a group from a famous improv troupe came to camp last year, and different campers were called up to participate.

Ari's sleeping over tonight and then we're starting our race training tomorrow morning. We're saving the spicy chip for another time. We can't do everything all at once.

I'm glad Amirah's doing the race with us and not just because I think it's super cool she's going to run a race in a hijab. I'm also glad because it means we've become more inclusive about our lists. And even though that wasn't a list item, it may as well have been.

It can't always be Ari and Kaylan.

I'm glad Ari was the one who asked Amirah to run with us; at least she likes someone at the table other than me.

I get downstairs for breakfast on Saturday morning and find my mom at the kitchen table, researching something on her laptop. I'm not totally sure what's going on with her and Robert Irwin Krieger these days. I don't think they talk as much as they used to, but maybe I haven't been paying close attention.

"Morning," I say, pulling one of the wooden kitchen chairs away from the table and sitting down. I wait for my mom to ask me what I want for breakfast but she barely looks up.

I look over at her, and get a sudden pang of the deepest sadness I may have ever felt in my whole life. She doesn't even notice me staring at her, but I look away because the pain is too great.

I don't know why this was such a slow-moving realization. It just didn't hit me at first, and now it's hitting hard—a boulder to my head.

My dad gets to just pick up and marry someone new, while my mom is forced to accept it. I don't even think that's fair. My mom didn't want the divorce, my mom didn't want him to leave, and my mom definitely doesn't want him marrying a different person.

I picture her the way she always looks on Christmas morning, getting all dressed up, wearing her pearls even though she cooks all day. I imagine the way she dabs little drops of perfume behind her ears and on her wrists.

I know she's been trying her hardest to be calm about it for Ryan and me, but deep down I think she's really hurting. No one plans to get divorced. On someone's wedding day, they're not imagining that it will just end and the whole thing will be pointless.

I don't understand how my dad just gets to do whatever he wants, and we're stuck dealing with it.

He can have his new Arizona lady-wife, but he's not going to have me.

I run upstairs to my computer.

Dear Dad,

Thanks for helping to pay for comedy camp. I really appreciate it. I'll pay you back when I'm famous. I'm sorry but I can't go to your wedding. I am still hurting so much from when you left. I miss you. I wish you were still here. I hope you can understand.

Love, Kaylan

"Kay, want cheesy scrambled eggs?" my mom asks when I get back down to the kitchen.

“Yeah, sounds great,” I reply, feeling a sense of relief that I was honest with my dad. *Be Me*. Truly. “I told you Ari is sleeping over tonight, right?”

“Yup.”

She goes to the fridge and gets out the eggs and the milk and the cheese, salt and pepper from the pantry. She puts a few pieces of bread in the toaster, scrambles the eggs, adding the cheddar cheese at the last minute, and voilà, I have the breakfast of a queen.

“Thanks, Mom.” I smile.

She sits down at the table with me, does one more thing on her laptop, and then closes it.

“Ryan and I are planning to have the basement cleaned out within the next few weeks,” I tell her. “And then Mrs. Etisof can start painting.”

She slow-nods. “Okay.” The way she says that, it sorta seems like she doesn’t care all that much, but I decide not to dwell on it. I guess a basement mural isn’t as exciting for her as it is for me.

I finish breakfast and then read on the couch for a few hours and before I know it, Ari comes over, looking all gloomy.

“What’s wrong?” I ask her once we’re up in my room.

She sighs, and hesitates before answering. “Ugh. Bub. She’s not doing great.”

When Ari’s upset, she always talks in short sentences.

“How? In what way? What do you mean?” I ask.

“It seems unlikely she’ll walk again,” Ari explains. “I don’t even know what’s happening. I thought, like, once she got home from the hospital she’d bounce back. But it doesn’t seem like she’s bouncing.”

“Well, she doesn’t have to bounce. She could just slowly move in the right direction.” I pause. “Y’know?”

Ari nods. “Yeah, but that’s not happening. It seems like she gets worse each time I see her.”

I scratch the top of my head, sort of hoping that will give me an idea of what to say back to Ari. Nothing seems right. My mind is blank.

“That doesn’t mean she’ll never get better,” I say finally. “I mean, just because it’s going in one direction doesn’t mean it’ll always go in that direction.”

“I guess.” Ari shrugs. “Anyway, it just feels depressing.”

“I get that. What can we do to cheer ourselves up? We need something good.”

“I don’t know.” Ari sighs. “Listen, though, I feel like we need to have a conference about something on the list. We have barely discussed this one item in depth; it just sort of pops in and out and it’s been bugging me. Like, gnawing away at my mind.”

“Um, okay. Which one?” I ask.

Ari gets up to make sure my door is closed, and my stomach starts to rumble, thinking this conversation is going in a super-awkward direction.

"The *Be Me* thing," she whispers.

I laugh a little. "Wait, why are you whispering?"

She cracks up. "I have no idea. It just seemed like one of the most kinda personal things on the list and I didn't want Ryan to hear."

"It's not that personal," I tell her.

"Anyway, *Be Me*. So, like, I thought I was 'being me' with the whole Jason thing and stuff, but it kinda seems like it was a bad idea. I've been trying to be more open about what I want to do and what I don't, in terms of our lunch table crew and stuff." She pauses. "But it's not so easy. Because everyone has opinions."

I nod. "Yeah, I know what you mean. I finally told my dad I'm not going to his wedding. I mean, I emailed him, but it was super hard to do. I don't think it's supposed to be easy."

"Yes it is," Ari disagrees. "Being yourself should be the easiest thing in the world because you're literally, like, being yourself."

I throw myself back on the bed, feeling a headache coming on. "No, that's why it's hard, because you're doing things that may be unpopular in an effort to be yourself. So it's not easy. For example, the Jason thing. You're doing it because it feels right, but that doesn't mean everyone's just gonna love it just because it feels right to you."

"Yeah," Ari replies. "That's true. So then why do people

say 'just be yourself' like it's the easiest thing ever? It's totally not."

"No idea. But of course it's not the easiest thing ever. That's why we put it on the list."

Ari shakes her head and flops over onto her stomach, burying her face in my stack of pillows. "This is giving me a headache."

"Ari," I say. "Just because you're doing what feels right to you, you think everyone automatically has to like it. That's not true."

"So what about your dad then?" Ari asks. "He's being him, or whatever. He feels like he's *being me*, with his decisions."

I'm quiet after that because it feels like I just got hit in the stomach during a violent game of dodgeball.

"That's different," I tell her, curling up on my window seat. "Totally different. Because he has a family and people who depend on him and rely on him and he made commitments and then broke them. Totally different." I feel myself getting all fired up, so I take some deep breaths to calm down.

"Okay, I'm just debating this with you." Ari defends herself.

"Well, that was way harsh. Don't bring my dumb dad into this. We're talking about teenagers here, not, like, grown adults who should know better." I sniffle a little but force myself not to cry. I'm not letting my dad make me cry. He's already done that enough.

We're quiet for a few moments and then I say, "Also, it's important to Be Me, especially when it's not popular for a big group. This is cheesy, but what about when someone stands up for someone being bullied? Or fights injustice and stuff? That's Be Me, too."

"Maybe we need to make a list of all the things that can fall under *Be Me*," Ari suggests. "Hey, I have an idea. Something that will def cheer us up! I'm craving garlic bread with cheese. Want to see if your mom can drive us to Mario's and we can make our list and eat a thousand loaves of garlic bread at the same time?"

"I could go for that," I reply. "But only if we can go out for ice cream after. I just realized I'm super hungry."

"I am too," Ari says. "But I think we're onto something with this *Be Me* thing. Do you feel like you've been doing it?"

I think a minute. "Um, kind of. Especially with the email to my dad. But also, I didn't just give in to what Cami wanted. Basically she wants me to commit to being her BFF one hundred percent and she wants me to be super mad at you for the Jason thing. And let's see, what else? I don't know. Also, I think I've been open with you about how I'm feeling. So that's *Be Me*, too."

Ari nods. "I feel like it's something bigger, though," she says as we walk down the stairs.

"Mom," I call out. "Can you drive us to Mario's, please?"

She doesn't answer.

"Mom! Where are you?"

"Sheesh, Kaylan. Chill. She's in the basement doing laundry," Ryan yells from the den, shouting over the beeping sounds from his video game.

"Ryan, shut up. I'm not even talking to you." I roll my eyes at him, even though he can't see me.

A few seconds later, my mom comes up the stairs from the basement carrying an overflowing laundry basket, and I get that sadness pang again, especially seeing how tired and worn-out she looks.

"Let me take that for you." I grab the basket. "I'll run this upstairs, okay?"

She nods, looking slightly confused. "Kaylan and Ryan, this basement still needs tons of work. You know this, yes?"

"Yes," I yell from upstairs.

Ryan doesn't respond. His version of *Be Me* is basically just *Be Only About Me*, and that's a totally different thing.

We're quiet on the drive over to Mario's. The air in the car feels thick with everyone's swirling thoughts.

When we get there, we sit at the best table in the whole place—the little booth for two in one of the front windows. The waitress brings us cups of water and then we order garlic bread with cheese, two root beers, and an order of mozzarella sticks.

"I'm starving," I say. "I feel like I could eat every single thing on the menu."

"Me, too." Ari nods. "So *Be Me*. The thing is, it's more than just the two of us. I mean, who suggested it when we were first making the list with our friends? I can't remember."

"Me neither," Kaylan adds. "Oops. But anyway, go on."

"So it goes beyond just us. It's also, kind of like a battle cry of teenagehood."

I crack up. "Ari! You sound like some kind of preacher. Are you becoming a rabbi or something right now?"

She shakes her head. "Maybe. Who knows. Anyway, though, hear me out. We're all trying to figure ourselves out all the time, while also trying to fit in. It's like we're trying to do so many things all at once. It came to me the other night when I couldn't fall asleep because I was worrying about Bubbie. Our movement."

"Yeah?" I ask, a little confused. "What about it?"

"Our movement is *Be Me*. It's not just about you and me being ourselves. But take Cami, for example—she's all over the place because she's always trying to be something. It's like she has some kind of hidden plan of the person she wants to be, but she could just be herself, and then it would all come together."

I pause and think a minute, looking to the back of the restaurant, hoping that our garlic bread comes soon. When Ari mentioned it, I started salivating right away.

Nothing in the world (except for maybe sushi at Hibino) can compare to the garlic bread with mozzarella at Mario's.

"So what do you think?" Ari asks me. She takes a sip of root beer.

"It sounds amazing," I say. "I think it can definitely be our movement. But how do we make it a movement?"

Ari shrugs. "No clue. We put *start a movement* on the list without any idea how to really do it."

"Sounds like us." I burst out laughing.

A few minutes later, our garlic bread arrives and we tear into it, still discussing the *Be Me* thing.

"Oooh," I say. "Maybe we can hang posters at school that say *Be Me* and we can have people's photos, just of them looking natural and stuff?"

"Yes!" Ari screams. "Maybe it's a hashtag! Like #BeMe! And we write that everywhere!"

I finish chewing my piece of garlic bread. "I think we'll need to get the administration involved."

Ari rips off another piece. "Yeah, so? We can do that."

"I'm in." I grab a mozzarella stick off the plate. "Look, we learned to unicycle. We can so do this, too."

"We *are* doing it," Ari adds.

34

ARI

KAYLAN FINDS A WAY TO bring up the Jason thing at least once an hour. I'm not counting exactly but I'm keeping track enough to notice. It's not bugging me that much, though. And the weird thing is that it's not really taking away from our fun at this sleepover. She just sort of mentions it, I reply, and then we move on.

Maybe that means we're growing up. Like we don't dwell on stuff as much as we used to, or something. Hard to say.

"I never showed you this," Kaylan says. "I meant to take a picture and text it to you, but then I forgot." She hands me a square-shaped airline napkin, and I read it over.

Dear Ari, I'm writing you on the back of this airplane napkin to solidify our thing about God on the list. I don't know if you'll ever see this note.

I may die.

I keep reading and then I look up at her.

"So how did you feel about God after the plane landed?" I ask. "Sure about her existence? Or no? You didn't die." I smile.

"I know. That's why I'm showing this to you." She motions for me to move over on her beanbag chair and she reads the note over again, too. "I am one hundred percent a believer."

I laugh a little. "You sound like you just joined a cult or something."

She cracks up, too, falling onto me a little. "I know. But I mean, God was always this concept that we learned about in church and Sunday school and I never thought about it so much. It was just not that meaningful to me. But then things got sort of hectic. I mean, not only on that plane. But in life, too. And I found myself needing someone to help me, but not a real person who would give me advice or tell me what to do. Someone who would just sort of listen, but I almost didn't want to see the person nodding or making faces. And that was God. You really do feel like someone's listening," she says. "Even though you can't see anyone."

I put my arm around her and rest my head on her shoulder. "I agree. It's like, without talking to God, who do you ask for stuff? The actual big stuff in life? Those desperate moments. The times when all you can do is hope and pray and stay positive. God helps you through that."

Kaylan stands up and starts pacing back and forth in her room like she's on the cusp of figuring out something really big and important. I start to wonder if we're the only thirteen-year-olds in the world who think about this stuff. Maybe there are others out there but we don't know them. My camp friends are kinda like this, too, I guess, now that I think about it. Maybe I'm drawn to deep, introspective thinkers.

Is Jason like that? Kinda, I guess.

Golfy definitely was.

Kaylan's still pacing and I'm still thinking and we're so quiet, I can hear the grandfather clock chiming downstairs.

"It's sort of unfair how we only come to God when we're desperate, though," Kaylan says, finally, sitting down on her bed. "When we are literally so stressed we think we're going to die or we think a relative is going to die and there's nothing we can do, so we're like 'God, please help. Wahhhh.'" She makes a crying face and I burst into laughter. "We should all write God a note sometimes. 'Sorry I'm so rude. I never ask how *you're* doing and I never say thank you, and I take you for granted and I just ask so much of you.'"

My mind flashes ahead twenty years and I picture her on the stage at Madison Square Garden, in front of thousands of people, making everyone laugh. And I'll be in the front row because I'm a VIP and I'll think back to this moment. I'll be able to tell everyone that I always knew Kaylan was funny, and she made me laugh first.

I catch my breath and Kaylan says, "Do you know what I mean, though? I'm serious."

"I do. Totally. You're right." I inch back on the beanbag chair so I'm sitting up straighter. "But Judaism is all about gratitude, though, too. Thanking God for stuff. So we don't totally take him or her for granted. And you guys, Christians, I mean, do that, too. Saying grace and stuff—that's all appreciating God. It's not all take take take."

She considers it for a minute. "Yeah, I guess."

"How are there people who don't believe in God, though?" I ask her. "Do you know any?"

She thinks. "Yeah, I don't think my brother does. And my dad always told us he was an atheist."

I laugh again. "We should take a poll at school. It would be interesting. Don't you think?"

"Yeah, it's kinda personal," Kaylan says. "But maybe."

We stay up really late continuing to debate this, and also entering as many online contests as we can find and searching for dogs on Pet Finder. We fall asleep after one in the morning, still in our clothes, with Kaylan's laptop between us.

I'm pretty sure those are all signs of a successful working-on-a-list sleepover.

When Kaylan's alarm goes off at eight the next morning, we're so asleep it feels like the middle of the night. It takes me a minute to remember why we even set an alarm, and then I remember.

Training!

For the race!

I flop over onto my stomach, hoping to sleep for a few more minutes, but then Kaylan's phone rings.

It's Amirah.

"Hiiii," I answer, groggy, not totally sure I should be answering Kaylan's phone, but she's still asleep, so I figure it's okay.

"Hi, Kaylan?"

"No, it's Ari." I laugh. "I slept over last night."

"Oh, um, okay. I'm running late. I'll be over in a few. But you guys know it's kind of rainy, right?"

I close my eyes, trying to sleep and talk at the same time. "Ummm. So we'll just do a short run and wear raincoats maybe. I think we just want to feel like we started the training."

"Got it. See you soon."

Kaylan mumbles "Who was that?" still mostly asleep.

"Amirah. She's coming soon. We need to get up, Kay."

"Five more minutes," she grumbles again.

When Amirah gets here, she does these high-knee warm-ups and jogs in place while we get ready to go outside and start running.

"Is it bad to run on an empty stomach?" I ask them. "Should we have breakfast first?"

Kaylan shakes her head. "It's fine, we're not doing that much. Just drink some water and then maybe we'll walk over to Martin's after we run. It's super close to the track at the high school. Mmmm. Bacon, egg, and cheese. How good does that sound?"

I smack her arm. "Kay! You're making me hungry. Now I really want breakfast first. Should we do Martin's and then run?"

Amirah laughs, and falls back on Kaylan's bed. "Girls, come on. For real, people. You two always think about food. Let's do this training! I'm pumped up! I'm wearing my best running leggings. Let's do this, people!" She does some fast jumping jacks.

A second later there's pounding on Kaylan's door, and Ryan busts in. "What the heck is going on in here? You guys know it's not even nine a.m., right? You're so loud!"

"Sorry," I groan, as Kaylan rolls her eyes.

"Oh, hey," Amirah says to Ryan, like they sort of know each other in more than a Kaylan's-dumb-brother kind of way.

"Oh, hey, Amirah. I didn't realize it was you." He looks down at his shorts and his dirty socks. "Later."

We all stare at each other after that, and I'm wondering if something's going on with Ryan and Amirah. I thought he was still going out with that girl Maura, but maybe not. We don't exactly spend a lot of time talking about Ryan's love life, or lack of a love life, I should say. That's the case most of the time.

"You guys ready? Come on!" Amirah says, running in place again. "I'm fired up! Let's do this!"

"Do we need raincoats?" I ask. "Is it too rainy to just run in a sweatshirt?"

I look to Amirah since she seems to know what she's doing here, with her fancy running gear and everything.

"Nah, you'll be fine, it's not that bad, just wear your hoodie. You guys are wayyyy overthinking this." She pauses. "Aren't we just running a few laps at the high school? Come on, peeps."

We finally make it outside and Kaylan's mom drives us over there.

She says, "Please don't stay out too long, girls. It's kind of a nasty day. Amirah, your parents are okay with this?"

"They've already been out for a jog this morning!" She laughs. "Don't worry!"

We all giggle after that and soon we're at the track, running around. I tell myself that it's not that rainy, even though I have to keep brushing the water out of my eyes. I assure myself that we'll be done soon. I imagine myself eating the Egg McMartin—oozy eggs and oozy cheese on a flaky roll, and maybe I'll get a hot chocolate, too.

It's not that bad, I repeat to myself again and again as I run around the track.

I just need to do this four times. Four times is a mile. That'll be enough for today and we can hustle over to the warm restaurant and sit in a cozy booth and have that happy-the-hard-part-is-over-and-now-we-rest feeling.

I feel the wind and rain slapping my face as I run. It slows me down a little but I try not to focus on it. As I run, I think about all the things in my life—the Jason thing, how my camp friends are a little disturbed that I ditched Golfy, how Kaylan feels about stuff, Kaylan's dad, Cami, and Bubbie, too.

But as I run, it all kind of flows together and then melts away. Like the running is literally clearing my mind, letting me have a break from the stress and the worry and, in Kaylan's language, agita.

I think back to camp and the whole mindfulness thing and this may seem obvious, even though it never occurred to me—but running is a super-easy way to clear your mind, to truly and completely be mindful.

As I run, I can't really focus on anything except for the actual running. I can't think about anything else except for the basic movement of one foot in front of the other, one foot in front of the other, and again and again and again.

I look over at Amirah and Kaylan as they run. Kaylan

looks to be struggling, slowing down her pace, a little bit like she may cry at some point.

But Amirah glides like some kind of Olympian. Her hijab is around her head and her leggings have this glittery reflector panel along each leg.

I watch Amirah run some more and I try to catch up with her.

I don't think she really needs to train for this race; she'd probably be all set to run it tomorrow. Maybe she just wanted running buddies. Maybe she just wanted an excuse to hang out with us.

It doesn't matter—I'm glad she's here.

I run and run and run some more and soon I've completed the four laps. I plop onto one of the picnic tables, not even caring that the bench is wet.

Amirah's on the side doing some stretch where she pulls her foot up to the back of her thigh and then puts it down. A few minutes later, Kaylan finishes her run. She sits down next to me, and rests her head on my shoulder.

"Holy cannoli," she says, gasping for air. "That was hard. We basically have to do that run three times for the race?"

I nod. "I think so. But it will be nice and warm out then!"

"You promise?"

I rest my head on her head. "Yes. I promise."

“Race you to Martin’s?” I hop up from the bench and take off.

Kaylan slumps over onto the table, but I know she’ll follow behind me soon enough.

This is all part of the training.

35

KAYLAN

Me: u sure u don't want 2 invite the girls today

Ari: yes sure

Ari: be over in 10 min

I read over the Laurel Lake packet that just came in the mail—with the packing list and parent handbook and directions to camp—and then I set up the spicy chip on the kitchen table. It's pretty small and it's kind of unbelievable that it's really that hot. Also that Ari and I are literally sharing one chip. That we had to wait this long for one chip to arrive in the mail.

"I can't believe you're doing this," Ryan says. "People have died from eating those."

"No they haven't!" I yell, but my agita feelings start to creep in. He may be right; I haven't researched it that much.

"They have, Kay." He walks away, and I sit there at the table, trying to quickly search on my phone. I have the yogurt ready and the milk and I have gloves for Ari and me—all the stuff that I've heard helps to make the experience a little easier.

A minute later, Ari walks in, slumpy and bored-looking. "I can't stay long. My parents are annoyed that my room is so messy. I started another donation pile and now everything is everywhere."

"Oh, sorry," I mumble, still reading on my phone. "Why are you giving so much away?"

"I just don't need so much stuff."

I feel her staring at me.

"Are you ready?" Ari asks, sounding impatient.

I hesitate because we've waited so long for this chip to come and it feels so anticlimactic now. It would have been way more fun with the lunch table girls. Now this just feels boring and lame and like something we have to get done. We never wanted our lists to be like that.

I nod. "Sure. Put on the gloves."

So she does and we each take half a chip between our fingers.

"As soon as you're done, drink this glass of milk and then eat the yogurt and then we can take these Tums," I instruct. "Okay?"

"Sure."

"You ate before this, right?" I ask her. "We can't eat

this chip on an empty stomach!"

"Yes, Kay!" Ari yells. "This chip is turning you back into the old Agita Kaylan, you know that, yes?"

I roll my eyes. I don't want to tell her that she yanked all the fun out of this in the least Chill Girl Ari way imaginable.

"Ready?" she asks again. "I'll count to three!"

I nod, pouring two tall glasses of milk. I set out pieces of bread to help absorb the spice. I read somewhere that can help.

"One." We stare at each other, talking with our eyes. I think we're both wondering why we agreed to do this. "Two." We pause again and there's a longer space between numbers. "Three!"

We take the chip pieces and move them to our lips and Ari takes two nibbles. Her face is the angriest face imaginable but she takes the whole piece of chip in her mouth. I turn away to eat my piece because if I look at her, I won't be able to do it.

"Oh my God. Oh my God! I'm dying!" Ari screams. "I'm dying!" She pours the whole container of yogurt into her mouth and then the milk. "I need ice! Help!"

But I can't help her because my mouth is an inferno and she ate all the yogurt. I pull open the freezer and put my whole head in, finding the pint of ice cream, taking the lid off and literally putting my face into it, licking the whole top with my head still in the freezer.

Anything to cool my face down.

It hurts deep in my throat, all the way down my esophagus to my stomach.

My whole body is singeing.

"What are you doing?" Ryan yelps. "Ew! That was my ice cream! You guys are so gross."

Ari throws the empty yogurt container at him and moves over to the sink, literally putting her face under the faucet and drinking like it's a water fountain.

She stays like that for the next ten minutes while my head is in the freezer.

Finally, things start to calm down.

"Holy mother of pogo sticks," Ari says. "That was mind-blowingly, insanely the most awful thing I've ever eaten in my life." She pours a few Tums in her mouth, directly from the bottle.

I shake my head, crying, tears dripping from my eyes like a leaky pipe. When will this pain end? Maybe never. Maybe I'll spend the rest of my life feeling like my entire body is on fire.

"Holy mother of anchovies," I say, not sure where we're getting these sayings but kind of enjoying it. "What if this taste never leaves my mouth?"

"I was wondering the same thing," Ari says. "And I have to go home now. Pray for me."

"Same," I reply, pulling Ari into a hug. "We did it, though."

"We did it," she says, leaving the kitchen. "Smooches forever."

I sit at the table and finish the ice cream and drink water, but nothing really helps. My mouth is on fire for the rest of the day.

Loyal to the List.

We may have taken it too far with this one.

After we complete the spicy chip eating, the weeks really start to fly by in that *spring is finally here* kind of way. Everything feels lighter and more manageable. We shed our heavy coats for hoodies and it gives me the feeling that everything (okay, maybe not everything) is right in the world.

Ari, Amirah, and I train for the race every weekend—either Saturday or Sunday—and every week it's a little warmer and we run a little farther. Ryan and I usually work on cleaning out the basement on the other weekend day, and Ari and I squeeze in a Bubbie and Zeyda visit, too.

Some days Bubbie seems like she could run for public office and other days she seems like she could sleep for a month and still not feel rested. There's never really an in-between.

My mom doesn't say much about my dad's wedding. Not to us, anyway. But sometimes when she thinks I'm doing my homework in my room, and I've left the door open, I hear her on the phone with her friends. She talks super quietly, almost whispering, but I can hear enough to know that she's hurt.

She'll say "I just can't believe it" again and again. It stings.

I don't want my mom to be hurt.

Sometimes I wonder if I think more about my mom's feelings than other kids do about theirs. I guess there's no way to know for sure.

Ryan's planning to go, and that's fine with me. He has a different relationship with my dad, and also he's not going to comedy camp. He's also kind of a doofus, so there's that, too.

I can't worry about what he does.

Be Me. That's what matters.

And ever since Ari and I had that God talk, I think about God a lot more. I talk to God a lot more, too. And I try to figure out if God is a woman or a man. The more I think about it, the more I think woman.

Only a woman would be able to handle listening to so many people's problems all at the same time.

I'm down in the basement finishing the final touches of clean-out so Mrs. Etisof can start on the mural next week when my phone rings. I never really turn the ringer on but I knew I wouldn't feel the vibrations while cleaning.

"OMG, Kay," Ari says. "Did you check your email?"

"No. I'm cleaning. What's up?"

"There's a dog for us. He's a rescue from Massachusetts and he's so cute, and hypoallergenic, and he's only nine months old but already trained so he won't pee and poop all over. Eeeee." Ari pauses. "Check your email. I want you to see the pic."

I put her on speaker so I can click on my email while she's still on the phone and I look at this picture of this little furry, orangey-haired poodle (I think) that's just so cute I want to scoop him up right through my phone screen.

"OMG. Cutest ever."

"Right?" Ari *eeeees* again.

"Your parents said yes?" I ask her.

"Yes. And get this—they finally agree that it would be good for Bubbie's health to have a dog around. They checked with one of her doctors, who said that certain dogs have healing powers. We were right!"

"Really?" I yelp. "I love to be right!"

"Yes. We're getting a dog! We're getting a dog!" she sings again and again.

"When?" I ask.

"We're driving to get the dog next weekend. I can't even believe it. My parents said spring and it's definitely, finally spring and this is happening!"

I sit down on the dresser and lean against the wall. "But a name! We still don't have a name! That was the main thing on the list for this. Well, convincing your parents, too, obv. But we need a name!"

"Yes, I am so excited. Brainstorm sesh after training tomorrow, K?"

"K. Sounds fab. Okay, back to cleaning for me." I pause, debating about asking her something. "Am I the first person you told about this news?"

Ari laughs. "Um, yeah. Why?"

"Just checking." I smile, even though I'm down here alone and no one can see me.

Something occurred to me the other day.

We all have a first person: the girl or woman or boy or man or whomever we contact when we want to share a funny story, or tell someone good news, or express a particular kind of sadness.

I want to be Ari's first person because she's mine.

I want her to always be my first person and I want to always be hers.

Even though friendships change all the time (and they really, really do) I hope we can always be each other's first person.

Maybe someone's first person is also their unicorn.

I'm not sure.

She laughs. "You're so weird, Kay. But I love you so much."

"Right back atcha."

At the same time, we start to recite the words we saw

on this print in an art gallery by this artist named Brian Andreas, the summer before fifth grade.

You're the strangest person I ever met, she said & I said you too & we decided we'd know each other a long time.

We crack up after we say it.

"Remember when we first saw that and thought it was honestly so weird?" Ari asks me. "But truthfully, it kinda makes sense now. Don't you think?"

"Totally," I reply. "I think about that all the time."

"I wonder why it stayed with us so much," Ari considers. "Like, we saw tons of stuff that day when my mom thought it would be fun to take us to an art gallery. Um, no thanks. But for some reason, that one thing stuck in our minds."

"I know. I don't get it. But I still love it."

"I do too," Ari says. "Okay, start thinking of names. I'll call you later."

"Okay. Smooches."

"Smooches."

I keep cleaning after that even though Ryan only joins me for the last twenty minutes.

"Why are you so lame about this project?" I ask him.

He throws a soft basketball against the wall. "Because I don't care about a stupid mural. You're lucky I'm even helping at all."

"You're so rude, Ryan."

He doesn't answer.

I keep sorting toys into a giveaway pile and a garbage pile and when I reach the top shelf where all his old Hess trucks are, I pause.

"Are you saving these?" I ask him. "Maybe you can just put them on a shelf in your room. Like a cool display. They may be worth money one day, you never know."

He stares at the trucks and then back at me.

"What?" I ask him when he doesn't say anything.

"Just donate them. I don't want them." He grabs a bunch and shoves them in a big, black garbage bag.

"You used to love these," I remind him.

"Well, I don't anymore. I don't play with trucks. Get over it, Kay. Things change and people move on. That's it. Stop being so dramatic all the time."

I fold my arms across my chest, about to say something, but I stop myself. I don't think we're talking about Hess trucks anymore.

I sit down on the floor and pull my knees up to my chest. "Are you sad about Dad?" I ask him.

"I just said stop being so dramatic! God! Why are you like this? You're the one who's sad about it, the one who won't go to his dumb wedding." He throws the last of the trucks in the bag and then stomps up the stairs. "Get a life."

I wonder how long it will take him to learn that it's better to express your feelings and get them out instead of just pushing them way down deep.

He'd feel so much better if he just talked about stuff.

Maybe I should suggest God as a listening ear for him. Or Mrs. Etisof could be helpful, too.

Either way, talking to someone would do him some good.

36

ARI

Me: U guys guess what?

Alice: ?

Zoe: what

Hana: What? Tell!

Me: we r getting a dog 4 real

Me: & best part is it's a rescue from right near camp

Alice: OMG

Hana: what r u going to name it

Me: IDK still thinking

Zoe: r u open to suggestions? ☺

Me: possss

Mei: miss u guys

Alice: dittttoooooo

Alice: don't be mad but we r all going to golfy's for a camp reunion

Alice: I didn't want to keep it from u

Me: oh ok ☹

Zoe: we still love u ari obvs

Hana: not even a question obvi obvi

Me: k good

Me: but still ☹

I slump down in my chair at the table after reading all of those texts. The dog happiness fades away a little bit. I mean, it makes sense that I wouldn't be invited to Golfy's for a camp reunion but it still sort of stinks.

A minute later, Jason's sitting at the table with me, taking one of my mom's apple-crisp muffins out of the basket and biting into it.

"Hey, where'd you come from?" I ask him.

"Across the street. Duh."

I shrug, half smiling. I stare at him as he eats his muffin. His hair is sticking up in a million directions. He has a constellation of crumbs in the corner of his mouth. The neck of his T-shirt is so stretched out, like he's always pulling on it, and he has a scab on the knuckle of his right thumb.

This is Jason.

I don't even know what to say, or how I ended up here, really.

I like him. At least I thought I did. But then right now, the like doesn't feel quite so strong. I guess it's good people don't get married at thirteen. There'd be no way for me to make up my mind. And my opinions change way too often.

"So what's up? We're going to visit your grandparents today, right?" he asks after slurping some orange juice. "Where's your fam? Why are you sitting alone at the table?"

I look around. To be honest, I hadn't realized I was alone here. I got so lost in that group text about the Golfy camp reunion and then Jason showed up and now here we are.

"No clue where anyone is, truthfully," I say. "You don't have to come with me to visit them, ya know."

"Dude!" Jason yells. "I want to! Zeyda's my man."

I laugh a little, realizing again why I like Jason. "Okay, sounds good."

We put on our shoes and head over there.

"It's gonna be fab that you can walk over here in the summer and swim in this pool," Jason says as we walk into their development.

"But we have our own town pool," I remind him.

"Yeah, but still. This one looks sick." He nods for emphasis.

"It does? It's covered up. Jason!" I swat his arm. "Stop being dumb."

We walk up the path to my grandparents' apartment and ring the bell. When no one answers, I knock. Still no answer. I start to get a panicky feeling. What if something happened to them? I don't want to be the one to discover they're dead. Maybe that's selfish of me, but it's true.

"See if the door's unlocked," Jason says.

"Should I?" I ask. Sometimes I feel like Jason has all the answers, even though he's just a dumb seventh-grade boy and really knows nothing. He gives the impression that he has answers, though. I'm not sure how or why. But he does.

"Yeah. We're not gonna just stand here forever." He flicks the top of my hat and shakes his head. "Oh, Nodberg."

Then he leans his forehead against mine and pulls away, giving me a quick kiss.

This boy is an enigma. He can be so dumb and mildly gross when he eats and then so cute and romantic.

I turn the doorknob and call out a singsongy, "Hello?"

No answer.

Okay, they're dead. And I'm going to be the one to find them and then have to report it to my parents and the police. This is a nightmare. I don't know why I started coming here alone, without my mom or dad or someone. I always take on too much. Way more than I can handle.

"Hello?" I call again.

"Ari?" Zeyda asks in a sort of confused yelling tone.

I run back to the den and find both of them in their

recliners. Bubbie's asleep, her head back against the cushion, the blue oxygen cord firmly in her nose. Zeyda's watching some game with the volume low and reading the newspaper at the same time.

A minute later, their aide Sally pops in, a dish towel over her shoulder.

"Oh, hi." She smiles. "I was just fixing them some lunch. Want anything?"

I shake my head. I feel like I'll never eat again when I come here. It's the combination of the oxygen and someone else in Bubbie's kitchen that really irks me. It's like no food will ever be appealing in this space for the rest of my life.

"How ya doing, Zeyda?" Jason pulls over a folding chair and turns to face the TV so he can watch the game with him.

"All right." Zeyda offers a halfhearted smile, like he's not even sure he's met Jason before. I guess they haven't really talked that many times—just at my bat mitzvah and a few visits last year. "You?"

"Can't complain," Jason replies, like he's suddenly a forty-five-year-old dad of three.

"Good. And you, Ar?" Zeyda asks, turning to me.

"Okay." I choke back tears. I want Bubbie to wake up. I know she's alive because I see her breathing, but it's not good to sleep in the middle of the day like this. It feels depressing. Like it's a sick day. I guess it is a sick day for

Bubbie, though. Does this mean all of her days are sick days? I push the thought away.

"She didn't sleep well last night," Zeyda says like he can read my mind. "Truthfully, I didn't either."

"Oh, maybe you guys sleep too much during the day," I mention. One of our counselors at camp told us that if we skip activities to nap we won't sleep at night and then we'll be on a perpetual tired cycle. In all fairness, she was the lamest counselor, but maybe she has a point.

"I don't know," Zeyda says, like he's too tired to debate the issue.

I want him to tell me that I can wake Bubbie up, the way he used to do when I was little and I'd sleep over and they'd still be asleep first thing in the morning. He doesn't, though, and I'm too scared to ask. I don't want the answer to be no.

So we sit there, and Jason watches the game with Zeyda. I think it's a rerun of a baseball game, which also seems kind of depressing.

Sally brings over a plate of cheese and crackers and I nibble on a corner and pray that Bubbie wakes up and is alert right away, exactly like the Bubbie lioness I know and love.

This isn't Bubbie, sleeping in the middle of the day, with the oxygen whirring and whirring endlessly.

I think back to the God conversation Kaylan and I had.

Please, God, let her get better.

Let her get back to her old self.

I want to come here in the summer and sit by the pool with her, and go to Martin's for breakfast. I want her to meet our dog (whatever his name is), I want her to write me letters at camp this summer and I want to write back.

There's so much more we have to do.

37

KAYLAN

"OH, I'M SO HAPPY YOU'RE here," I say to Mrs. Etisof as I open the door. "Mural painting day! Mural painting day."

She smiles and hangs up her jacket. "But you still haven't told me what you want. I have all my supplies, but I'll need to know what you have in mind before I begin."

"I know," I reply. "Ryan and my mom don't care. So I think it's really my call."

"Well, what's been on your mind?" she asks me, setting up all of her paints on the dresser and sitting down on the couch in the basement.

I think for a minute. About the Ari and Jason thing, and the Cami weirdness, about the list and God and unicorns and unicycles and my dad getting married. I have a lot on my mind, too much to mention, really.

"Um, friendship. And the universe and life, I guess," I add, laughing.

"You're so young to be thinking about such heavy things." She laughs too. "You must enjoy life, my dear."

"Oh, I am," I reassure her. "I just like to think about deep stuff."

"Uh-huh."

"Unicorns, too, though," I tell her. "I think a lot about unicorns."

"You do?" she asks.

"Yup. Because they're pretty, but also the concept of that far-fetched, hard-to-find sort of miraculous thing." I pause. "I'm trying to find my unicorn."

"We could do a unicorn mural," Mrs. Etisof suggests. "Something subtle with pale colors, maybe a rainbow, too. Something that gives the feel of a whole, wide, expansive universe just waiting to be explored."

"Ooh," I say. "I like it."

"Yeah?"

"Yeah. Can you add two girls on unicycles, too?" I start to wonder if this should be our list in mural form. Not everything, really. Not the spicy chip, or the race, or the movement. Just a few of the things. "Actually, can I show you some of my and Ari's doodles? We doodled every day for a bunch of months. Maybe we can incorporate some?"

"Sure. I'd love to see them." She smiles. "I'm going to

start with the background and then we can discuss again when I'm ready to add the details."

I nod and then I sit there and watch her paint for a little while until she says, "Hon, you can go do what you need to do. It's hard for me to work with someone watching me. I hope that doesn't hurt your feelings."

I shake my head. "Not at all."

When I get up to my room, I decide to call Ari and update her on the mural situation.

"Hey," I say as soon as Ari answers.

"Hey," she replies, and I can tell by the sound of her voice that something is off.

"What's wrong?" I ask.

"Eh, nothing. I don't feel like getting into it." She pauses. "What's up?"

"Mrs. Etisof is painting the mural now. I just wanted to see if you wanted to come over and check it out. Also I wanted to continue discussing *Be Me* and make up our unicycle practice schedule." The more I talk, the more I realize how intense I'm sounding. I'm starting to stress myself out.

"I don't feel like it today, Kay," she replies. "I'll see you in school tomorrow and we can work on the unicycle thing and also the *Be Me*. I have ideas on that but I'm too tired to discuss it now."

"Okay." I'm quiet then, waiting for her to say more, but she doesn't.

I stay in my room for a while, debating about calling Cami or June for plans, but I don't really feel like doing much of anything.

Mrs. Etisof paints for a few hours but then she stops. "I need to let this base coat dry before I add more," she tells me. "But have no fear. I'll be back tomorrow."

"I'll be at school tomorrow," I remind her. "But you can always come in. You know where we keep the extra key."

She laughs. "I do."

At school the next day, Ari and I meet in the gym early to practice the unicycling. Mr. Kohnmi meets us there.

"Girls, I have some bad news," he starts.

We stare back at him, waiting to hear more.

"The administration said no about adding unicycling to the PE curriculum," he says. "They don't think it'll get enough kids active at the same time. And it's too costly to purchase so many unicycles. Not everyone has their own, like you!"

"But we had it all planned." I try to stay respectful but something in my tone comes out annoyed and impatient. My art of persuasion clearly didn't work in this case.

"We tried to get it through, but the administration wasn't into it." He shrugs. "I'm sorry. Sometimes plans don't work out. Sometimes schools aren't as innovative as we'd like them to be."

"Is there anything else we can do, though?" Ari asks,

totally in a genuine way but also sounding a little rude.

Maybe we shouldn't have these meetings so early in the morning. We're not really morning people.

"Not really," he says. "Girls, this isn't for you to worry about. I'm happy to help you practice for your New Year's resolution or whatever this is, but please, enough questions about school matters. Get started. Okay?"

We nod, and Ari hops up on the unicycle. She's actually pretty good at it now and she can circle around and around the gym with no trouble. She can even do it with her arms folded across her chest, like she doesn't need them for balance.

"Amaze," I say. "Ari, you can join the circus. For real."

She rolls her eyes. "Okay. Your turn."

Something's up with her. She looks messy—her hair is in a bun, like she didn't have time to wash it, and she's wearing the same faded gray hoodie she wore last week when she hates to repeat outfits too often.

I nod and hop up on the unicycle, steadying myself with one foot on a pedal until I'm all the way balanced.

I'm not as good as Ari but I do make it around a few times, which is good enough for today.

"Think we're ready to add Hula-Hoops tomorrow?" she asks me.

"I think so. You?"

"Def."

She turns to Mr. Kohnmi. "Can we meet again

tomorrow morning? Same time. Same place. But with Hula-Hoops?"

He shakes his head a little, laughing. "Knock yourselves out, girls." He sounds defeated.

We thank him and walk back to our lockers.

"I don't think he gets us," I tell Ari.

"I don't think so, either."

I wait for her to tell me what's on her mind but she launches into an entirely different conversation.

"So for *Be Me*, aka our new movement." She laughs. "I think we need to get the lunch table girls on board today and see if they'll let us take pictures of them looking super casual and natural and then we hashtag #BeMe and ask the administration if we can hang them around school and then it'll catch on and then we can photograph everyone." She looks at me. "What do you think? It'll be great to have them on board from the start, since they're like our friends and stuff, and they can help us get things going."

"Um." That's a lot to take in. I just think it's funny that she's all about including the lunch table girls now when she's barely hung out with them this year. I don't want them to feel like we're using them or whatever.

"You hate it?" Ari asks, after I don't really say anything.

"I don't hate it," I tell her. "It's awesome. I just feel like you don't really like the lunch table girls so it's a bit awk to ask them to be all into this and stuff."

"Who said I don't like them? I love Amirah. And Marie and I have our own thing . . . I mean, not like you and me. But we still have something."

"You never hang out with them outside of school."

"So?" she asks. "We hang every day at lunch. Don't do this, Kay. Like the second I have a good idea, you have to pick it apart."

I pull back a little. "I'm not."

I don't even know why this is bugging me right now. It's a great idea, and I should be happy Ari wants to include the lunch table girls. But sometimes it seems like Ari gets to have everything: parents who are still married, a camp she's obsessed with, all the boys who love her, a little sister who adores her.

The one thing I had was that I was closer to the lunch table girls. I bet they'll love this plan so much, she'll have them, too.

It's not fair for her to have everything.

38

ARI

AT LUNCH, I BRING UP the *#BeMe* thing to the table.

"Which one of you suggested it when we had our first brainstorm list-making meeting?" I ask. "So sorry I can't remember."

"Um, me." Amirah smiles, raising her hand a little. "Your running buddy!"

Everyone cracks up and then June says, "Hey, did you get the donation I sent in?"

"And mine?" M.W. asks.

I look over at Kaylan, who was keeping track of all that.

"Yup. We got 'em all," she replies. "We reached our goal of two thousand dollars thanks to all of your generosity and family friends' generosity. And my neighbor Mrs. Etisof's generosity. She gave a thousand on her own." Kaylan pauses. "Wait, was this supposed to be anonymous?"

We all shrug at each other and I'm glad we can check the donation stuff off the list. "So, anyway, back to #BeMe . . ."

"Yeah?" Cami asks, looking and sounding annoyed, one cheek raised slightly higher than the other. "What about it?"

"We want to make it a movement," Kaylan jumps in, sort of taking over. "It was cool for it to be about us individually, but we want to make it, like, a collective movement all over the school, and then maybe the town and the county and the state and on and on and on. . . ."

I jump in, "But we need your help. We want to take photos of you guys and hang them all over the school with the hashtag #BeMe, and you can post online, too."

They all stare back at me, confused.

"Um," June interjects. "That's sort of awk, no?"

"Not at all," I answer her. "It's all about highlighting our individuality, being our truest and best selves, not conforming to fit in with others."

"I feel like I could get into this," Cami says slowly, like she's considering it. "I feel like this could be really huge, guys. Like it could get onto a morning news show. . . ."

"Well, I don't know about that. But it's a good idea." Amirah slow-nods. "Kinda like me running in a hijab. I want that to be my photo, okay?"

"Sure!" Kaylan yelps. "Brilliant."

We continue discussing this for the rest of lunch, and

I think we have them all on board.

It's kind of amazing how willing they are to get into our ideas. They show a ton of enthusiasm. I think I took that for granted up until now.

After school, I'm upstairs in my room procrastinating on doing my homework by searching baby name websites for dog names and checking my email a zillion times waiting for Countdown to Camp Silver emails.

I refresh again and then a new email pops up!

You've won a PoshPalace towel set!

I click on it and the email reveals that I actually won an online contest! Sure, it's not the trip to Japan I really wanted, or the Disney cruise, or even the two-night stay at an amusement park in New Jersey.

A deluxe set of Posh's most posh bath towels: two bath sheets, two robes, two hand towels, two washcloths, two pairs of slippers, and two super-fast-drying hair towels.

Click here to claim your prize and pick your color!

I forward the email to Kaylan and wait for a response.

Nothing.

I go back to searching dog names but still nothing feels quite right and we need to decide soon.

When Kaylan still doesn't reply almost an hour later, I decide to call her.

"Did you check your email?" I ask as soon as she answers.

"No. Why?"

"We won!" I sing. "An online contest!"

"Wait! Really? What did we win?"

"A towel set," I admit. "But it's still fancy. And we can share it. And whatever—we won! Who knows, maybe we'll win more contests?"

"Yeah," she replies. "Fab, we are slowly but surely finishing this list!"

"I think the only things we really have left to do are think of a name for the dog, and thank our teachers," I tell her. "Or at least figure out how we're going to thank them so we're ready for the end of the year. And hula-hoop on the unicycle."

"Cool, sounds good."

Kaylan's quiet after that and I know something's up with her.

"Are you okay?" I ask.

"Not really," she says quietly, and I wait for her to elaborate.

She doesn't, so I ask, "What is it? What's up?"

She sighs and then I start to hear crying on the other end of the phone. "It's just," she starts, and then stops again. "It's just that I feel like you have everything, Ari!

And I've been chill about it for so long but I just don't feel chill anymore."

"Have everything? What do you mean?"

"You have your camp crew, and your parents are happily married, and you have a little sister who adores you, and all the boys in the world fall in love with you!" she yells. "Jason barely even talks to me anymore! And the one thing I had was the lunch table girls. Like, I was closer to them than you were. But then with the whole #BeMe thing, it's like you're using them when you need them! And then you'll probably end up BFFs with them, too." She pauses, sobbing. "You can't have every single thing! And I think I care more about you than you care about me! And friendship is supposed to be even." She goes on and on, saying these same things again and again.

I listen to her even though it truthfully sounds like nonsense.

No one has *everything*.

When she finally stops ranting, I say, "Kaylan, first of all, I'm really sorry you're so sad. And I don't even know how long you've been feeling this way."

"Since, like, winter break!" she yelps. "You get to pick and choose what stuff you come to with us, but then the girls are always there when you want to hang. You decide you don't like Golfy and immediately Jason loves you! You can't have everything!"

"Stop, Kaylan." I roll my eyes, thankful she can't see me.

"First of all, you don't even like Jason, and you admitted that. And you're the one who got to go on a trip with Cami!"

"Yeah, and it kinda sucked," she says. "And you know that."

"Whatever." I stop talking, trying to think about what to say. "I can't convince you of this stuff. If you want to be mad, be mad. I really didn't want to get into a fight with you. We've gone so many months without a fight. And we have the race coming up."

"We can still do the race. We don't need to be in a fight. I just had to tell you how I feel." She pauses. "Be Me. Remember?"

"Okay."

"Okay."

We're quiet on the phone, I guess debating who will be the first person to hang up.

"Congrats on the contest," she says.

"Congrats to you, too. We entered them together, remember?" I huff.

"Right."

"Talk to you later, Kay."

She hangs up after that and I'm a little confused if we're in a fight or not in a fight or if it really even matters. The older I get, the more I realize that friendships are always evolving and changing. We're always hurting each other and then making it right again.

But if it's a true friendship, it'll be able to weather all of that. Survive it. Maybe even come out stronger.

I look over the list again, feeling pleased with our progress.

13 Must-Dos to Keep Crushing It as 13-Year-Olds

1. Hula-hoop on a unicycle. (still working on it)
2. Start a movement. (getting closer)
3. Figure out how we feel about God. (lots of deep talks)
4. Spend more time with Bubbie and Zeyda. (quality time for sure)
5. Perfect the art of persuasion, especially with Kaylan's mom. (crushing this)
6. Train for and run a race. (yes!)
7. Come up with many varieties of fruit-infused water. (SO GOOD)
8. Properly thank our teachers before the end of the year. (soon)
9. Find a unicorn. (hmm)
10. Win an online contest. (TBD)
11. Be Me. (on it)
12. Eat one of those super-spicy chips. (DONE!!)
13. Convince Ari's parents that they need a dog and come up with an awesome name for said dog. (soon)

So we do still have a bunch of things to do. But not totally. Only partially.

I feel good about our progress, even if this unexpected fight sort of got in the middle of it.

After my conversation with Kaylan, I feel a medium sense of slumpiness.

I'm up in my room, lying flat on my bed, staring at the ceiling. There are things I could do, but nothing seems overly appealing.

Gemma yells from downstairs, "Ari! Jason is here!"

I close my eyes tight, wishing he'd have texted or called or anything. I'm just not in the mood for unexpected visitors.

He sits down on my desk chair, throwing my rubber-band ball up in the air and catching it. "I'm bored," he tells me.

"Okay." I shrug. "Well, I still have homework to finish." It's a little bit of a white lie since all I have left to do is long-term stuff.

He nods, and keeps throwing the rubber-band ball.

I look at him with his mismatched socks and the chewed-up string of his hoodie and I realize I don't think I like him anymore.

I don't know why I change my mind so much about boys.

Maybe I need a complete boy break for a while until I figure it out.

39

KAYLAN

IT TAKES US A FEW more weeks but we finally master the hula-hoop on a unicycle thing.

"It's all about the side-to-side motion!" I yell as Ari pedals around the gym and hula-hoops at the same time. "Keep going! Keep going!"

When she hops off, she pulls her sweaty hair back into a ponytail.

"You did it," Mr. Kohnmi says, clapping. "Unbelievable. Maybe you two want to do this for the fall talent show next year?"

"Hmm, maybe," I say. "We'll think about it, but thanks for all of your help."

"Will you keep unicycling?" he asks us.

Ari's quiet.

"Maybe," I tell him, laughing at myself. It seems I'm

not really sure of anything he's asking me at the moment.

"Are you girls all right? You've hardly said three words to each other."

"We're fine," Ari says. "Thanks for everything. See you later for gym."

"Um, okay. Well, this has been fun. . . ." It seems like he has more to say but we don't stick around. We leave the gym and head to our lockers, silently. I don't think we're really in a fight—we're just in a kind of quiet period.

Mrs. Etisof is finishing the mural after school today and she says that I can watch her since it's the last day and she's just doing finishing touches.

I talk to her as she paints.

"Thanks so much for doing this," I say. "I love it so much."

"I'm glad, Kaylan." She turns around and brushes some hair away from her face. "I'm pleased with how it turned out."

"Me too. I love how you put in some of our doodles, especially that hot dog one." I smile. "Did I tell you my dad's getting married?" I'm not sure why I bring this up to her, or why right now, but every time I'm down here I think about Ryan and me cleaning out and the Hess trucks and Dad's old treadmill in the corner, and I don't want to be alone with these feelings. I have to share them.

"No, you didn't," she says softly. "That's news."

I nod, wondering what she means by that.

"How are you doing with it?" she asks, finishing the last details of the unicorn.

"Not great," I tell her. "It feels so final. Like a death in a way. A death of our family. I mean, I know a lot of people get divorced and remarried. But, like, it's still sad for me. Ya know? And Ryan too. And my mom even though she tries to be positive about it, and most things."

"You have a great mother," Mrs. Etisof adds. "And you and Ryan make her so happy."

"Yeah," is all I can think to say.

"This is hard," Mrs. Etisof says, her back to me, and I think she may be talking about the mural but then I realize she's talking about the my-dad situation. "Hard things are hard. That may sound obvious, but we need reminders of it sometimes."

"It is hard," I admit. "Really, really hard. I don't want him to get married to someone else and live in some other house forever and do trips with this person and come home after work to this person and make French toast on the weekends for someone else. He was supposed to be doing that with us."

"That's true," she says. "Life doesn't always go the way of *supposed to*. And that's really one of the main hard things. I'm not sure we ever get used to that."

She turns around and adjusts her painting apron,

setting down the brush for a moment. I reach over and hug her tight.

"Thank you for getting me, Mrs. Etisof," I say.

I start to think that maybe Mrs. Etisof really is my unicorn and even though she was right there all along, it's still a magical feeling to discover it. But I still have that nagging feeling like maybe it's too easy, too obvious.

Maybe the key to finding a unicorn is the challenge of the discovery.

That night, our lunch table crew emails each other with the pictures and the #BeMe hashtags they've all added in.

Ari responds right away.

Ari: Awesome photos, guys. We'll take them to the administration first thing Monday.

Ari texts me separately: We're doing this together, you know that, right?

Ari: Also my bubbie's in the hospital again. We're on our way to get our dog now and we still don't have a name.

Ari: I'm sorry if you think I have everything. But I don't. Not at all.

Ari: Especially if I don't have you.

I don't respond because what I want to say is way too much for a text and I don't want to have a call if her whole family is around.

I lie awake all night imagining Ari coming home with

the dog, and praying that her bubbie will be okay, and talking to God about hard things being hard, the way Mrs. Etisof said it.

I pray that one day I'll be okay about my dad leaving and getting remarried and that one day everything will make sense and that the hard things won't feel as hard, or that I'll at least be better at managing them.

40

ARI

I LOOK AROUND OUR CAR as we pull into the driveway of the person who's been fostering our new dog, realizing that in a matter of minutes we'll have that dog in here with us and that dog will be ours.

Our life will never be exactly like it is now, ever again.

"Ready, guys?" my dad asks.

"Um, yes!" Gemma yelps. "Even though we still don't have a name."

"Give it time," Mom says. "Sometimes you need to meet the dog first."

She stares at her phone, distracted, and then whispers something to my dad. I bet it's about Bubbie. I know it is because that's what they always whisper about these days. I don't even want to ask because I don't want anything to spoil this moment.

We get inside the little house where the foster dog mom lives and it smells terrible—like wet dogs and wet dogs and wet dogs forever. It takes all my effort not to gag.

"Hi, guys," she says, all cheerful. "I'm Barbara. Ready to meet your new puppy?"

"Yes, yes!" I smile.

She leads us over to the corner where there are a few dogs sleeping. She shows us which one is ours—an orangey-red-haired small poodle—and Gemma and I play with him on the floor while Mom and Dad get all the instructions.

He cuddles up to us and licks our cheeks and it's sort of hard to believe but he looks even cuter than he did in the pictures online.

My phone buzzes in my pocket and I almost don't check it because I'm so consumed with this little bundle of love.

But then it buzzes again.

Kaylan: Lion! That's the name for your dog!

Kaylan: In honor of your bubbie!

Kaylan: And based on the photos with his reddish hair, he sort of looks like a lion!

Kaylan: I know we're sort of in a fight and haven't been talking a ton but I had to tell you because you're getting your dog today! And that's big!

Kaylan: ok bye

"Hey, Gem," I say.

She looks up.

"What do you think about Lion as a name for the dog? Because, like, Bubbie loves lions and lions are fierce and loyal and strong and passionate and he has red hair and . . ." My voice trails off and then I add, "Isn't it the most perfect name in the world?"

She thinks about it for a minute. I feel like she's going to say no because she always likes to disagree with me.

"Hiiii, little Lion," she sings, right into the dog's ear. "Hi, little Lion baby."

He looks up right then and moves closer to me and licks the top of my cheek.

"Oh, Lion, I love you." I smoosh into him. "You're ours forever."

In the car, Gemma and I go on and on about how Lion is the perfect name for the dog.

I'm not sure if Mom and Dad really agree but they seem okay with it. Lion sits on the seat in between Gemma and me and we pet him the whole ride home.

"Is Bubbie going to die today?" Gemma asks, all matter-of-fact. I don't know why she talks like this.

"Stop, Gem. That's awful."

Hearing those words aloud make my whole body tense up. Like even knowing they're out there, that they've been uttered, is too much. Obviously, dying is a fact of life, but when it comes to Bubbie and Zeyda, I can't face it. I don't want to face it.

They're immortal to me.

"I don't think so," Dad replies.

"Can we please bring Lion to Bubbie so she can meet him?" I ask. "Remember the healing powers. The doctors agreed."

"I don't think dogs are allowed in the hospital, Ar," my mom says. "She'll meet him when she comes home."

Back at our house, I take a zillion pictures of Lion and text them to the camp girls.

Hana: OMG he is SO CUTE

Zoe: Plllllleaaaaase bring him to drop off

Alice: LOVE HIM SO SO MUCH

Me: isn't he the best dog in the world? Btw I broke up with Jason

Alice: OMG ARI, ur nuts

Me: no boys 4 me 4 a while

Me: except for Lion LOL

Zoe: LOL LOL

Bubbie ends up coming home from the hospital a few days later and it feels like we narrowly escaped tragedy. She had a minor infection but it cleared up and she's back in her recliner. She still has the terrible turquoise oxygen cord in and she still sleeps most of the day, but at least she's home.

“This is Lion,” I tell her, holding our perfect little puppy in my arms.

“Oh, Lion,” she says softly, reaching out to pet him. I set him down on her lap. “My first granddog.”

“Yup,” Gemma says, scooping Lion up right away. “Time to take him out. I think he has to pee.”

Gemma takes her dog responsibilities very seriously.

We stay at Bubbie and Zeyda’s for the rest of the afternoon, playing with Lion and watching old home movies and ordering Chinese food for dinner. Bubbie even eats a little bit of soup.

I try to imprint this moment on my mind in a way I’ve never done before. Like if I think really hard about it, I’ll always remember it exactly the way it was and I can go back to it again and again.

I stare really hard at everyone as if I’m taking pictures of each of them with my eyes. Bubbie home and eating soup, Lion running in circles around the dining room table, all of us talking and laughing together.

I try as hard as I can to study every little thing, each detail etched on my brain. This way, the moment will last forever.

Monday morning rolls around and we find ourselves in the new assistant principal’s office explaining the #BeMe movement.

“I like the thing about highlighting individuality,” Ms. Therault says. “And we already have signed releases from all the parents on photos. The one thing I will say is that if people don’t want to participate, they don’t have to.”

“Okay,” I answer. “That makes sense. But you’re okay with it?”

“I’m more than okay with it. It’s creative. I like it.”

We talk to Ms. Therault for a few more minutes, and then Kaylan and I leave, feeling pretty proud of ourselves.

“We are starting a movement,” I say. “This is big, Kay.”

She nods. “Yeah.”

“Thanks again for the dog name suggestion,” I tell her. “It’s perfect.”

“I’m glad,” she replies. “I think so, too.”

We’re quiet on the rest of the walk to our lockers.

“I’m sorry about the Jason thing,” I say, finally needing to get it off my chest and clear the air. Maybe it never really felt right to me because there was still a part of Jason that was sort of Kaylan’s. Maybe he was meant to stay as a neighbor/friend for me. “It wasn’t cool of me. And I’m sorry for being so wishy-washy about the lunch table crew. And I’m sorry about all the stuff you’re dealing with about your dad.”

She sits down in front of the lockers and buries her head in her knees.

I put an arm around her.

"Hard things are hard," she says. "Isn't that so smart?"

I nod. "Yes, it sums up everything basically, in the simplest way."

"I'm sorry about your bubbie," Kaylan says.

I shrug. "She keeps bouncing back."

I'll never admit that something's wrong and her days are fading and that every time I see her, I imagine it will be the last time. I will never allow myself to believe that there will come a time when Bubbie won't be on this earth.

It's impossible.

"That's good," Kaylan replies.

She knows not to debate it or give me a sympathetic, sad smile that reveals we both know she's dying.

Kaylan gets me.

She knows me.

You don't need a million people in your life like that.

If the person is Kaylan, one is enough.

41

KAYLAN

IT'S ALREADY MAY AND THE #BeMe movement hasn't taken off like we'd hoped, but there's still some time. We have about thirty photos of kids hung around the school and people stop to look at them. But no one's really posting their own photos yet.

The day Ari decided to explain the movement over the loudspeaker during morning announcements really made people talk about it. At least for that day.

Movements take time, I think.

Plus we just put "start a movement" on the list, not "complete a movement," if that's even a thing.

"And we can't expect to succeed at everything we try," I tell Ari after a run.

"Yes, we can. We're the best and we will crush

everything," she answers, standing up to do some more running in place.

"At least it's not freezing," I say.

"Kay, it's May. Duh." She starts laughing.

"We made it to May," I remind her. "We survived the winter. We're almost at the end of the year and the end of the list."

"Thank our teachers, though," Ari reminds me.

"I know," I reply. "And find a unicorn. Still working on it."

She nods, stretching her legs from side to side.

"Ooh, I just had an amazing brainstorm," I tell Ari, sitting back on the grass while she continues to stretch and run in place. "The #BeMe thing can also be a way we thank our teachers," I say.

"How?" Ari asks, doing jumping jacks.

"We can make each teacher a poster with the #BeMe hashtag and then on the bottom some awesome facts about them."

Ari thinks for a minute, and sits back down next to me. "Um, I like the poster thing, but why would it say *Be Me?*"

"Because they're all being themselves in their unique teaching styles," I explain.

"Maybe," Ari replies. "I think it needs some fine-tuning. And what if teachers feel bad if we don't make posters of them? Like, we're only gonna do the teachers we have, ya know?"

I hold a finger in the air. "Oh! Another brainstorm! Another movement!"

Ari crinkles up her cheeks and laughs. "Huh?"

"The #ThankATeacher movement," I yell. "We make sure all teachers are covered and we recruit other people to do it with us and the last week of school, we have posters up for every teacher!" She smiles. "It's literally called the #ThankATeacher movement and maybe it catches on nationwide! Maybe not only at the end of the year in some places . . . maybe all year. Who knows?"

"So we've started two movements?" Ari asks.

"Think so!" I drape an arm over her shoulders. "We are on fire!"

We stretch our legs out in front of us on the grass and start to do a kick-line-style dance. After a few seconds of that, we fall backward on the grass, laughing.

I flop onto my side to face Ari. "We may have out-listed ourselves with this list. It's just so amazing."

She laughs. "We'll never out-list ourselves."

42

ARI

“WHO DID THIS?” WE HEAR Ms. Phipps muttering to Ms. Lincoln when Kaylan and I are cleaning out our lockers, brushing sticky strands of hair away from our faces. We finished our last final and school is so close to over. We can smell summer break, or maybe that’s just the stench of super-sweaty boys in a building without air-conditioning. “The administration is finally starting to appreciate us!”

“I know, about time! You think they told the kids to do this? Or what?” Ms. Lincoln shakes her head. “Did you see my poster? It thanked me for really taking the time to connect and talk to all my students.”

Ms. Phipps smiles. “And mine says how focused I am on keeping the school safe and orderly and productive.”

It would be too much to really high-five right now, and

they'd see us, so Kaylan and I tap pointer fingers, a mini high five.

A high *one*, really.

One list.

Two movements.

Unbelievable.

"Kay, hurry," I tell her, slinging my heavy backpack over my shoulder. "Finish getting your stuff. We gotta go!"

"Why? We're done studying," she reminds me, as if I don't already know that. "I want to make sure I don't throw anything super important away."

I shake my head. "None of this is that important. I have a surprise for you! Come!"

She shoves the rest of the papers in the backpack and follows me out to the parking lot, where my mom is waiting for us.

"What's going on?" Kaylan whispers to me in the back seat.

"I'll tell you at my house." I drum my fingers together so she knows I've concocted something amazing.

When we get there, we drop our backpacks in the mudroom and sprint up the stairs.

"Wait, don't go in yet." I open the door slowly and peek into my room to make sure Gemma didn't mess anything up, and everything is ready to go. I quickly light a few candles.

I smile, about to open the door for her. "Okay. Now. Come in."

Kaylan puts a hand on my arm. "Is something going to jump out and attack me?"

I laugh. "No. Nothing like that. Come on. Go in."

She walks inside and I follow behind her, waiting to see her reaction. My room is set up like a spa with aromatherapy candles and the robes we just won from the contest spread out on my bed. The slippers are set up by the door so we can slide our feet in right away. Tranquil music is playing from the speakers and I have a stack of postcards and fancy pens set up on my desk.

"Ooh la la, Ari." Kaylan shimmies. "What's this all about?"

"The Arianna Simone Spa and Wellness Center, dahling . . ." I drape an arm over her shoulders and we survey the scene. "Lovely, right?"

"Beyond," Kaylan replies.

We put on our robes and sit down on the throw pillows I've set up on my floor. I get up to pour Kaylan a tall glass of cucumber water.

"These candles smell so good," Kaylan says. "I think I need one."

"You do," I agree. "Also, we're writing each other postcards now. I mean, not writing them, addressing them, so we're all set with our correspondence plan before camp."

"Correspondence plan!" Kaylan slaps my leg. "Ari,

where do you even get this stuff?"

"No idea." I shrug. "Do you know the Laurel Lake address by heart yet?"

"Um, yes." Kaylan smiles. "I've memorized the whole website."

"Perfect. Oh, and after we address the postcards . . . pedicure time!"

"You've thought of everything, Ar." She leans over and rests her head on my shoulder, pulling me close.

"I know how you are with rituals, Kay." I clear my throat, feeling myself getting a little choked up. "The whole thing with the kayaks and the lanterns and stuff. I mean, you're all about this stuff."

"That's true." Kaylan uncaps the pen and copies down the Camp Silver address again and again on twenty postcards. "This is genius, Ari. An amazing pre-camp ritual."

"I thought of it on my own," I declare. "And it wasn't even on the list. Okay, go pick your pedicure color! I lined up all the bottles on the shelf in my bathroom."

I finish addressing Kaylan's postcards and I imagine them all traveling through the mail and getting to Laurel Lake. I picture Kaylan reading them on her bunk at camp, and laughing. And we'll think back to this day, and this ritual and this moment, and the postcards will keep us together.

Together always, even when we're apart.

43

KAYLAN

"YOU KNOW IT'S ONLY A 5K," Ryan says, pounding down the stairs on race day. "That's like an average jog for most people and doesn't require training or an audience or anything."

"Ryan! Shut up! Why do you always ruin every single thing?" I shake my head in his direction. "You're such a jerk."

"I'm just stating a simple fact."

"Ryan, leave her alone. I'm proud of her for doing this," my mom says, pulling a cardigan out of the closet. "Ready to go, guys?"

I nod, virtually patting myself on the back for training for this race and actually running it. If there was ever a situation that truly symbolized leaning in, this would be it.

We drive over to the start of the race—at the village hall in Shelby Green, a town twenty minutes from us.

"How did you even find this race?" Ryan asks on the way over. "It's so random."

"It's for stroke awareness and research and Ari's bubbie had a stroke and you'd know that if you'd donated or ever listened to me or read the emails I sent you!" I scoff.

"Why do you have to email me? We live in the same house!" He laughs.

"Ryan," my mom warns, sounding annoyed. "Stop."

We get stuck in a little traffic but finally get there. Ari and her family are all talking to the lunch table girls. They're holding signs that say RUN, GIRLS, RUN! Go, Ari! Go, Kaylan! Go, Amirah! Gemma's holding Lion's leash tight and every time he tries to jump up on someone she says "No!" in a very authoritative tone.

"Hiii," I sing, walking up to them. I bend down to pet Lion and he licks my hand.

"I still can't believe you're doing this," Cami says, shaking her head. "I mean, it's great and everything. But, like, it seems super intense."

"I'm ready for it, Cam." I smile, not really getting what she's even saying. Sometimes she talks just for the sake of talking.

Cami leans over and whispers in my ear, "I've already written you three letters and mailed them to comedy camp. They'll be there when you arrive."

I smile. "Thanks, Cam. I'll write you back. I promise."

"Oh, yay, you're both here," Amirah says, stretching her arm back over her head. "We need to warm up." She takes my hand and Ari's hand and we go off to the side right near the starting line.

"Good luck," all the girls yell. "Go, Ari! Go, Kaylan! Go, Amirah!"

We're mid-stretch when we hear more screams and cheers. "Go, Ari! Go, Kaylan! Go, Ari! Go, Kaylan!" I look over, wondering why they're not cheering for Amirah, too, and I realize it's because Alice and the whole crew of Ari's camp girls are the ones who are cheering.

"Ari!" I yell. "Did you know they were coming?"

She pulls out an earbud. "Who?"

"Your Camp Silver crew." I turn around again and point so she can see them, and that's when I notice that Golfy is there, too. What a guy to come out and support her in this race, after she broke his heart.

Maybe he's trying to get her back.

"Oh my God," she yelps. "I had no idea! And Golfy too!" she says under her breath. "This is so awkward." She clenches her teeth. "They all donated but I didn't expect them to come! I don't even know if they're all done with school yet."

"Guys, focus," Amirah says. "You need to make sure you're all stretched out."

I laugh. "We're like those ooey-gooey slimy hands that

we used to get as prizes at the fall fair. Remember?" I move my body in this slippery, stretchy way and they all crack up.

The three of us hold hands at the starting line but then Amirah lets go. "Sorry, too sweaty," she says.

I squeeze Ari's hand and she squeezes mine and I breathe in and breathe out, scared out of my mind, even more than I was on the day we ate the spicy chip.

The mayor of Shelby Green makes some long-winded speech that I can't focus on, and then there's a quick countdown and finally a loud boom and we're off running.

Amirah is with us for the beginning of the race, but then she sprints on ahead and we lose her entirely.

"She's so fast," I say.

"I know," Ari replies, out of breath from talking and running.

We keep an even pace and stay together the whole time.

"So what are we going to do now?" Ari asks. "When this race is over, the list is over, summer is here, we're going to be apart."

"I don't know," I answer. "I guess just keep crushing it. And write all those postcards to each other. Duh."

Ari laughs. "Wait, the unicorn thing. Have you figured it out?"

"Yeah, the unicorn thing." I pause. "Well, I have a

unicorn mural in my basement now."

"That doesn't count," Ari huffs.

"I know." I stop talking to catch my breath but after a few minutes I'm ready to start talking again. "The unicorn is the most obvious thing on the list."

"It is?" Ari asks.

"Run!" I yell, and we sprint the last hundred yards through the finish line, holding hands, finishing at the exact same time.

We hear cheering—my mom and Ryan, the Camp Silver crew, the lunch table girls, Ari's family. Even Lion is barking.

People hand us bottles of water and medals and even those metal warming poncho things.

Again, probably a little overboard for a 5K, but still cool. It makes it all feel official.

We're off to the side by ourselves, catching our breath and sipping water, when Ari says, "What did you mean, the unicorn is the most obvious thing on the list?"

I hesitate. "You're my unicorn, Ari. My first person. My truest friend. The one who always gets me, no matter what, who lets me get mad and angry and have a fight and then welcomes me back with open arms. Friendships like that don't come around every day, ya know. I know we're only thirteen, but we'll be friends for life. No doubt whatsoever."

Ari takes a piece of paper out of her shorts pocket. It's

wet from sweat and crinkled and ripped along the edges. She hands it to me.

It's an original copy of the list, maybe even the first typed-up rough draft. I wonder if she takes this copy everywhere she goes.

I scan it until my eyes get to the important part, the reason she's showing this to me.

11. Find a unicorn. (Duh, already completed this one the second we made the list. Kaylan. My BFFFFF. Forever.)

My eyes well up with tears. "When did you write this? Why didn't you tell me?"

"I wrote it the first day we printed out the lists. It says it right there." She laughs. "No-brainer. My feelings about literally everything are changing all the time. You're the one thing I can be sure of. Even if our friendship changes, the way I feel about you will never, ever change." She pulls me into a sweaty hug. "That's unicorn material right there."

"Why didn't you tell me earlier?" I ask. "I spent all this time searching. Every time I brought it up, you made it seem like you were still searching, too."

"Just because you're my unicorn doesn't mean I'm yours." She shrugs, crinkling her nose. "Plus, you like searching."

I nod, agreeing with her.

"Some things are just so pure, and real, and good and true, there's no way to debate them, to not see them, to even question they exist," Ari says. "And a unicorn is a magical, once-in-an-eternity discovery, but that doesn't mean it can't be someone who's always been there."

I'm completely bawling at this point and the other runners are staring at us, confused and also mildly concerned. I have no idea where Amirah is. She probably finished an hour ago at this point.

"Plus, aren't you glad I didn't tell you?" Ari asks. "And this way you know it's mutual and really, really true. I have proof on this paper. And you came to the realization on your own."

"Definitely." I pull her into a hug.

She stacks her fists together and puts them on the top of my head like a unicorn horn.

"Wait," I say. "There's one more thing we have to do . . . now that school's over and the list is complete and it's finally summer . . ." I look at Ari, wondering if she'll catch on.

"What?" she asks. "Pack for comedy camp? Yes, I'll help. And yes, you can take my polka-dot bikini with you."

"Oh, thanks. Okay, well, all of that, yes, but something else, too." My eyes bulge. "The pool! Today is opening day! And we're sweaty! Let's go!" I grab her hand and start running. "Spontaneous pool party!"

"We can't run to the pool from here." Ari laughs. "I know we did train for a 5K, but come on, Kaylan . . ."

I nod. "Right. Okay, let's go ask our parents to drive us. The Camp Silver girls can come, too, and the lunch table girls. We can all jump in together!"

"Yes!" Ari reaches over and hugs me again.

It takes a few minutes to cajole everyone and get them in cars to Brookside. But once that happens and we're on our way, the most peaceful feeling washes over me.

We finished seventh grade.

We finished our third list.

I'm going to comedy camp.

My best friend for life is sitting beside me and her brand-new puppy is licking my face.

I turn to Ari and whisper, "Thank you for being my unicorn."

She replies with a sniffle, "Thank you for being mine."

ACKNOWLEDGMENTS

Dave, Aleah, and Hazel—the lights of my life, my loves, my cheering squad, my everything! How can I ever fully thank you for being the awesomest?

All the Greenwalds and all the Rosenbergs—I'm stuck with you and you're stuck with me, but it's a good stuck. Thanks for all the love and laughs!

BWL Library & Tech team—my people at my home away from home! Thanks for all the support.

Caroline Hickey and Lisa Graff—you two are the best writing-retreat partners in the universe! We've known each other for thirteen years already. How crazy? Mwah!

Alyssa Eisner Henkin—thank you for your wisdom, honesty, kindness, and passion. I am beyond grateful.

Maria Barbo—a unicorn of an editor, a unicorn of a person! You are brilliant, and I thank the universe every day that I get to work with you!

Stephanie Guerdan—thank you so much for your patience and dedication. You make all my books sparkle.

To the incredible people at Katherine Tegen books: Katherine, Haley, Vaishali, Aurora, David, Amy, Liz, Emily, and Mark—you are truly the best in the business. Thank you for everything you do. I am so lucky to be part of the KT Books family.

A zillion thanks to all the readers who submitted list ideas through PopJam! They were all extraordinary!

Last but never least, to all the kids who've read my books and all the kids who've emailed me and written me letters—thank you, thank you, thank you from the bottom of my heart! Keep reading!

Ari and Kaylan's friendship continues
in Friendship List #4:

13 AND ¾!

1

KAYLAN

IT'S KIND OF AMAZING HOW the human brain works. I am here, in this moment, at the pool, having fun with Ari and the lunch table girls, but inside I'm completely and totally freaking out about leaving home for a full month. Freaking out in a way I've never freaked out before. And I'm pretty used to freaking out. It's basically my middle name(s).

"We were thinking something interactive," M.W. tells all of us. "Go up on the diving board and yell out your list ideas and then jump in and swim over to the group. K? But quick, one after the other."

Ari and I are about to start our fourth list to help us

stay close while we're apart this summer. Of course, she's sooooo happy to be going back to her favorite place on earth, Camp Silver, while I'm a looming skyscraper of agita. I mean, I know it was my choice to go to Laurel Lake Camp for the Arts and focus on comedy. I applied and everything. And I was beyond excited when I got in.

But right now? I'm scared out of my mind. I'm regretting all of that.

Ari and I made our first list of Eleven Fabulous Things to Make Us Even More AMAZING Before We Turn Twelve before sixth grade because we were so nervous about starting middle school and we thought it would calm us down to have a project. Then we just couldn't stop making them. The thing is, we hadn't really planned on doing another list so soon since we just finished the last one, but, well, we couldn't resist. And of course, the lunch table girls want to share some of their brilliant ideas with us.

"I'll go get my phone in the waterproof case so I can record everyone jumping," June suggests. "And then I'll text you guys the video so you'll remember all of our amazing ideas."

"Everyone at the pool will hear," I say, biting my pinkie nail. "But I guess who really cares? We're leaving!"

I laugh my nervous laugh and look over at Ari, praying we can unpack some of this leaving-home agita tonight at our sleepover.

I lean closer to her and rest my head on her shoulder.

She whispers, "Kay! So amazing you're not stressing about people hearing this. You've come soooo far since freeze dance at the pool two summers ago."

"I have, right?" I raise my eyebrows and pull her into a sideways hug. "OMG, Ari, I'm out of control nervous about leaving home and going to camp for a whole month. A month is a realllly long time. Completely freaking out right now."

"Shhh." She tries to soothe me. "We'll talk tonight. I kind of can't believe they came here with all these list ideas, totally surprising us. Can you?"

"Guys! Stop whispering to each other," Amirah scolds. "For real. Join the group. We planned this day! We even got you a balloon arch!"

It's true that they really did go all out with the decorations. They wrapped the lounge chairs in streamers too and got a gold foil A balloon and a gold foil K balloon and an arch of gold and silver balloons that they tied to the trees. It's all pretty remarkable. I guess they're really gonna miss us.

"And we love it!" I yell. "Really and truly love it!"

Cami stands up and walks behind me and wraps her arms around my neck. "Kay! I can't believe you're leaving. What am I gonna do without you?"

I turn around to face her and whisper, "Don't say that; it makes me feel bad."

"Why? You don't want me to miss you?" Cami asks.

I clench my teeth; I need her to stop. "I don't know. I'm a jumble glob of emotions right now and truthfully anything can send me over the edge."

"Hey, guys!" Cami turns and shouts like she wants everyone at the pool to hear her. "Can we discuss that we're going into our senior year of middle school in the fall? I mean . . . this is big-time stuff, people."

"We know," June groans. "But school just ended and it's summer. Let's not talk about the fall. K?"

"K." Cami rolls her eyes. "I'm going first!"

She runs over to the diving board and stands there for a few seconds like she's about to make some kind of acceptance speech. Then she says, "Ready? Here are my three brilliant ideas. Actually, wait, I have four. I forgot. Okay, ready?" She pauses for a second before she jumps. "Sneak a gigantic pool float into your bag and use it in the camp pool, dye your hair blue, teach the entire camp a dance you've made up, and . . ." She jumps in and screams, "Make a difference!"

We all clap for Cami. She gets out of the pool and grabs her towel off a lounger and comes back to sit with us.

June finishes recording Cami and then hands her phone to M.W. to record. She calls out her list items as she jumps. "Keep a gratitude journal, have a conversation in another language, and this is a no-brainer: get a younger kid at camp to start their own list!"

I look at Ari and she looks at me. Brilliant. All three of June's ideas are keepers. I know they'll make it on the list. Cami's? Not so much. But maybe we'll keep *make a difference*. That feels like us.

M.W. hands the phone back to June and goes up on the diving board, looking sheepish and embarrassed. I'm not sure if it's because her bathing suit is too tight or because she doesn't like talking in front of groups. "I only have one," she says. "But it's a good one. Get two counselors to fall in love." She jumps in and stays underwater for a few seconds and then pops up.

"Ooh!" Cami yells. "I love that one. Wowie!"

I love how Ari and I are on the side of the pool, watching and listening to all of this like it's a show they've prepared for us. I guess it kind of is. I'm still shocked they organized it and got it together. I mean, we didn't ask them to come up with ideas for our fourth list, but we also didn't expect to be working on another list so soon and, well, we are. It's happening. We might as well go with the flow.

"My turn!" Marie says, hopping up from the side of the pool.

"Take it away, Marie Mundlay Burns." I laugh. For some reason, I'm obsessed with saying her full name.

"Write to each other once a week," she says as she jumps. And when she pops up from the water she adds, "And draw a portrait of each other from memory!" She swims over to us. "The second one can be done while you're apart or when you're back home, either way." She widens her eyes. "Amazing, right?"

"Amazing!" I stand up and shimmy from side to side. "Ah-may-zing!"

Amirah is the last to go. Before she walks over to the diving board, she says, "I'll admit, I had trouble with this. I feel like I had good ideas for the last list, but this one was tough because I don't know anything about what it's like to go to camp or even what happens there or whatever, so I only had two but anyway." She climbs up the ladder, all chic in her hijab swim cap, and yells, "Do something daring. Master the art of tie-dye." She jumps and swims over to us. "Also, can this please be the last list? I know I'm not really part of it but it kind of stresses me out. I'm always a little worried you won't be able to complete all the stuff."

"For real?" I ask her, giggling a little. "But it's not even your thing to worry about."

"I know." She bobs under the water and hoists herself up to the side of the pool. "But still. How do you always manage to get it done?"

Ari and I look at each other. "We just do," we say at the same time. "Jinx." Everyone cracks up.

"I like your ideas, though, Amirah," I say. "Don't you, Ar?"

"Yes!" Ari picks at a cuticle. She seems like she's ready to be done with this.

A minute later, she gets up to do some jumping jacks off to the side, away from the pool. "Guys, I have so much nervous, happy, excited energy! Can we pause the list stuff and just have fun? All of your ideas are amazing, but I need your help . . ."

"You do?" Cami tightens up her face. "You never need help with anything."

I don't know how it's possible, but even Cami's compliments sound mean sometimes.

"Yes, I do," Ari says, all matter-of-fact. "And I need help now."

She stops the jumping jacks and sits down on the edge of the pool with everyone else, dangling her feet into the water again.

"Fine. What do you need help with?" Cami asks, leaning back on her elbows.

"Okay, so, don't hate me because of my feelings that change minute to minute, but here's the thing." She pauses and pushes her sunglasses to the top of her head. "I'm in love with Golfy. I never really stopped being in love with him even though, ya know, my brief love of Jason thing. And I'm so nervous and so excited to be back at camp with Golfy, but what if he doesn't like me anymore?"

We all stare at her because obviously we don't have an answer. We don't even really know Golfy. How can we know if he loves her now or if he ever loved her or anything at all really?

June tilts her head to the side like she's waiting for someone else to respond, but then when no one else does, she says, "Ari, hate to break this to you, but I'm pretty sure everyone would like you—boys and girls. You're gorgeous. You know this, right?"

Ari's cheeks turn red. "Um, thank you, but I don't think that's true."

"It is." June smiles. "Also, hello, remember the giant bear thing? That Golfy sent to school on Valentine's Day? He's obviously still going to like you when you're back at camp together. I mean, he just came to see you run the 5K for your last list only a little over a week ago! I feel like you don't have to worry *at all* about that boy. He is one hundred percent pro Ari Nodberg."

"Maybe. I don't know. I just feel like I messed things up," Ari says. "We didn't really talk that much when he came for the 5K. And now I'm going to camp with all these expectations and then what if he likes someone else this summer? What if he just wants to be friends now?"

"That would be terrible, I guess," Marie says, "but how can we possibly know the answer? And what's the point in worrying about this ahead of time?"

"Yeah, you're right," she says, not looking entirely pleased with this help.

I raise my eyebrows, telling her in eye-speak that we'll hash all of this out at the sleepover later.

She scrunches her eyes back with a half smile.

The lunch table girls are awesome, and so kind to plan this pool day for us, but we need a one-to-one sleepover to prepare for this monumental summer. That probably should have been on the last list, but I guess it didn't need to be.

It's one of those things that goes without saying, without listing.

2

ARI

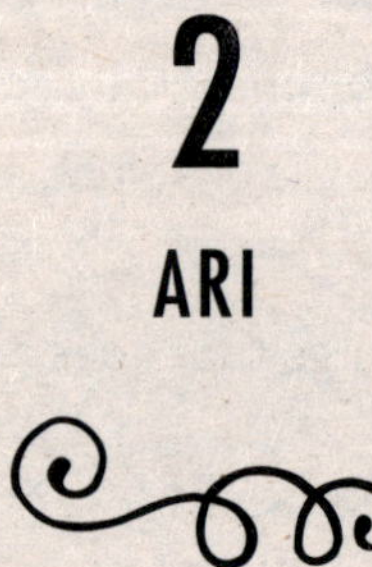

WE DON'T TALK ABOUT THE list for the rest of the day and it's kind of a relief. Since we just finished a list and we're starting a new one right away, it almost feels like too much to have all the lunch table girls weigh in. I'm glad we got their ideas, but I just couldn't debate and analyze it all with them. I didn't have the energy.

After snack bar lunch (Kaylan and I shared our favorite: a combo platter of mozzarella sticks and chicken fingers), some swim races, soft serve from the ice cream truck, a zillion hugs and sniffles and goodbyes, Kaylan and I walk back to my house just the two of us.

When we get there, Lion follows us up the stairs, licking our ankles on the way. He rests on my bed as Kaylan and I take turns showering. We change into comfy clothes and hang out in my room, surrounded by my camp stuff. It's all pretty much packed up in my giant duffels and my chest of plastic drawers and I like seeing it in the corner of my room, ready to go. It's like even my stuff is excited to be back at Camp Silver.

"I don't get why you have to bring your own drawers," Kaylan says. "Should I be bringing plastic drawers to Laurel Lake?"

"It's just a thing we all do," I tell her. "We only get one cubby that has three shelves. So I like to put my undies and bathing suits and pj's in these drawers. Keeps them neat and protected a little." I lean back on my bed. "You may not need to."

"And what's with all the nail polish?" Kaylan asks, swiveling around on my desk chair. "You never do your nails."

"It's a camp thing." I put my arms behind my head and stretch my legs out as far as they can go.

I need Kaylan to stop asking questions. I love her, and I'm happy she's here, and I'm happy we're having a sleepover, but I can't handle the questions right now.

We're quiet for a minute as I read over the packing list for the millionth time to make sure I didn't forget anything. Kaylan's staring out my window. I know she spies on Jason whenever she's here, even though I never admit that I realize she's doing it. It's just one of those things, a secret kind of BFF code where we both know what's happening but we don't discuss it.

I'm not even sure she likes Jason; I think she just likes to spy on people, him especially, and know what he's up to. He was her first kiss, and even if feelings change, the fact of the matter never will. He's a big deal in her life for that reason.

"Is someone crying?" Kaylan asks.

I crinkle my eyebrows because I hear it, too. We move closer to my door. My heart pounds because every time anyone cries, or the phone rings at an odd hour, or I hear my parents whispering, I always assume the worst.

Bubbie.

"If I don't like it, can I come home?" I hear my little sister say between sobs.

Okay, phew. Nothing happened to my grandmother. It's just Gemma being scared about camp. Again. Not that I want her to be scared and crying, but I'll take that over a tragedy two days before I leave for the summer, or any-time, really.

"What's not to like, Gem?" my dad says softly. "Sports and arts and crafts and carnivals and swimming and singing . . ." His voice trails off and then he adds, "I loved camp as a kid!"

"I don't know," Gemma says. "I don't think I'm ready."

"She sounds like me," Kaylan whispers, coming over to sit next to me on my bed and resting her head on my shoulder.

"Maybe you should've had a sleepover with her!" I crack up and she smacks me with a pillow. "Okay, enough of this eavesdropping, enough of the agita—for you, for

Gemma, for me about Golfy—we need to just get to camp already. Too much anticipation."

"You're right." Kaylan sniffles and curls her body up tight. "List time. Let's finish this thing so we can play Best Case Scenario in your backyard!"

"Yes!"

"Ya know how the last list was all organic and stuff and everything just kind of came to us over time?" Kaylan asks, adjusting herself on my bed. "We have so little time with this one, it's kind of like an extra list since we didn't plan to do it. For this one, we need to go with gut instinct."

"Totally! A gut instinct list," I agree. "And also that makes total sense because this is our fourth list! We have this down to a science."

"Right."

We grab snacks from the kitchen, then cuddle together back in my room and watch the video of the girls jumping. We crack up over and over again, so loud that we can't even hear their ideas and then we need to watch it again and again to jot everything down.

Lunch Table Girls' Ideas for our Fourth and Fabulous List

Cami:

Sneak a gigantic pool float into your bag and use it in the camp pool.

Dye your hair blue.
Teach the entire camp a dance you've made up.
Make a difference.

June:
Keep a gratitude journal.
Have a conversation in another language.
Get a younger kid at camp to start their own list!

M.W.:
Get two counselors to fall in love.

Marie:
Write to each other once a week.
Draw a portrait of each other from memory.

Amirah:
Master the art of tie-dye.
Do something daring.

"Okay, let's do a yea or nay," Kaylan says. "I'll say yea to both of Marie's ideas—write to each other once a week and the portrait thing. You?"

"Yes." I crack my knuckles. "Yea to both."

She nods, and writes a check mark next to both.

"No to most of Cami's." Kaylan rolls her eyes. "Except maybe the make a difference. I like that one."

"Totally. I don't even really know what that means, but I like the soul-searchy element of it."

Kaylan nods. "Yeah, same. I think some of my favorite list items are the ones that start out vague, when we don't even really know what they mean and then we figure them out as we go."

I rest my head on her shoulder and breathe in her coconut papaya shampoo. "You smell so good," I say. "Do you have an extra bottle of that new shampoo you got that I can take to camp so I can use it on my hair and smell good but also feel like you're with me? Smells are the most important triggers of memories, did you know that?"

"I'll see if I have an extra bottle," Kaylan says with her eyes bulged like I'm going a little loony tunes, but also kind of into it.

I look over our notes. "Okay, and yea to both of Amirah's, right? I feel like she nailed it—master the art of tie-dye and *do something daring*? It's like she has a soul-searchy one and a totally camp one."

"Yeah, she seriously nailed it the most of anyone, and she was the one who said she didn't know anything about camp," Kaylan reminds me. "Kind of amazing, right?"

"Totally."

"M.W.'s seems kind of tricky, though, no?" I ask.

"Kinda. No clue how to do that one, but I feel like we need to include it. She only had one idea." Kaylan crinkles her eyes, unsure.

We watch the video three more times, and review the notes, and then we come up with a somewhat formed list.

“Definitely yea to all of June’s,” I say. “She pretty much crushed it, too. The language one will be tricky, though. We’ll need to agree on a language.”

“Yeah,” Kaylan says. “We’ll figure out a language when we write back and forth at camp. Or maybe we’ll even save that one until we get home. Too much to do now, and we need some quality hang time.”

“Duh.” Right now, I feel like I’m in two places. Or maybe even more than two places. Part of me is here, with Kaylan, in my room. Part of me is already at camp. And part of me is just lost in my thoughts. It feels like a literal jungle that I’m climbing through. Voices are muffled and I can’t really hear what’s going on. My thoughts are taking over.

I think back to all I learned about mindfulness and letting thoughts pass and being in the moment. I try as hard as I can.

Kaylan flips the notebook to a fresh page and starts writing.

Great books by LISA GREENWALD!

The Friendship List

TBH

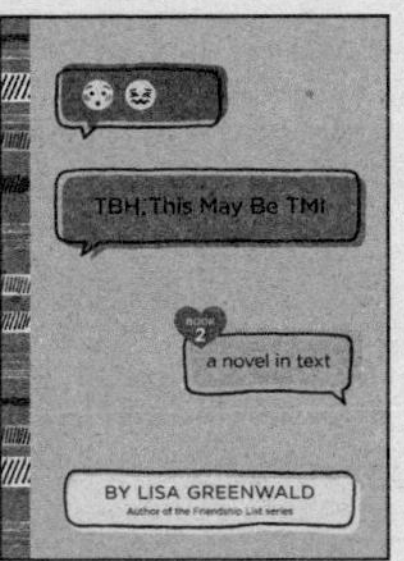